FICTION

Daughter of Fortune

Summer Campaign

Miss Chartley's Guided Tour

Marian's Christmas Wish

Mrs. McVinnie's London Season

Libby's London Merchant

Miss Grimsley's Oxford Career

Miss Billings Treads the Boards

Mrs. Drew Plays Her Hand

Reforming Lord Ragsdale

Miss Whittier Makes a List

The Lady's Companion

With This Ring

Miss Milton Speaks Her Mind

One Good Turn

The Wedding Journey

Here's to the Ladies: Stories of the Frontier Army

Beau Crusoe

Marrying the Captain

The Surgeon's Lady

Marrying the Royal Marine

The Admiral's Penniless Bride

Borrowed Light

Coming Home for Christmas: Three Holiday Stories

Enduring Light

Marriage of Mercy

My Loving Vigil Keeping

Her Hesitant Heart

The Double Cross

Safe Passage

Carla Kelly's Christmas Collection

NONFICTION

*On the Upper Missouri: The Journal
of Rudolph Friedrich Kurz*

Fort Buford: Sentinel at the Confluence

Stop Me If You've Read This One

IN *Love* AND WAR

A Collection of Love Stories

A Hasty Marriage
The Light Within
Something New
The Background Man

CARLA KELLY

Sweetwater Books
An Imprint of Cedar Fort, Inc.
Springville, Utah

ISBN 13: 978-1-4621-1226-5

Published by Sweetwater Books, an imprint of Cedar Fort, Inc.
2373 W. 700 S., Springville, UT, 84663
Distributed by Cedar Fort, Inc., www.cedarfort.com
Originally published by Signet in four anthologies

LIBRARY OF CONGRESS CATALOGING-IN-PUBLICATION DATA

Kelly, Carla.
 [Short stories. Selections]
 In love and war : a collection of love stories / by Carla Kelly.
    pages cm
 ISBN 978-1-4621-1226-5 (mass market : alk. paper)
 1. Short stories, American. I. Title.
 PS3561.E3928I5 2013
 813'.54--dc23

                                    2013025966

Cover design by Erica Dixon
Cover design © 2013 by Lyle Mortimer
Edited and typeset by Melissa J. Caldwell

Printed in the United States of America

10 9 8 7 6 5 4 3 2 1

To those who have waged war
and do not fear love

$\mathcal{C}$ONTENTS

*D*EAR READER,

In Love and War is an anthology of four of my short stories that were published years earlier by Signet. I'm delighted to see them as a quartet now, in a book of their own, ready for new readers via Cedar Fort Publishing.

Some writers enjoy the Regency period of British history because of Jane Austen, magnificent author of *Pride and Prejudice*, from which all modern Regency romances have sprung, including my own. The Regency was a colorful era of good manners, witty conversation, lively plots, and romantic potential.

As a military historian, I've been drawn to the Regency for an additional reason—war. The Napoleonic Wars set Europe aflame for nearly a generation, ending with Waterloo in 1815. The War of 1812 involved the fledgling United States in a second conflict with England. Two of these stories—"The Light Within" and "A Hasty Marriage"—introduce American characters on British shores. "Something New" features two British Army artillery officers returning to England after Napoleon has been exiled to Elba. "The Background Man" covers that heady summer of celebration in London after Napoleon's exile.

My reward for writing romances set during the Regency of George IV (1811–1819), is the pleasure of writing about soldiers and sailors—some royal, some ordinary—and their lovely ladies. It was by no means a simple time at all, but even in the middle of a grinding war, it was a time of elegance and courtesy sadly missing in our own era. Maybe we'd like to revisit such a time. Now we do it through stories.

Sincerely,

Carla Kelly

The Light Within

⌐⌐

*T*HE SCURVY PLOT THAT SET IN MOTION the elopement of the season was precipitated by the deposit of kittens upon the doorstep of 11 Albemarle Road, the City, two days before Valentine's Day, in the Year of Our Lord 1816.

Perhaps to call it an elopement is to put too strong a face upon the matter, although many insisted that Thomas Waggoner had last been seen in a fervent embrace with a beautiful woman. But no one really knows. There are those in London's best houses who still wonder whatever became of Lord Thomas Waggoner, second son of the late Marquess of Cavanaugh and brother to the biggest rake who ever cheated his tailor.

Among the *ton* who discounted the elopement theory were those who believed the rumor that Tom Waggoner had taken holy orders and thrived, shriven and shorn, on some remote isle of Micronesia. Others declared that he had taken the king's shilling yet again and served this time as a mere private in one of his majesty's far-flung regiments.

Absurdities mounted among those who still remembered Lord Thomas. One family friend even claimed, years later, that he was sure he had seen Thomas, Quaker from his broad-brimmed hat to his plain black shoes, striding

1

bold as life down a street in Nantucket, America, with a small boy perched on his shoulder, an army of stairstep children behind him, and a pretty lady at his side.

"And we remember how susceptible all Waggoners since Adam have been to a pretty face," the man had insisted. "She was a beauty, what I could see of her around that Quaker bonnet."

It was a piece of nonsense, everyone agreed. No one considered it for a moment. Still . . .

* * *

"He will ruin us, Chattering," Thomas Waggoner declared to his valet, who was surveying Lord Thomas's wardrobe and frowning. "It distresses me no end. I swear I would take to the bottle if the vile brew were not so expensive."

"It does seem that Lord Cavanaugh is making serious work of the family fortunes," the valet commented, his eyes still on his master's outmoded clothing. "Sir, by a glance in this closet, one can see how long you have been soldiering."

"Oh, I do not care," Thomas said, flinging himself back on his bed and propping his hands behind his head. He smiled to himself. "Look at that, Chattering! I can put my arm behind my head now. And you thought I would never be able to do that again."

"Pardon, sir, it was the regimental surgeon who said that, not I," the valet declared firmly. "I, for one, have infinite faith in your capacity to come about."

Thomas grimaced and gingerly straightened his arm. "But it does hurt." He held his arm up over his head and opened and closed his hand. "How nice to still see fingers at the end of this pesky arm."

He folded his arms on his chest, corpse-fashion, and eyed his valet. "I would have left the brigade, had I known the seriousness of Charles's idiocies."

The valet turned to fix the same look of concentration on his master that he had awarded the outdated waistcoats and jackets. "You would never have left your men, my lord, and you know it. It took a saber cut of iniquitous proportions to do that."

Thomas nodded. "So it did." He sighed. "I shall not dwell on that, Chattering, for it only makes me dismal." He managed a slight smile that rendered his face young again, as long as one did not look too closely at his eyes. "Do you think Charles's latest dolly-mop would scare off if I acquainted her with his precarious finances? And I do have a little money of my own. Perhaps she would remove her hooks from Charles for some coin of the realm."

The valet shrugged. "You could try, my lord," he said, the doubt evident in his voice.

"Perhaps I shall," Thomas Waggoner said. He closed his eyes and rubbed his arm.

"Lord Cavanaugh's man let it drop to me only this morning that he is taking his ladylove to the opera tonight."

Thomas opened his eyes wide. "Charles at the opera? I wonder what it can mean?" he murmured. "It sounds to me that he is tiring of his honey and means to inspect the opera dancers." He closed his eyes again. "But even Charles would not take his current amour on a hunting expedition. We have some breeding, Chattering."

"Of course, my lord," the valet said, even as he inspected the ends of his fingernails.

Thomas raised himself to rest on his good elbow. "Do you know, I could waylay his fair damsel. Of all things, Charles hates to be kept waiting. If he is already less interested, this could put an end to the affair, if I know my brother."

Chattering nodded. "But there would only be another one to follow."

Thomas lay down again. "I am sure of that, my man, but even Beelzebub himself must surely pause a bit between dirty dealings. Perhaps I could reason with Charles, and if not I, then our solicitors."

He sat up. "I shall do it! I shall write a pretty note to . . . to . . . Have you any idea what her name is?"

The valet recoiled and shook his head emphatically. "Really, my lord! Probably any flowery phrase will do. And while I am thinking of it, shall I order flowers to accompany it?"

"Gracious, no!" Tom said firmly. "What a waste of money!" He thought a moment. "I have a better idea. A stroll through the kitchen only this morning put me in mind of it, and it's something dumb that Charles would do. No, my good man, no flowers. Prepare a basket, though, and I shall kill two birds with one stone."

"Very well, my lord."

Thomas Waggoner rubbed his hands together.

"Perhaps I shall kidnap her and deposit her in some remote part of the landscape."

"I am sure that would be illegal, my lord."

Thomas nodded. "Then I shall have you do it, Chattering."

"My lord!"

* * *

Blessing Whittier did not answer the doorbell for some moments. She had removed her shoes and was lying on her bed, staring up at the ceiling, when the doorbell jangled. She felt remarkably disinclined to answer its summons.

Her feet ached from standing upon them all day, and all day the day before, waiting for an audience with a lord of the Admiralty, any lord of the Admiralty.

She sighed and sat up, rubbing her ankles. No matter how early she and her mother-in-law arrived at the building with the three massive pillars, there was always a crowd before them, composed mainly of naval officers and others with petitions.

No one ever offered them a chair. "It is because we are Americans," Patience Whittier had whispered to her at the end of that first endless day.

"Perhaps they are not Friendly," Blessing had said, her small joke bringing a dimple to her cheek, even as her feet ached and her mortification grew.

"Thee is a trickster," Mother Whittier had said, a smile on her own face. She raised her chin. "We can outwait them, my daughter. It is a talent we Friends have. And it is not as though we have a choice, is it?"

And so they had waited, day after day, for an audience. Her spine straight, her eyes demurely lowered, Blessing had counted over and over the black and white tiles in the floor of the Admiralty antechamber. She ignored the rude stares of the officers, the jokes not quite loud enough for their ears but meant for them all the same. When she felt light-headed from all that standing, she leaned against her mother-in-law and considered the Light Within.

So great had been their weariness that afternoon that they had splurged for a hackney. They sat in silence, side by side, on the journey from the Admiralty House to one of the City's shabbier streets. Blessing touched Patience's hand as they neared their rented rooms.

"Does thee think we have come upon a fool's errand?"

She was startled to see tears in her mother-in-law's eyes. "I begin to fear it, my dear. They will not see us, that is obvious, and it is our poor fortune that our ambassador is not in the country right now."

Patience looked down at her clasped hands. "But we will not surrender yet, Blessing. We have come too far, and the issue is too important. We will wait in that ante-chamber until someone will see us."

Blessing recalled her thoughts to the moment and raised her eyes to the ceiling again. It was not as though they were asking for the moon, stars, and George Washington's teacup. "It is only a paper, my lord admiral," she said out loud. "You need merely direct some piddling clerk to search the records and bring us written verification that the British Navy did sink the *Seaspray*, whaler out of Nantucket."

Tears came to her eyes, and she wiped them on the hem of her dress. "My lord admiral," she whispered, "it was only a small ship on a great ocean. My father-in-law captained, and my husband was his first, but you need not concern yourself with that. We only need a paper."

She lay back down and stared up at the ceiling again, her hands tight fists at her sides. "Aaron, I can scarcely remember thy face," she said. "Has it been so long?"

To the best of their knowledge, the *Seaspray* had been blown out of the water—try-pots, harpoons, and all—in the first year of the war with England. Another whaler, the *Jennie Birdsong* out of Boston, had watched from a prudent distance at the Arctic whaling grounds, and then grabbed for the weather gauge and beat a hasty retreat when the warship swung about. "Mind, we're not sure, Mistress Whittier," the captain had told her months later, "but it looked like the *Seaspray*."

And then the lawyers had descended on her and her mother-in-law, spouting their "whereases" and "therefores" and Latin until Blessing wanted to escape the room. All she remembered was that they stood to lose their home and the Whittier Ropewalk to the ship's partners unless they could confirm that it was an act of war and not mere accident.

The doorbell jangled again and Blessing got up, straightening her cap, tucking her hair under it carefully. *I am sure there is no place for lawyers in the kingdom to come*, she thought. *I am wicked to think that, but I expect it is true.*

She hurried down the grimy hall and opened the front door upon a neighbor lad who held a basket with two kittens. With a sigh of relief he thrust it into her arms.

"Coo, but I'm glad you're home," he said. "I dislike the idea of dumping these, or surprising me mum."

"Oh, I cannot . . ." she began as she stared down into two whiskered, inquiring faces, all white and gray perfection. Blessing smiled and tucked the basket on her hip so she could touch their velvet ears. "There must be some mistake."

The boy shook his head vigorously and clapped his cap back on. "There was gent, a nice-looking gent, walking up and down at the head of the street. He asked me if I knew of a beautiful lady on Albemarle Road." He blushed and looked down at his feet. "The mort next door, she's a pretty tart, ma'am, begging your pardon, but she's not an eye-popper like you."

"Heavens!" Blessing exclaimed, her face as red as the errand boy's. "No one has ever called me beautiful before," she said, even as she thought of Aaron and his words of love murmured from such a distance of space and time that she couldn't even be sure he had ever said them. "Well, no one recently."

The boy grinned at her. "And I like to hear you talk, ma'am, even if me mum warns me not to speak to the Americans." He tugged at his cap and looked down into the basket. "The gentleman, he said I was to make sure that you saw the note. Good day to ye."

"And to thee," Blessing said as she smiled and closed the door, the kittens in her arms.

Patience was coming from her room, her hand rubbing the small of her back. "What has thee there?" she asked, coming closer, and then laughing out loud at the kittens, which by now had taken exception to the basket and were scrambling up the front of Blessing's dress.

"I will share this blessing," Blessing said as she handed the white kitten to Patience. "I am sure it is someone's idea of a joke," she said and then sat down on the floor, the other kitten in her lap. She let it go, and it wobbled on unsteady legs.

"The lad claims there is a note." She looked in the basket and pulled out a note, sealed with a dab of wax and inscribed with a strong hand. "Here is the answer to our mystery."

As the kitten climbed into her lap again and dropped immediately into slumber, Blessing broke the seal and stared at the short note. "'My dear,'" she read, "'come walking at the end of Albemarle Road at seven of the clock, and we will settle this little matter to your advantage, I am sure. Cavanaugh.'"

She looked up at her mother-in-law. "Cavanaugh? Cavanaugh? Mother, is that one of the Admiralty lords? I seem to recall the name."

Patience sank down onto the low stool beside Blessing. She took the note from her daughter-in-law's hands. "I am not rightly sure. Does thee think so?"

"I cannot imagine what else it would be," Blessing said, her practical nature in charge once again. "Perhaps the Admiralty feels that diplomacy is best served by this kind of discretion."

Absently Patience removed the kitten that was attempting to climb her cap. "How odd these British are!" she exclaimed. "Is there any wonder that we thought to separate from them?"

"As to that, I do not know, Mother," Blessing said. "As I think of it, I am sure that there is a Cavanaugh numbered among the lords of the Admiralty, and I will be there this evening." She touched her mother-in-law's face. "Don't thee be so alarmed! If this is how the British choose to carry out delicate matters of state, I say let them, if it means we could be on a ship bound for Boston in a few days."

Patience nodded. "I am so anxious to be home!"

Blessing gently replaced the slumbering kitten into the basket, got to her feet, and held out her hands to her mother-in-law. "Then remove that frown, dearest. What could possibly happen that is worse than standing day after day on marble floors?"

* * *

If she had any doubts of her own, Blessing Whittier kept them to herself through their frugal dinner and their moments of silent contemplation in the sitting room. She was meditating upon her own sins, wondering why a ragbag neighbor boy's assertion that she was an eye-popper should cause her such pleasure. *I am only grateful Patience did not hear him*, she thought, and the dimple came to her cheek again.

She stroked the gray kitten, its stomach bulging with pabulum, which had found its way to her lap again. The little beast purred and rolled onto its back. "Think how good they will be for mice in this wretched place," she said to Patience, who also contended with a similarly well-fed kitten in her lap.

Patience smiled and rubbed under the chin of the white one. "I will remind thee that the mice that are part of these furnished rooms are bigger than these kittens." She glanced at the clock. "And now it is hard upon seven, Blessing. Does thee think thee should go?"

Blessing set the kitten on the lumpy sofa. She tucked her hair carefully under her cap again and settled her bonnet firmly on top. She pulled her cape about her shoulders and peered out the window. "I wish it were not so foggy, Mother. I shall be swallowed up in this pea soup the moment I leave."

"Don't go, my dear," Patience urged.

Blessing kissed her cheek. "Only think how fine it will be to feel a heaving deck and know that this paltry round of seasickness will be carrying us to Boston!"

In the narrow street, she looked back at the house once, marveling how rapidly the fog settled about her. She nearly turned back once, then shook herself for her want of spine and set out at a brisk pace to the junction of Albemarle and Hose.

The street was deserted. *Everyone with any sense is indoors,* she thought as she pulled her cloak tighter about her. *And so I should be. I will give this quixotic Lord Cavanaugh five minutes and no more.*

The words had scarcely crossed her brain when she heard horses' hooves. A carriage with a crest on the door loomed out of the fog and stopped before her. A man, black-cloaked like herself, opened the door and pulled down the step.

"Come, madam," he said, holding out his hand.

"Are you Lord Cavanaugh?" she replied, stepping back from the carriage and wishing all of a sudden that it was bright daylight and the street crowded with its usual complement of vendors.

"Come," the man repeated. "Lord Thomas will make this worth your while."

As she hesitated, Blessing wondered at the tone of disgust that entered the man's voice. *Are we Americans so hated abroad?* she thought as she hesitated a moment more and then held out her hand and allowed the man to help her inside.

The horses leapt into motion, and Blessing grabbed for the strap that swung so wildly. She hung on, her eyes growing accustomed to the gloom.

As she watched, wide-eyed, the man seated across from her removed his hat and swabbed his face with an immaculate handkerchief. When he finished, he shook it at her. "I told Lord Thomas it must be illegal to kidnap young persons, but he did not listen."

Blessing stared at him. "What!" she managed as the horses careened around the corner and she clung to the strap.

He ignored her outburst and folded his arms. "So I told him, miss, I think too much war has addled his brain."

"Let me out at once," Blessing ordered. "Thee has no right to do this. I am an American citizen," she declared, raising her voice to be heard above the horses. "That ought to mean something to thee."

The man stared at her and groaned. Out came the handkerchief again for another vigorous swab of his head. "And now we have created an international incident," he said, his tone much put-upon. "But no one told us Cavanaugh's light-skirt was a Yankee!"

Blessing gasped again. She administered a ringing slap to the little man's face, looked out the window, decided against jumping, and curled herself into a ball in the far opposite corner.

She rode for hours, or so it seemed, cocooned as they were by the fog and the artificial stillness it created. Other than a sniff and a wounded look in her direction, the little man in black ignored her after muttering something about looking for employment elsewhere.

The horses raced on through the foggy streets. The sound changed, and she knew they were in the country. The fog lifted, but she could see no more than the dark outlines of trees and houses spaced farther and farther apart.

When she could force herself to think beyond her immediate fears, Blessing considered her situation in rational Quaker fashion. *I cannot lose my virginity,* she thought. *That's been gone these three years and more. If they kill me, I know there is a much better world beyond, and Aaron is there. If they mean to hold me for ransom, they will soon see their mistake. I only wish I could give a reassuring report to Patience.*

They careened down a narrower lane, one where the bare branches of February trees brushed against the carriage. The lane showed signs of neglect, being graveled here, muddy there. They lurched along and Blessing held her breath, waiting to be overturned. Tears stung her eyes as she thought of the high hopes with which they had sailed for England. She glanced over at the man who crouched in the other corner of the carriage.

"Does Lord Cavanaugh mean mischief?" she asked hesitantly.

"Lord Cavanaugh always means mischief."

"Oh, dear."

They must have traveled a mile at least before the carriage rolled to a stop. Blessing peered out the window at a small house, brightly lit, with the door wide open despite the chill in the air. A tall man stood on the steps, silhouetted black against the light. She gulped. *And to think I believed that Lord Cavanaugh would help me,* she said to herself.

"Come, miss," said the man in the carriage. He held his hand out to her.

"No," she replied, her voice quiet but filled with determination.

The valet lunged for her as she hurled herself from the carriage, gathering her skirts for a run down the road.

"Please, miss!" the valet wailed, even as the man on the steps ran to the carriage. The tall man grabbed her by the arm and she shook him off, wondering as she struck out at him how someone with such an open, friendly face could plot so nefariously against a widow with only a small bone to pick with the British Empire.

She squeaked in surprise as he grabbed her and threw her over his shoulder. She dragged her fingernails up both sides of his neck and then clutched at his hair.

When he would not let her down, she flailed out, striking him on the arm. His breath went out of him in an *oof!* as his legs buckled under him, and he sank right down on the driveway.

Her knees scraped the gravel, but Blessing was on her feet in a second, her hair wild about her face, her bonnet flung somewhere in the dark. She sucked in her breath and drew back her leg to kick him, when she remembered with a start who she was.

Blessing looked down at the man who clutched his arm and writhed on the driveway, the bloody tracks of her fingernails across his neck. She put her hands behind her back in embarrassment and came closer, to find herself pushed aside by the valet.

"Are you all right, my lord?" the little man asked, his face pale and anxious in the moonlight. "Oh, let me help you." He bent closer. "My lord, she is an American!"

"That explains a lot," gasped the man on the ground. He stared up at her and allowed the little man to help him into a sitting position. "Woman, was that entirely necessary? I'm sure you needn't fear for your virtue."

He looked at her closer then, his unbelieving eyes taking in her plain black cloak, her gray dress, and the demure fichu of white linen twisted now about her neck. He stared down at the linen mobcap that he still held tight in his hand.

"Thee is a very bad man," she said, her hands still behind her back.

"Oh, mercy," he breathed.

"And I will thank thee not to indulge in wooden swearing," she said as she took hold of him by the arm and tugged him to his feet. When he swayed on his feet, she gave him another shake. "Thee should know better than to kidnap helpless widows." She took the cap from his fingers and dabbed at his neck with it. "Our founder, George Fox, enjoined us not to resort to violence, Lord Cavanaugh," she said, "but I gladly made an exception in thy case!"

He could only stare at her, his mouth open, then transfer his gaze to the little man in black who stood in miserable silence beside her. "Chattering, remind me never to send you on an abduction again," he murmured, taking the cap from her hand and holding it to his neck to stanch the bleeding. "You have botched it."

To Blessing's amazement, the little man burst into tears. "But there she was, sir, standing at the corner of Albemarle and Hose."

The tall man touched his arm and winced, holding it steady by the elbow. "Obviously, Chattering, there is more than one beautiful woman on Albemarle Road." He shook his head and held out his left hand. "My dear Miss . . ."

"Mrs. Whittier," she replied, taking his hand.

He rolled his eyes. "Worse and worse! Mrs. Whittier, there has been a dreadful mistake. Will you permit me to explain?" He motioned toward the house.

Blessing released his hand. "What is this place?" she asked, suspicion high in her voice.

To his credit, the man did not flinch. He took a deep breath and grinned. "It is the iniquitous love nest of Lord Cavanaugh, who, I profoundly assure you, I am not. The only danger you will encounter within is that certain numbness that comes from staring overlong at really poor art reproductions."

She smiled. "I had hoped to find a lord of the Admiralty here."

He offered her his good arm. "And I had hoped to

have a serious discussion with my brother's . . . ah, yes, Lord Cavanaugh . . . my brother's latest amour. Obviously we are both doomed to disappointment."

She nodded. After a moment of contemplation that the tall man did not interrupt, she took his arm.

"Let us discuss this turn of events, Mrs. Whittier. I hope your husband will not call me out. I am a dreadful shot these six months and more."

"He will not call you out," she replied, suddenly shy. "Let me help you, sir."

She grasped him more firmly by the elbow and steered him up the stairs and into the sitting room, where he sank onto the sofa, his eyes closed.

He was handsome in a rangy way that appealed to her, his hair black as an Indian's, his cheekbones high. His nose was arrow-straight and there were creases about his rather thin mouth. He was dressed quite casually in buckskin breeches and an open-throated linen shirt. His fingers were long, and the veins on the backs of his hands stood out distinctly, as though he had lost weight in recent months and not yet regained it.

"Sir?" she inquired when he did not open his eyes. "Are you all right?"

He looked at her then, a slight smile relieving the severity of his face. "I am well enough," he replied. "I was just wondering where to begin. Perhaps if you went first, we could get to the bottom of this quicker. Chattering, do you think my dratted brother keeps anything as prosaic as tea in this bordello?"

"I am certain he must, my lord. After all, he is an Englishman, even if he is a rake."

Blessing laughed out loud, and then put her hand to her mouth in embarrassment.

"We do have our standards," the tall man murmured and reached into his pocket. He removed a small penknife, which he tossed into her lap. "I never thought I was squeamish, but do me the favor of cleaning out those devilish sharp fingernails of yours, Mrs. Whittier."

She busied herself with removing the bits of bloody tissue from under her nails. "Do tell me your name, sir," she said when there seemed to be no end to the silence. She peeked a glance at him to observe him gazing at her, a half-smile on his face. "Sir?"

"Oh! Yes." He put his hand to his heart. "If you do not mind, I will remain seated. I am Thomas Waggoner, brother to Charles Waggoner, Earl of Cavanaugh."

"And is he a lord of the Admiralty?"

Thomas shook his head. "He has been called many things, my dear Mrs. Whittier, but lord admiral is not among them."

"I thought he was, does thee see, else I never would have answered that note."

He nodded. "The note I remember well, because I wrote it. But I do not understand your obsession with lords admiral. One scarcely meets a stuffier lot."

Over scalding tea, Blessing told Thomas Waggoner what had brought them from Nantucket, Massachusetts, to London. Her voice faltered when she mentioned Aaron Whittier and his father, and the *Seaspray*, lost these three years and more.

Lord Thomas touched her hand. "I am sorry, Mrs. Whittier."

"It is not thy fault," she replied quickly. "The Lord works in ways we cannot discern."

"So he does," Thomas agreed, taking a sip of tea.

"When I received that note that said I would be given what was due me, I thought . . . Well, we thought perhaps this Lord Cavanaugh chose not to go through official channels. I am sure this matter is an embarrassment to the British government." She looked up at him. "Foolish, wasn't I?"

He nodded, but his eyes were kind. "The Admiralty lords are much too prosaic for kittens, Mrs. Whittier. Tell me, are they a burden? I can reclaim them."

She laughed and shook her head. "So far, they are the one bit of real joy in this whole wretched affair, Mr. . . . er . . . Lord Thomas." She set down her teacup and folded her hands in her lap. "And now you tell me there is no Lord Cavanaugh on the Admiralty Board."

He thought a moment. "There is a Lord Ravenaugh," he said.

"Ravenaugh, Cavanaugh," she said. "Yes, that was my mistake." Blessing rested her chin on her hands. "But I am no closer to solving my problem, am I?"

He set down his cup and folded his arms across his chest, contemplating her. "It could be that you are closer than you think, my dear Mrs. Whittier. Have you heard of Thaddeus Calcingham, Lord Renfrew?"

She nodded. "He is another, is he not?"

"In very deed. He is my late mother's uncle. I think I can solve your problem tomorrow. A note to Uncle Calcingham will grease the wheels of naval inquiry amazingly."

He looked up when the valet entered the room. "Chattering, allow me to introduce Mrs. Whittier to you."

"Blessing Whittier," she added and held out her hand. "I am sorry I was so rude to thee."

"Blessing, is it?" Thomas said, his eyes merrier than she had seen them yet that evening.

"I was the first daughter after five sons," she explained. "We Friends value our daughters as well as our sons, Lord Thomas."

He smiled. "Well that you should. Have you any children of your own, Mrs. Whittier?"

She shook her head. "Are you married, sir?"

"No." He leaned forward, resting his elbows carefully

on his knees. "And it's just as well. I am certain my brother is taking the Waggoners down to utter financial ruin. Thank the Almighty I do not have a wife and children to muddy the waters."

She reached out impulsively and touched his arm. "Oh, sir, discomforts are less unpleasant when they are shared."

He blinked and stared at her, the smile coming back into his eyes. "I never thought of it that way. Seriously, Mrs. Whittier, beyond a small sum which I had hoped to tempt Charles's beautiful doxy, I am worthless."

Blessing tightened her grip on his arm. "No one is worthless. Thee cannot be serious." She shook his arm. "I do not wish thee ever to think so again. Promise me," she said, her voice urgent.

Startled, he nodded. "I promise thee," he said softly. He looked up at Chattering, who had been watching him. "Are we ready for the return trip, my man?"

The valet yanked out his white handkerchief again and, in the gesture rapidly becoming familiar to Blessing, dragged it across his bald head. "My lord, we must have jarred the axle on the way down that wretched lane. The coachman says he can fix it in the morning, when the light is back."

Thomas Waggoner sighed. "You know times are harsh for the Waggoners when Charles can't even afford to maintain the road to his love nest." He looked at Blessing. "I am afraid we will be spending the night here, Mrs. Whittier."

She got to her feet quickly. "I dare not leave my mother-in-law wondering what has become of me." Tears came to her eyes. "We have only each other, and she will be prostrate with worry if I do not return." She reached for her cloak. "I am sure I can walk."

Thomas Waggoner took the cloak from her. "We are

some little distance from town, madam." He looked at Chattering again. "What do you say to the postboy riding my horse back to London with a message for . . . for . . ."

"Patience Whittier," she supplied.

"I am sure that he would, my lord." Chattering broke into a rare smile. "He would like to ride that hunter of yours."

"I am sure he would too!" Waggoner stood up. "It's the only item of value I possess anymore. Very well, then. Chattering, see if you can find pen and paper somewhere about this den of iniquity, and we will let Mrs. Whittier compose a satisfactory note."

"I suppose I have no choice," she said, far from satisfied.

"I wish you did," he answered apologetically, "but events would dictate otherwise."

"Very well, then. I shall write," Blessing said.

The note was less than satisfactory, she decided after two attempts and coaching from Lord Thomas, who seemed, to her irritation, to find the situation amusing. She stabbed the badly mended pen in his direction.

"Thee claims thee is not a rake, but I say thee is too easily entertained!" she muttered as she began again.

He looked at her with wide eyes. "Madam, I am not a rake, but I am still a Waggoner, and we are easily entertained. It's in the blood," he offered as further explanation.

"Then take thyself off so I can finish this. Thee is a serious annoyance."

He threw back his head and laughed, then propped his feet on the dining-room table where they sat and folded his hands in his lap. "I have finished my composition to Uncle Calcingham," he said, unable to keep the note of injured virtue from his voice. "I do not know what is so difficult about informing your mother-in-law that you must spend the night in a love nest with a rake's brother. And so close to Valentine's Day," he added for good effect.

Blessing laughed in spite of herself. "Well, as long as the news does not travel to Nantucket," she said at last.

"How could it possibly?" he replied. "Some of us I could name seem to relish making mountains out of molehills."

A smile on her face, she addressed herself to the note again, remembering how Aaron used to say much the same thing. *I suppose it is true,* she thought as she wrote, reread, and then folded the missive with a sigh.

Thomas left with both notes. In another moment she heard a horse galloping down the lane. She got up from the table and went in search of the bedroom.

It was a small house, and she found it quickly. A candle burned on the bedside table. Gingerly she felt the mattress.

"I am certain that the mattress is in excellent working order," came Thomas's voice from the doorway.

She could tell without even looking around that he was grinning from ear to ear. Her face fiery red, she returned some noncommittal answer.

He came closer. "Beg pardon?" he murmured. Blessing leveled him with a frosty stare that only made the smile wider.

Thomas went to the bureau and opened a drawer. "It appears that you will find any number of nightgowns."

She came closer and gasped. "I would never wear one of those iniquitous gowns!" she exclaimed, staring at the little patches of lace and silk.

He closed the drawer, his back to her as his shoulders shook. "Mrs. Whittier, I am sure that is the reaction of many of the women who have been here before you. They probably never wore these either."

She burst into laughter. "Thee is not good for me!" she protested.

"Ah, but thee is good for me!" he said and bowed himself out of the room.

She closed the door and locked it with a click, listening to Thomas's laughter on the other side. "Some people . . ." she said out loud so he could hear.

Blessing knew that she would never sleep, but she undressed, found a nightgown a little less iniquitous than some of the others, and crawled into bed. The mattress was perfect, she had to admit. She snuggled herself into the bed and was asleep in minutes.

She woke an hour later, thinking of Thomas Waggoner and his injured arm. She pulled the pillow against her stomach, resting her chin against it. *I suspect there is no other bedroom in the house, and so he must be contending with that sofa,* she thought. *Mother Whittier would say I am thoughtless indeed.*

Blessing lit the candle and went to the dressing closet, where she found a wrap. She tied it firmly around her and went to the door, unlocking it and tiptoeing into the hall.

Thomas Waggoner, his eyes haggard, was sitting on the sofa, holding his elbow with his other hand. He looked at her in surprise and straightened the sheet about his bare legs.

"What on earth?" he began.

"Get up," she said. "Thee may take the bed and I will sleep here. Thee cannot rest this way on a narrow sofa. I am sorry I did not think of this sooner."

"I won't hear of it," he said.

She sat down on the sofa with him. "Then I will sit here until thee comes to thy senses."

He glared at her and then leaned back. "I would be more comfortable in a bed," he admitted, "but I hate to wish this sofa on you."

"It is of no concern to me, Lord Thomas," she said, getting to her feet again. "I am much shorter than thee, and the only pain I feel is when thee cracks thy miserable jokes."

He smiled. "Very well, Mrs. Whittier," he said. "I capitulate. Now, close your eyes and I'll do a better job with this sheet."

She saw him settled in the bed and reached across for the extra pillow. "Would this be better tucked under thy arm?" she asked. "How should I do it?"

"Chattering usually helps me," he said. "Yes, yes, just prop it there." He relaxed and closed his eyes. "Much better. I fear you will not do as well."

She only smiled and blew out the candle. "Good night, Lord Thomas."

Blessing woke in the morning to the fragrance of bacon cooking. She sat up and stretched, rubbing the small of her back. It was a wretched couch indeed. She pulled on her wrap and tiptoed to the bedroom to reclaim her clothes.

It was empty and the bed was made. She dressed quickly and followed her nose to the kitchen, where Lord Thomas was concentrating on the bacon. He looked up to see her in the doorway and waved the bacon fork at her.

"Crispy or chewy, Mrs. Whittier?" he asked.

"Crispy," she replied, tugging at the curls that would not behave and wishing that she had not sacrificed her cap to Lord Thomas's wounds last night.

"An excellent choice, madam," he said, "considering that I have long since passed the chewy stage. Chattering, is that bread toasted yet?"

"Yes, my lord," the valet replied. "Mrs. Whittier, if you would set the table, I think there is silverware in the dining room."

"We have discovered that Charles and his lady-loves don't spend much time in the kitchen either," Thomas said and turned back to the kitchen stove before she could scold him. "Chattering had to borrow a frying pan when he went to the farm nearby for bacon and eggs."

Blessing set the table, wondering how Patience was faring in London, and spent a moment at the window in silent contemplation, staring out at the bleakness of February. She thought of Aaron, something she rarely did, because remembering him was too painful. Hugging herself with her arms, she recalled other mornings—too few of them—when she and Aaron would read to each other from the Old Testament after breakfast.

She closed her eyes and leaned against the window frame, wishing herself home, back where friends and neighbors would greet her and not ignore her and look away because she was Quaker and an American too. She longed for the fragrance of the sea and the sound of water lapping on pilings . . .

"You may be able to ignore bacon and eggs, but I am constitutionally unfit for such asceticism," said the voice behind her.

She whirled around in surprise. Thomas Waggoner was seated at the table, a napkin in his lap. He grinned at her, and then his face became serious.

"But you weren't thinking of bacon and eggs, eh?" he asked, his voice gentle. He glanced out the window, where bare branches scrubbed the glass. "Dreadful useless month, my dear Mrs. Whittier. Thank heaven there is Valentine's Day to relieve it."

She took a cue from his light tone and joined him at the table. "It is not a holiday we Friends celebrate, Lord Thomas," she said, taking the platter from him and sniffing it. "You are certainly good with eggs, my lord."

"I can cook over campfires in caves, in abandoned Spanish monasteries, and in dens of iniquity."

She laughed. "And I can pray over it, sir, just in case."

Her blessing on the food was soft, his "Amen" hearty. They ate in companionable silence. Thomas finished first.

He pushed his plate back and leaned back in his chair, crossing his long legs and contemplating her.

"Mrs. Whittier, this has been frightfully inconvenient for you," he commented. "Any other lady of my acquaintance would have shrieked and fainted last night."

She looked at him over the rim of her teacup.

"And are *you* such an antidote, sir?" she asked quickly, before she thought how improper it sounded.

He laughed out loud, bringing the chair back to the floor with a thump. "You are a bit of a rascal, my dear, aren't you?"

"I am not," she protested. "Sometimes I speak before I think."

He grinned at her, and she blushed.

Thomas got to his feet and stretched. "Well, I, for one, am grateful for your kindness." He pulled her chair back for her. "Neither of us realized a successful outcome from this venture, but I have met my first American, and you might yet be satisfied by my Uncle Calcingham."

He saw her into the parlor and then went outside, whistling to himself to check on the progress of the carriage.

He was back before she had opportunity to tidy the room beyond straightening one or two of the poor art reproductions that he had disparaged last night, and wondering where she might find a dust cloth.

"Mrs. Whittier, your carriage awaits. If you do not object, I will ride with you. Indeed, I must, considering that the postboy left last night with my horse."

"Of course I do not object," she replied as she allowed him to help her into her cloak. "If your Uncle Calcingham fails me, you can suggest some other avenues I might attempt. Bribery is out, I must add. I have scruples." She made a face. "And little cash, anyway."

"I shall put my mind to the matter, Mrs. Whittier," he

replied and promptly fell asleep when the carriage began to roll.

Blessing sighed and settled herself, wondering where Chattering had taken himself off to, and deciding that he had chosen to ride with the coachman. *How odd,* she thought. *He should have known he would be welcome in the carriage.*

The ride back into London seemed to go much faster on the return trip. Lord Thomas Waggoner woke up, winked at her, and then directed his gaze out the window.

It should have been an embarrassing ride. Blessing had never been alone before with a man who was not a relative, but even in silence Thomas Waggoner seemed to give off an air of warmth. *I wonder, sir,* she thought, *are thee used to taking care of people?* He had mentioned the army, and his wound had obviously been a result of last year's horrendous struggle at Waterloo. She shuddered, unable to imagine war.

And then she was struggling to stay awake, thinking herself intolerably rude as she nodded and dozed and then jerked awake again.

In another moment Thomas had left his seat facing her to sit at her side. "Mrs. Whittier, I insist that you rest your head upon my shoulder before you pitch forward and crash onto the floor," he said firmly, and she opened her mouth to protest. "I fear I would be in serious trouble with your mother-in-law, and probably the American embassy, should I return you in less than impeccable condition."

Blessing did as he requested, burrowing comfortably into his shoulder. She thought to object when his arm went around her, but it seemed a waste of good breath.

"Tell me, Mrs. Whittier, what is Nantucket like?" he asked finally as they struck fog again and the carriage slowed.

She considered Nantucket. "It is all blue sky, white dunes, sea gulls, and the coldest water, even in summer," she replied. "And there is always the smell of hemp and tar and salt herring."

He made a face. "You miss the smell of rope?"

She nodded, her head against his shoulder. "I miss the ropewalk, Lord Thomas," she said. She sat up to see him better. "Have you ever seen a ropewalk?"

He nodded. "Once before in Portsmouth, before we shipped out for Spain. I never saw such a long, narrow building. Fascinating, I might add, how the strands twist and twist and produce the most prodigious cables. Noisy, too, with all that rope turning."

"I run the Whittier Ropewalk," Blessing said, unable to keep the note of pride from her voice. "Patience has not the constitution for business, and one of us had to take over when . . . Well, it is the other family business. Not as prosperous as the *Seaspray* was . . ." Her voice trailed off.

"You run a business?" he asked, his voice filled with respect. "I have often thought such a thing would be great fun." He chuckled. "Don't tell any of my relatives. They would sniff and call me baseborn."

Blessing's chin went up. "Work is a very American enterprise, Lord Thomas. I can recommend it to anyone." She moved away from him a little. "After a day of supervising in the ropeworks, I am too tired to repine over my situation."

"Who runs it now?" he asked quickly, to fill in the silence that threatened to choke her.

"My cousin William Peabody," she said, her voice light again. "But he was to have returned to Harvard, and only stays on in sufferance now. We had thought to have this matter cleared up much earlier."

"And now you shall," Waggoner said. He put his arm

around her again and pulled her to rest against him. "You'll be on the next ship bound for Boston, I'll wager."

"Yes, I expect so," she agreed and wondered why the notion did not inspire total delight.

She slept then, to be shaken gently awake later. The carriage had stopped. The door was already open, and Chattering stood there. Blessing allowed Lord Thomas to help her down. He walked her to the door, looking around him.

"Not a very promising street, Mrs. Whittier," he commented. "I am sure Aaron would not have approved."

"'Twas cheaper than hotel rooms," she explained. "No, I do not think Aaron would have approved either."

He was in no hurry to leave her at the door. "Tell me, do you know where this other beauty on Albemarle Road lives?" he asked.

"I wish thee would not call me a beauty," she scolded, feeling the spots of color in her cheeks.

"Well, the other antidote, then," he said with a laugh. "My dear, do you ever look in mirrors?"

"No!" She stared at him in confusion. "*Who* is the family rake?" she asked pointedly.

He staggered back as though she had shot him, and she laughed. "I have never had the slightest inclination to be a rake, Mrs. Whittier, but I do have two functioning eyes! All this aside, I would still like to find this damsel and talk to her."

"She lives next door with a veritable dragon I can only assume is a chaperone," Blessing replied. "I am not so sure she is a lady. She wears overmuch powder and rouge, and her laugh is memorable, to say the least."

Blessing stopped. It was hardly necessary for Lord Thomas to know that she had heard that laugh, and other sounds, any number of times through the thin walls of her bedroom. The sounds should have repulsed her, but they only left her hugging her pillow and feeling lonelier than she could have expressed in words. No need for Lord Thomas to know anything of this.

He looked at the house next door, vaulted the iron railing that separated the two doors, and knocked. He cocked his head toward the door and listened, and then knocked once more. No answer. He joined her again. "Well, I shall think of something," he murmured and took her hand again, kissing it. "Good day, Mrs. Whittier. I trust you will have good news from the Admiralty House before this day is over."

He saw her into the house and then waved to her from the carriage window as she stood there in the entrance watching him depart.

Patience hugged her and cried, then blew her nose and demanded an explanation over tea and biscuits.

"I told thee it was a strange scheme," she reminded her daughter-in-law when Blessing finished her recitation.

Blessing sighed. "So it was. I was foolish and God was merciful."

Patience nodded and kissed Blessing again.

"But now thee thinks we might hear at last from the Admiralty?"

"That is what Lord Thomas says."

"Can he be trusted?" Patience asked, her eyes anxious. "I am desperate to be home again, daughter."

Blessing nodded, remembering the strength of his arm about her. "He can be trusted."

By mutual agreement, both ladies retired to their respective bedchambers. "Even after that letter last night, I am sure I did not sleep above twenty minutes," Patience assured her.

The fog had burned away and the sun was quite high in the sky when Blessing's rest was disturbed by another jangle at the doorbell. When it would not stop, she dressed quickly, tugging her curly hair under her cap as she ran down the hall.

She opened the door upon Lord Thomas Waggoner, looking fresh as the flower in his lapel and bearing one more kitten in his arms. He winked at her, to Blessing's acute embarrassment, and bowed as best he could with the kitten.

"I seem to have overlooked one more little nuisance, Mrs. Whittier," he said. "It was mewing and mewing all around the kitchen this morning when I went belowstairs to beg a snack from the cook. It would have wrenched tears from your eyes."

With a laugh she accepted the kitten and carried it inside, setting it down on the floor where the other two kittens had congregated when the doorbell rang.

"Sir, how am I to return with these to Nantucket?" she inquired, half-amused, half-exasperated.

"Perhaps you will feel compelled to remain here," he said, his voice offhand. "At least until they have grown."

"I will remind thee that I have a ropewalk to run," she said. "The strands do not twist by themselves! Shut the door if thee is coming in."

He closed the door behind him, looking about with some disfavor at the dingy hall and its faded, tattered wallpaper. "I wanted to tell you that I have been to the Admiralty House."

"And thee got in?" she asked, her eyes wide.

He widened his eyes in imitation of her. "I am an Englishman, my dear, with some good report from my army days. I won't say they exactly stood aside and bowed, but I did see my uncle, and he will help you."

Blessing clapped her hands. "Thee is a wonder!"

He smiled modestly. "We Waggoners have that effect on some. You may ask any woman within a fifty-mile radius."

"But that is thy brother," she accused.

He nodded. "I cannot pretend to trade upon his . . . his . . . skill."

"No need to say more," Blessing interrupted hastily.

Thomas Waggoner was looking about him again, an expression of dissatisfaction on his face.

"I have a much prettier parlor in Nantucket," Blessing said, reading his thoughts.

"I suppose you have a view of the sea?"

"Oh, yes, my lord. Everyone does."

They just stood in the hall, Lord Thomas with his hat in his hand, and Blessing wondering if her cap hid all her uncombed curls.

"Mrs. Whittier, you could do me a great favor," he said at last, after obvious hesitation. "How would you feel about attending a Valentine's Day costume ball this evening at my brother's house on Curzon Street?"

"I . . . I could never, Lord Thomas," she protested. "We Friends don't mind a gathering every now and then, but not in costume."

He thought about it a moment, eyeing her gray dress with its tidy lace collar. "Suppose I were to come in costume and you wore what you have on now. You do look fine in gray."

Blessing blushed. "I never think about it."

He smiled at her confusion and put his hat back on his head. "You probably never do. Do consider my offer, my dear. I will come by for you at nine o'clock."

"But . . ."

* * *

Thomas had to resist the urge to whistle as he strode down Albemarle Road and hailed a hackney coach. He considered the matter. Walking would be cheaper, but the victory of convincing beautiful Blessing Whittier to attend the costume ball deserved some reward.

By anyone's estimation, she was a beauty. He leaned back in the coach, a smile upon his face. *I have never seen such luminous blue eyes,* he thought, *although they were a trifle stormy last night.* His hand went to his neck, grateful that his high collar hid the worst of her nail scourings. *She's not a woman to rile,* he thought.

He had never seen such perfect skin. Blessing Whittier would never need to resort to potions and powders. She was one of those women, he decided, who would probably grow more beautiful with age and children. *I have always wanted a large family,* he thought, allowing his mind to roam freely. *Dashed unfashionable, I suppose, but there you are. I like children.*

He sighed and tugged his thoughts back to the present. *I couldn't support a family of sea bream in my present circumstances,* he thought, *and here I am mooning about a regular tribe of Abraham. Oh, merciful heaven, Charles has just got to be brought up to snuff.*

He tapped on the roof and the coach slowed. "Take me back to Curzon Street," he said.

Charles was awake and sitting up in bed as Thomas came into the darkened room and threw back the draperies.

"Have a heart, brother," he gasped as he covered his eyes with his hands. "Is it noon yet?" he asked.

"Noon and then some," Thomas said as he sat himself down on Charles's bed. "I wonder that you have not been jerked awake by all the servants scurrying around, making ready for your party!" He leaned closer. "And how you managed to convince our solicitors to advance you any blunt for a party, I cannot fathom. Charles, don't you comprehend that quaint old expression 'under the hatches'?"

Charles removed his hands from his eyes and gazed at his younger brother with an expression of serenity that made Thomas want to shake him. "You seem to think I have done nothing to bring us about," he murmured. "I wish you would trust the head of the family, dear boy."

Thomas laughed, but there was no mirth. "All I have noticed since my return from Belgium—on a stretcher, I might remind you—is you turning losing cards and sniffing after questionable women."

"Jealous, Thomas?" Charles said, his eyes narrow and his voice soft.

"Drat your worthless hide, Charles," Thomas said, his voice equally soft. "Don't you care what's happening to the family name?"

Charles sighed and stretched out his hand for the bell rope. "I was going to tell you tonight, you crosspatch, but I suppose it will not wait."

"*What* will not wait?" Thomas asked.

"I am to be married." Charles shuddered, and then smoothed the hair from his eyes. "So do not think I have been idly standing by wringing my hands and waiting for the creditors to carry us off to the workhouse."

"There's not a family in London with a father so dead to reason that he would allow even his most distempered daughter to come within a block of you."

Charles laughed and threw back the covers. "Thank heaven for Northumberland," he said. "I have met an earl's daughter from that wretched place, and she will have me."

Thomas stared at his brother. Charles laughed and threw a pillow at him. "Thomas, if you don't look like a trout hooked and tossed up on the bank! Angela—and she truly is an angel—agreed last night at the opera." He paused and raised himself on his elbow to look at his younger brother. "You may wish me happy, Thomas."

Thomas did no such thing. He frowned and paced to the window, where he stood, hands in his pockets, staring out at the activity on Curzon Street. As he watched, tradesmen staggering under the weight of potted trees and cases of champagne formed a veritable parade into the servants' entrance below. Charles joined him at the window. He clapped his hand on Thomas's shoulder. "I had no trouble convincing our solicitors to extend me credit upon my expectations." He gave Thomas a little shake. "And what better way to celebrate Saint Valentine's Eve than with an engagement party? Think how surprised my guests will be."

Thomas said nothing for a long moment. When he did speak, he tried to keep his voice casual. "And where does this paragon, my future sister-in-law, reside?"

"On Albemarle Road," Lord Cavanaugh replied promptly, and then laughed, his voice indulgent, as though he humored a much younger child. "And now you will tell me that Albemarle Road is not quite the thing for the daughter of an earl."

Thomas nodded, his eyes still on the street, not trusting himself to look at Charles. "Yes, that's probably what I would say. How perspicacious you are, Chuck."

Charles went to his dressing table. "Yes, I suppose I am. I wonder that Mother was always so insistent that you were awarded all the brains in the family." He turned around to regard his brother. "I did ask Angela Davenport—ah, yes, the Northumberland Davenports—that very thing. The dear girl assured me that it was her father's idea."

Thomas held up his hand. "Don't tell me, Charles, but let me guess," he said, his voice rising despite his efforts to control it. "Papa Davenport thought that such a humble address would surely shield his daughter—his super-wealthy daughter—from a legion of gazetted fortune hunters."

Charles nodded in perfect accord. "One would

almost think you knew the story, Thomas," he murmured as he turned back to contemplate his face in the mirror.

"Heavens, no!" Thomas said, failing utterly at control. "I'm sure that without overmuch exertion you could find this little faradiddle scratched on a clay tablet in Babylonia! Are you such a flat, Charles?"

"Jealous," was all Charles said. "Shut the door quietly when you leave, Thomas. I have a bit of a head this afternoon."

Thomas slammed the door behind him but took no satisfaction in Charles's anguished shriek. His face set, his complexion pale, he hurtled down the stairs and out the door, scattering tradesmen and hothouse flowers on Curzon Street.

In a fury at his brother, he walked, his head down, to St. James's Park, where he threw himself onto a bench. His stomach churned; he felt the burning sensation of unshed tears as he stared at the nursemaids strolling by with their little charges, and small boys braving a chilly wind to launch their vessels on the pond.

I am ruined, he thought.

* * *

Blessing Whittier had stood for some minutes at the door after watching Thomas Waggoner leave in the hackney. As kittens nipped and purred around her ankles, she asked herself again:

"Did I *really* tell Lord Thomas that I would attend a costume ball with him?"

She could never have done such a thing, she thought as she knelt to appropriate one particularly insistent kitten. "Has thee no manners?" she scolded, and then massaged the little one under its chin. "No more do I," she said. "Dear me."

Blessing was wide awake now. She walked slowly into

the sitting room, kittens trailing, and sat cross-legged on the sofa.

"I would like to be home in Nantucket. Rope is so uncomplicated," she announced to the kitten in her arms. "And I suppose thee will insist upon coming too."

The other kittens climbed the sofa and arranged themselves in her lap. *If we can truly save the ropewalk, I can let Mother Whittier know somehow that I would not object to marrying again,* she thought as she rubbed each kitten and increased the crescendo around her. *Of course, it will likely be to a widower with a ready-made family, but I can be content with that. I wonder, does Lord Thomas have blue eyes or gray?*

She was admiring the kittens in her lap and contemplating serviceable names for them when the doorbell jangled again. She was on her feet and down the hall in a twinkling, smiling to herself. *He must have found another kitten somewhere and means for me to keep it company,* she thought as she flung open the door.

It was the porter from the Admiralty House. "Oh!" Blessing exclaimed and stepped back, to the irritation of a kitten. She recognized him as the man who sat behind the high appointment desk. For almost a month she had watched him gaze out across the throng of petitioners and naval officers with a look of extreme distaste on his face that must have frozen into unpleasantness years ago and could not be altered.

"Mrs. Whittier?" he asked, removing the stocking cap he wore. There was nothing in his voice of disdain this time, and she came cautiously closer.

She nodded in acknowledgment, but did not let him in. He handed her a thick packet stamped with wax.

"Then this is for you, from Lord Renfrew," he said, and bowed as he backed away.

She watched, openmouthed, as he seated himself

again in the government vehicle outside the door and spoke to the driver. Slowly she closed the door and stared down at the package in her hands.

She wrinkled her nose. The packet was bound in canvas and sealed with tar, and she knew that it was a ship's log, or at least a part of one. She pulled it from the protecting canvas and traced the words on the cover with a hand that trembled. HMS *Dare*.

She ran down the hall, calling for Patience and tugging at the red cord that bound the log.

Soon she sat on Patience's bed and opened the folded sheet that accompanied the log. She held it out to her mother-in-law, but Patience, tears in her eyes, pushed it back.

"Oh, I cannot! You read it, my dear."

"'To the Mrs. Whittiers: This excerpt from the first and second weeks of August 1812 should satisfy your solicitors,'" she read. "Mother, it is signed and stamped!"

Patience was looking at the far wall. "Read the entries," was all she said.

Heads together, arms about each other's waists, Blessing and her mother-in-law read each entry of the log of the *Dare* during the very week that hostilities opened between England and the United States. Her voice faltering at times, Blessing read how the *Seaspray*, unaware, was caught in the Arctic whaling ground. In the dispassionate, spare style reminiscent of her own dead husband's log entries, she read the nameless captain's encounter with the whaler, the explosions, and then the men hunted down who had fled into the whaleboats. "Survivors, none," he had written with a bold flourish. "Salvage, naught."

Patience sat a long time gazing at the papers. She leaned against her daughter-in-law. "We are the better for knowing, Blessing," she said at last. "And we have proof for our creditors that it was an act of war. That should satisfy the solicitors." Tears welled in her eyes. "I only wish I felt better about it, my dear."

They cried together one last time; then Patience folded the papers, running her hand over the tarry bag. "Thee may sleep now, my husband and son," she whispered. "And we will run the ropewalk." She looked at her daughter-in-law for reassurance. "Blessing, can we make it turn a profit?"

"Mother, we can try," Blessing said, swallowing her tears. "I will continue to supervise the rope-making. We need to find a salesman."

Patience hugged her again. "Do you know, we owe thy young man such a debt."

"Mother, he is not my young man!" Blessing protested. "I only wish he would stop bringing me kittens."

Patience picked up the newest arrival, a striped mixture of the other two. "I suppose thee will yip and wail if we do not take thee along," she said, stroking the tiny kitten that purred so loud it shook. "Blessing, let us pack our trunks. We could even leave tonight for Portsmouth, if we hurry fast."

Blessing put a hand to her mouth. "Oh, dear, we cannot," she said. "Mother, you will not believe this, but I have promised to attend a Valentine's Eve costume ball at the Marquess of Cavanaugh's house this night."

Patience gasped, and the little kitten arched its back. She opened her mouth to protest and then looked down at the canvas parcel in her lap. She touched it. "Well, perhaps it is the least thee can do," she said. "A costume ball, did thee say? Blessing, thee grows quite wild with dissipation."

"I . . . I told him I should never," Blessing said. "He has a way of doing precisely as he wishes. It is a vexatious habit, Mother."

Patience only twinkled her eyes at her daughter-in-law.

"I cannot imagine anyone of our acquaintance behaving in such fashion. Can thee?"

"Mother!"

* * *

She was ready long before she heard the carriage outside the door and Lord Thomas's knock.

"Never?" he teased as he helped her into her cloak. "How glad I am you changed your mind."

"I owe you this," she said and then put her hand on his arm as she remembered. "Oh, Thomas! I mean, Lord Thomas. The note from Lord Renfrew came only this afternoon!"

"And?" he prompted.

"Mother Whittier has the log and a page proof, signed and stamped. It was the HMS *Dare* that sank the *Seaspray.*"

He was silent, watching. "It is hard to know," he said at last, his voice quiet.

She nodded and lowered her eyes. "They were hunted down like animals in their little boats."

He bowed over her hand and kissed it. "I am so sorry, my dear."

She let him continue holding her hand. "I need not spend any more of my nights wondering, and that is some consolation."

"I am sure that it is." He thought a moment. "Tell me, because Uncle Calcingham will ask me, I am sure. Was the porter who delivered the package polite?"

She opened her eyes wide. "Unusually so! Oh, when I think how rude . . ." She stopped in confusion. "Oh, but that is unimportant." She leaned closer. "How did thee know?"

"It was something you said . . . or maybe didn't say. Men who prey on helpless widows excite my censure. Even if you are American, and lately a belligerent," he added with a twinkle in his eyes. "I told him myself that if he did not treat you with good English courtesy he would never work again."

"Oh!" she said, her voice solemn. "I could never be so bold."

He only smiled and offered her his arm.

She took it and then took a good look at him for the first time. "Lord Thomas, thee looks fine as a new penny!"

He handed her into the carriage. "I wondered when you would notice," he said, climbing in beside her and tapping the side with the elegant ebony cane he carried. He seated himself and brushed at the front of his gray coat. "Since you would not—or could not—go in costume, I had to, of course. Tell me, my dear Blessing, did William Penn really wear a rig-out like this?"

She nodded, her eyes merry again. "I suppose he did. Thee would be a trifle outmoded now, but not by much. Thee would scarcely be out of place walking down Orange Street in Nantucket, nodding and tipping thy hat to my neighbors."

"So glad thee approves," he said, his eyes straight ahead, some lingering sadness or longing on his face. "I hope this costume ball is not a purgatory for you, but you will recognize Charles's light-o'-love, and I really would like a word with her before Charles is able to detach himself from his other guests."

"It is the least I can do, after all thee has done for us," she replied, her eyes on his face. "But what will thee do?"

"I had thought to pay her off to leave Charles alone, but what does my brother tell me this very day but that she is an earl's daughter from Northumberland, come to town. Do you think this possible?"

"No, Thomas, I do not," she said, forgetting his title at last. "She . . . she must be saying that to tempt him into an unwise marriage." She gasped as the knowledge took root. "She must suppose him to have a fortune!"

"This is odd, indeed, Blessing," he said, taking her hand. "She thinks to marry him for his money, and apparently he labors under the delusion that she is wealthy, if a trifle eccentric." He eyed her. "I wonder who will be the more disappointed?"

"Thee, I think," she replied slowly. "Thy brother is thoughtless beyond measure, but thee sought to save the family name, didn't thee?"

"I did," he replied. "I seem to have some memory, even if Charles does not, of days when Waggoner, Marquess of Cavanaugh, was a respected name and title."

"Perhaps thee will be able to avert some disaster," she said as they turned into Curzon Street and the carriage rolled to a stop behind others in a long line of guests. "My, for a rake, thy brother can command the attention of many people!"

He managed a wry smile. "We Waggoners have been well-known since William the Conqueror as impeccable hosts." He moved restlessly, stretching his long legs out in front of him. "If I can convince Charles . . ."

He turned to her, his eyes pleading. "Blessing, I am certain that it would take only a few years of judicious management. Perhaps Charles would have to sell his place in town, but what is that, if he can hang on to Cavanaugh? It is the prettiest estate in Kent, or at least it used to be."

"Oh, Thomas," she said, taking his hand.

"Waggoners have been born there since the time of Queen Bess," he said, his eyes on the carriage in front of them. "It is my home, and I mean to save it."

"I wish I could help. I truly do," she whispered.

He remembered himself and squeezed her hand. "What you're doing is enough. Just point out the fair damsel to me, and I will try my best to dissuade her."

The carriage moved forward. "And if thee does not succeed?" Blessing asked in a low voice.

"Then I am ruined, my dear," he said. "No self-respecting woman will have a second son with no prospects." He managed a crooked grin. "Even if Charles's amour throws him over, he'll find someone desperate enough, maybe a millowner's toothy daughter who'd like a title, no matter how shopworn. And then it still will never be the same again." He sighed and patted her hand. "It's a bit daunting to think of facing the world with a bad shoulder and no prospects."

Impulsively she kissed his cheek. "The worst has not happened yet, Thomas. Thee may very well be able to convince thy brother of his folly and save thy home. If I can help in any way . . ."

He smiled at her, his good humor restored. "Just stand by me, fair one, and I will feel a little more indomitable."

"Done, sir," she said as the carriage moved forward again and the postboy opened the door.

Clutching tight to Lord Thomas in his severe Quaker garb, Blessing entered the Marquess of Cavanaugh's residence at 11 Curzon Street. She looked about in delight at the winking chandeliers reflected in the expanse of mirrors, and the graceful sweep of the staircase that lifted to the floor above. Masked ladies and gentlemen strolled about and greeted each other. She sniffed deep of the perfume and pomade.

Thomas stared too. "I did not think that even our solicitors would be so generous," he muttered, holding her close to him as a party dressed as Napoleon's Life Guards strode through the hall, their bearskin shakos brushing the lower chandeliers.

He shuddered at the sight of them and then loosened his grip on her. "No one who was there that day at Waterloo would ever dress up like that. How I hate war," he said, more to himself than to her.

Blessing looked at him in dismay, powerless to erase

the desperation from his eyes. She stood in front of him a moment, straightening buttons that were not out of place, and then placed her hands on his chest. "But thee is a fine Quaker gentleman," she reminded him. "Thee can have nothing to do with war anymore."

He shook himself visibly and regarded her seriously. "Thee is right as always, Mrs. Whittier," he said. "How am I doing?"

"Excellently well, Thomas."

He bowed to her, an elegant bow that made her put her hands to her flaming cheeks.

"Does thee dance, Mrs. Whittier?" he asked.

She shook her head. "No! And do not think that thee can coerce me."

"I would never try," he protested, and then grinned at her. "Well, not above three or four times a day, I am sure."

She looked beyond him to the door, and there was the beauty of Albemarle Road.

In spite of her own stringent upbringing, Blessing Whittier blinked and stared at the spectacle before her. No matter that Angela Davenport had cluttered her face with too much powder and rouge; no matter that her laughter just edged on shrill; in that bit of silky gauze that clung to her generous frame, Miss Davenport was a sight to behold.

"Look over there," she said unnecessarily.

Thomas was already staring at the woman in the foyer. Blessing felt a momentary irritation. "But thee doesn't need to look so hard, William Penn!" she admonished and tugged at his sleeve.

"I am sizing up the enemy," he whispered back, not taking his eyes from the overblown sight before him. "Tell me, Blessing. Do you think that is one of the night-gowns you refused to wear last night?"

Blessing opened her mouth to protest and then

looked into Thomas's laughing eyes. "Thee is a rogue," she said, her voice low but distinct. Several guests did look around, and she blushed when they laughed. "Well, thee is," she insisted. "That is she, if thee ever had any doubts. And Lord bless us, she managed to shake off her chaperone."

Thomas nodded and watched the woman's stately progress from the door to the center of the hall, where she stood alone and stripped off her gloves, well aware of the eyes upon her, some appreciative, some wary. She looked around for Charles Waggoner, who stood across the hall at the card-room door, his back to her.

Thomas took Blessing's hand off his arm. "Wish me luck," he muttered as he stepped forward with a smile, holding out his hand to the woman.

"My dear, I am Thomas Waggoner," he said and bowed over her hand. "Charles's dull brother."

Angela tittered, her silly laugh grating on Blessing like fingernails on slate. *Well,* Blessing thought grimly as she watched Thomas Waggoner's graceful bow, *at least after this night I need not suffer that laugh through the walls of our apartment. I will be on a ship to Boston.*

In another moment Angela was hanging on Thomas's arm, leaning toward him as he made a joke, and then laughing louder.

"You needn't be so charming," Blessing murmured under her breath as the couple swept past her. She shook her head at her own discomfort. *Thomas, thee could probably sell tomahawks to Indians,* she thought as they moved down the hall.

Angela's laughter had captured Lord Cavanaugh's attention finally. With a bow to his gentleman friends entering the card room, he hurried into the hall to stand beside Blessing. He looked after his brother thoughtfully and then turned his attention to Blessing.

"Two Quakers, eh? Now, where would my slow-top brother ever dredge up a lady as tempting as you?"

He put his hand on her waist, and Blessing moved out of his reach. He reached for her again, his hand clasping her more firmly. "Let us follow them, my little Quakeress."

"Get thy hands off me," she said between clenched teeth.

Charles threw back his head and laughed. "Oh, and is *thee* an actress too? How far does this charade go?" He touched her under the chin, his fingers rough. "Where did my brother find you?" he murmured, his lips close to her ear.

When she did not answer, Charles laughed again and pulled her closer, tugging her along the hall after his brother. "I think he is up to no good, my dear. What do you say we find him?"

When she continued to pull away from him, he released her finally but continued in the direction his brother had gone. "Actually, I suspected that he would try to make my dearest Angela cry off even before we announced our engagement." He patted his coat pocket. "Let's see whom she believes."

He surveyed the closed doors. "Now, where . . ." he began. "I know. He has gone into the library. He knows that is a room I never think to enter." He opened a door and peered inside. "And I was right. Come, come, let us enjoy this little scene."

Angela Davenport and Thomas Waggoner stood close to the fireplace. Thomas was leaning forward and gesturing with some energy, but as soon as Charles Waggoner entered the room, Angela hurried toward him, awarding him a lingering kiss that made Blessing look away.

Her hands possessively on his shoulders, Angela stared back at Thomas, who stood with his lips tight together in an uncompromising line.

"Is he really your brother?" Angela asked.

"If I can believe my late mother," Charles replied and then sighed heavily. "Alas, every now and then there is a stuffy Waggoner. I cannot account for it, but there you are."

Angela formed her lips into a pout. "He claims that you have no money at all." She twined her arms around Charles's neck. "I told him that was silly. I mean, just look about this room!"

"I suspect even the books are mortgaged," Thomas said, his words clipped short.

Charles fixed a stare on his brother over Angela's shoulder that was not lost on Blessing. "Of course it's silly, dear heart," he purred.

Thomas made no move to come closer, but his voice carried, and Blessing felt a little shiver at the command in it. "I was merely suggesting to Miss Davenport that she might wish to visit our solicitors in the morning, Charles."

Charles yawned. "Thomas, you are too tedious! Angela has better things to do than visit a dreary solicitor's office." He kissed her. "We have so many wedding plans to make, don't we, my sweet?"

"Well, I suppose," Angela said after another glower at Thomas. "But he did say . . ." Her voice trailed off.

Charles patted his pocket again. "Besides, my angel, I have something here for you which ought to put a stop to any foolish notions about my worth."

Angela clapped her hands and then reached into Charles's pocket. She drew out a green velvet case. Blessing looked around in surprise as Thomas sucked in his breath.

"Charles, you wouldn't dare," he began and moved closer.

"Oh, wouldn't I?" Charles said. He opened the case and Blessing leaned closer for a look.

A many-stranded diamond necklace winked at her, all

fire and ice. As Blessing held her breath, Charles lifted it from the velvet nest and put it around Angela's neck.

"Diamonds for a lady," Charles said, his eyes on his brother.

"Blast your hide, Charles," Thomas said.

Blessing hurried to his side. "Not a scene now, Thomas," she urged.

He shook her off. "Yes, a scene now!" he shouted at his brother. "You would give the Cavanaugh diamonds away? Charles, you're certifiable!"

He was so angry he shook. Charles merely smiled at him serenely and then winked at Blessing.

"My dear, take Miss Davenport closer to the light of the fireplace. I think the clasp is not sufficiently in place."

"No," Blessing said as she took Thomas by the hand. "I won't."

Charles raised his eyebrows. "You're a managing baggage," he said, his voice soft.

She ignored his insult and leaned closer to Thomas. "And thee will control thyself," she said.

The brothers glared at each other. After a moment of vast discomfort, Angela shrugged her bare shoulders and flounced toward the fireplace, muttering something under her breath about "people of class with no manners."

"I have a mind to call you out," Thomas said to his brother.

Charles only smiled. "You can't even aim a pistol with accuracy anymore, Thomas dear, unless you've suddenly achieved ambidexterity." With a supercilious smile that made Blessing want to rend him from collar to boots, Charles came forward in conspiratorial fashion. "Besides, dear brother, they're only paste anyway. I am depending upon Angela's aging father, the earl from windy Northumberland, to cock up his crusty toes. Then I shall redeem them, and the devil of a lot more."

"Paste? The Cavanaugh diamonds?" Thomas gasped. "Merciful heavens, Charles! How long?" Charles attempted to stare down his brother's fierce gaze, but found himself regarding Angela preening herself in the mirror over the fireplace. "Oh, years and years," he said vaguely with a wave of his hand. "Tom, it's devilish hard to maintain horses the year around."

Thomas turned away, his eyes closed. He bowed his head, and Blessing found herself close to tears. She thought suddenly of the ropewalk that she had nurtured and led along through the days of her grief at Aaron's loss. *How would I feel if it were suddenly taken from me?* she thought as she rested her hand on Thomas's shoulder. To her surprise, he reached over and grasped her fingers. His hand trembled, and her heart went out to him.

"Then we are ruined," Thomas said, his voice scarcely audible.

Charles threw up his hands in exasperation and came around to face his brother. "Thomas, haven't you heard a word I have said? I am to marry into this juicy family." He frowned at Angela. "I suppose she is a little, well, less genteel than Mama would have wished. But, Thomas, she's rich."

How callous you English are, Blessing thought as she watched the brothers. She dabbed at the tears that spilled onto her cheeks and sniffed audibly.

For the first time, Lord Cavanaugh seemed to really take note of her presence in the room. His eyes narrowed as he watched her.

"And who, pray tell, are you, to intrude upon this tender family scene?"

Thomas turned around slowly, as if suddenly old beyond his years. "She is my friend," he said simply.

Charles grinned at his younger brother and raised his eyebrows. "So that's what you call them? Thomas, you needn't split hairs in such hardened company." He took Blessing's other hand, and before she could withdraw it, kissed her fingers. "I want to know how you convinced a Haymarket doxy to dress in Quaker gray. When you tire of her, just hand her down."

Before she could stop him, Thomas dropped her hand, hauled back, and struck his brother at the point of his jaw. Angela uttered an unladylike oath as Charles's eyes fluttered back in his head. A quizzical expression on his face, he sank to his knees and pitched forward, unconscious.

Angela threw herself on her knees beside the recumbent marquess. She shook him and then turned him over, hugging him to her ample proportions. "Charles," she murmured over and over. When there was no response, she began to sob.

Thomas regarded his bleeding knuckles ruefully.

"I have always wanted to do that," he said, more to himself than to Blessing. "I do not expect you to understand, but it felt so good." He grinned at her. "I won't do it again," he promised.

Thomas strolled to Angela and knelt beside her.

Humming to himself, he pulled back one of his brother's eyelids. "He's still in there," he said and turned to Angela. "My dear Miss Davenport. I don't know how to break this to you, but that necklace you are wearing is paste. Charles is truly to let. He had thought to marry you and replenish the family fortunes, but we both know that's a lie, don't we?"

Angela opened her eyes wider and pulled Charles closer to her. "Whatever do you mean?" she asked.

"I took a stroll to the registry office this afternoon. The only earl from Northumberland who could possibly be your father died five years ago and left his fortune to his housekeeper."

Angela raised her chin and tried to stare him down.

She looked away first. "That dratted housekeeper," she said between clenched teeth. "I thought the old scarecrow would at least mention me in his will." She looked at Blessing, her eyes imploring. "And he was me dad, even if it was not a regular affair."

Blessing shuddered and went to the window.

"You're petitioning the wrong party, Angela," Thomas said mildly. "Blessing is more scrupulous than the Waggoners, thank goodness, and obviously the Davenports too."

Charles began to stir, but he did not open his eyes. Thomas regarded him for a moment. "And you just picked Lord Cavanaugh out of a hat?"

By now Angela had lowered Charles Waggoner to the floor. "The old earl mentioned how rich you were." She touched the necklace. "Can you blame a girl for trying?"

Thomas smiled back, his affability restored. "I suppose not. Pity you picked someone so improvident." He helped Angela to her feet and directed her toward the door. "Don't be discouraged, my dear. There are any number of choice spirits present here this evening who would love to, ah, make you their valentine. Oh, and keep the necklace, by all means, my dear. Happy hunting, Angela . . . Angela . . ."

"Scrooby," she sighed. "That old buzzard never would admit I was his own flesh and blood." She poked Charles with her foot. "I hope I am a wiser girl, Lord Thomas."

"Glad the lesson was so instructive," Thomas commented as he closed the door behind her.

His expression thoughtful, Thomas turned to Blessing. "All's well that ends, my dear," he said. "Oh, and look, Charles is coming about. Well, thank heaven for that! I would hate to have disabled such a boil on the rump of humanity."

Hands in his pockets, he stared down at his brother

a moment. He sighed and turned away. "Come, my dear, and let me take you home. The emergency is over for the moment, I suppose."

They rode in silence. Thomas stared out the window, his thoughts miles away. Blessing knew that if she even made the smallest pleasantry, she would burst into tears, tears she would be hard put to explain away.

The carriage pulled up in front of 11 Albemarle Road. Thomas helped her down and stood beside her. "I suppose you are leaving soon?"

She nodded, careful not to look him in the eye. "Tomorrow we go to Portsmouth on the mail coach."

He held out his hand. "Glad I was able to be of service, Mrs. Whittier," he said, his voice casual, offhand.

She started to say something—what, she could never recall—when he grasped her by both shoulders, pulled her close, and kissed her soundly.

He needs consolation, was her first thought, and then she did not think anymore as she caressed the back of his neck and stood on tiptoe to make consolation easier. From her lips he explored her neck and then traveled up the line of her jaw to her lips again. She clung to him.

And then he was holding her away from him and looking at her as though he wished to memorize her face. She looked at his own dear face, more austere than she would have liked, and too solemn for his own good, but unspeakably important to her.

"May I write to you?" he asked finally, when he could speak.

She nodded. "Care of Whittier Ropewalk," she whispered and touched her fingers to his lips one last time.

Without a backward glance, she ran up the steps and into the house.

Hours later, morning found her still staring at the

ceiling, willing the sun to rise faster so she could leave sooner. Dry-eyed now after a night of tears, she contemplated her rope-bound trunk. *Patience must never know,* she thought. *It would make her so uncomfortable that I even considered for one minute what I have spent a whole night wrestling with. I dare not hurt someone so kind to me.*

Blessing was dressed and waiting for Patience to check through the house one last time when the doorbell rang. She leapt to her feet and ran to answer it.

The neighbor boy stood before her, cap in hand, holding out a package done up in frills and ribbons. He gestured with his head. "From that gentleman. You know."

Blessing smiled her thanks and tore off the wrapping paper. The boy watched, interested, and then sniffed and stepped back, muttering something about gentry and their strange notions of Valentine's Day.

Her heart marching at the double quick, she opened the box and burst into tears.

"I'd cry too, miss," the boy said.

A valentine, tarred and made of rope, lay nestled among tissue in the box. She dried her eyes on her sleeve and picked up the card. "'Happy Valentine's Day,'" she read out loud. "'A whiff of this every now and then ought to stave off the pangs of homesickness until thee is safely home in Nantucket. As ever, Tom.'"

The boy watched a moment in uncomfortable silence and then cleared his throat. "Ma'am, I think he's still waiting at the head of the street for a hackney."

With a cry, she dropped the box, picked up her skirts, and ran to the corner of Albemarle and Hose.

He stood where the lane turned, hands in his pockets, head down against the early-morning mist. He looked up and smiled as she approached but made no move.

"It's silly, I suppose," he said.

"It's beautiful," she assured him. "I've never had a valentine before. It's not something we Friends do."

He bowed in her direction, his voice light. "I will see that you have one every year, then. That should shock your neighbors."

She watched him. His tone was light, bantering, but his eyes reflected some new misery she had never seen before. She touched his arm. "Something has happened," she stated.

He nodded, at a loss for words. When he could speak, he gazed over her shoulder, as though he could not bear to look into her eyes. "I shouldn't have left Charles alone when I took you home last night."

Blessing drew in her breath and clutched his arm. "Oh, surely he did not . . ."

He shook his head again. "Oh, no, no! Nothing that dismal, my dear. Charles is too much of a coward to lift a hand against himself." He laughed, the sound bitter. "A hand!" He took a deep breath. "My brother lost the Cavanaugh estate and our house in town on the turn of a card last night at that dratted Valentine's party."

Blessing put her hands to her mouth. Speechless, she shook her head.

"He always swore he could turn a good hand. Well, now he has done it," Thomas said as he stepped into the street to hail a passing hackney.

The vehicle stopped and the driver opened the door. Thomas climbed inside before Blessing could stop him and closed the door.

"But what will thee do?" she managed to say as the driver seated himself again and looked down at her, no patience in his eyes.

"Stand away, miss," he ordered.

Blessing stamped her foot. "I will not!" She opened the door. "What will thee do?" she asked again, her voice more insistent.

"Pack, I suppose," Thomas said, not looking at her.

"Thee knows that is not what I mean!"

He took her by the hand. "I do not know, my very dear Mrs. Whittier. Do you know anyone who wants a broken-down soldier?"

I do, she wanted to say. Blessing let go of his hand but did not move away from the hackney. She took a deep breath.

"Thee must listen to thy Inner Light."

Thomas looked at her. "What?" he asked, his voice incredulous. "I tell you that the Waggoners have ruined themselves and you rattle on about 'inner light'?"

She backed away then, her hands behind her back, feeling all the embarrassment of her difference. All the humiliation of the last few months in England washed over her again, and she wondered what she was thinking.

"Yes, thy Inner Light," she repeated stubbornly. "Thee has one. It will tell thee what to do." She hesitated, her face red, and plunged ahead. "Does thee ever pray, Thomas?"

"Not since Waterloo," he muttered.

She raised her chin. "I recommend it."

She stepped back then and waved the driver on. Thomas did not look back. Blessing watched the hackney as it careened down the street crowded with early-morning merchants and the tattered sprites of Albemarle Road, staggering home after a late night.

Thee will likely never see him again, she thought as she started back to their rented rooms. Tears came to her eyes. She stopped and stood where she was until she had some measure of control over herself. It would never do for Patience to see how much Thomas Waggoner had come to mean to her in less than three short days. *She would call me impetuous, and she would be right,* Blessing thought. She sighed. *And he is not a Friend.*

Patience, well-covered in cloak and bonnet, stood

on the doorstep, holding the wicker basket of kittens. A hackney waited in front, their luggage already inside.

Silent, her face composed, Blessing retrieved her rope valentine where she had dropped it in her hurry to chase after Thomas.

"He is certainly an Original Item," was Patience's only comment. A smile lurked around her lips. "Does thee think it is a good length of cable?"

Blessing forced herself to enter into the spirit of Patience Whittier's gentle joke. "Not as good as Whittier Ropewalk can do, Mother," she said.

Patience was too kind to continue her scrutiny. She set down the kittens. "Unless thee has some additional pressing duty in London, I suggest that we shake the dust off our boots and go home."

Blessing nodded. She put on her own cloak and bonnet. Taking up the kittens that mewed in their basket, she followed her mother-in-law to the hackney. "And I will try a bit of my own medicine and listen to the Inner Light," she whispered under her breath.

* * *

If she felt disinclined to speak much on the journey by mail coach to Portsmouth, and to say still less while they waited in the inn for the *Josiah Dabney* out of Boston to finish stowing cargo, Blessing could only thank Providence for Patience's forbearance. Several times her mother-in-law seemed on the verge of conversation that could only prove difficult. Each time, she stopped and did not ask questions. Her soft-spoken reminders to Blessing to eat her dinner and not stand on the dock so late contemplating the waves, carried no reprimand.

Patience's voice was gentle as always, her eyes full of sympathy. Blessing knew without saying a word that Patience was fully aware of her personal agony. *Someday when I have passed this difficult point, I will thank her for her circumspection,* she thought as she leaned on the ship's rail finally and watched the topmen lower the mainsail.

She gazed seaward and took an appreciative sniff. The smell of hemp and tar was all around her now, reminding her of home, but even more forcefully of Thomas Waggoner.

"What will thee do, my dear?" she whispered. "Where will thee go?" She waited for the captain to give the command to weigh anchor. The sailors on the deck waited too, resting their arms on the capstan, their eyes on that worthy who stalked the poop deck.

"Why do we not go?" she asked Patience crossly.

Patience had turned her gaze to the far shore. "I think there is a Johnny-come-lately passenger," she said, her hand shielding her eyes from the sun on the water. "Thee would think he would know about winds and tides and urge the waterman to row faster."

"Perhaps he is a lubber, Mother," Blessing said, her eyes on the water.

In another moment she heard Patience chuckling to herself. Patience touched her arm, her voice filled with amusement, and tremulous with another emotion.

"Look, my dear, oh, do look!"

Mystified by Patience's curious insistence, Blessing crossed the deck to the lee side. Patience was leaning over the rail now, waving.

"Mother, whatever . . ." Blessing began and then stopped, her eyes wide. She clung to the rail and stared at the sight below her.

Clutching his saddle, an expression of real preoccupation on his face, Lord Thomas Waggoner sat in the harbor dinghy that pitched beside the *Dabney*. He was looking dubiously at the chains hanging over the *Dabney* as the waterman gestured to them.

Blessing could only stare. Patience took in the

situation and turned to the boatswain, who was motioning impatiently for Thomas to hand up his saddle and then climb the web of chains.

"Thee does not understand," she was saying calmly. "He cannot climb the chains because of an old injury. Waterloo," she added for good effect.

"I've already stowed the chair," said the boatswain, one eye on the captain, who glowered down from the poop deck.

"Then throw him a bowline," Patience said. "He has the wit to know what to do with it."

The boatswain did as Patience Whittier suggested. In another moment, Thomas Waggoner, his arms still tight around his saddle, was deposited on the deck. His duffel followed, and the captain boomed out, "If his worshipful lordship is happy now, we will weigh anchor." His Yankee voice was heavy with sarcasm.

Blessing took the saddle from Thomas and handed it to a seaman, who whistled at it and took it below. "Thee'll have to excuse the captain," she said, her attempt at calm undone by the quaver in her voice. "I think we Yankees can be every bit as rude as ye British."

Thomas straightened his coat. "I expect so." He nodded to Patience, who smiled back.

"Blessing, I had best go belowdecks and comfort the wretched kittens," she said, a twinkle in her eyes.

"Lovely lady, is your mother-in-law," Thomas said. "I wonder, do you think she likes me?" He led Blessing to the rail that faced the open water. "I'd rather not look back," he said as the sails boomed and the ship began to move. He looked down at the water.

"I did what you recommended," he said at last and took hold of her hand. "I listened to my Inner Light."

Blessing let out the breath she had been holding and squeezed his hand. "And . . . and what did it tell thee?"

He laughed. "You won't believe . . . well, yes you will. Something very distinctly told me to sell my horse." He put his arm around her. "It gave me a pang, I can tell you. I rode her to Tatt's for the last time and got my passage money."

"I'm sorry thee had to sell thy horse," she said. She hesitated a moment and then put her arm around his waist. "I thought . . . Didn't thee say thee had some money to bribe Angela Davenport with?"

He nodded. "I did, but I thought Charles could use it." He scratched his head. "Which brings me to a delicate bit of negotiation here, Mrs. Whittier of Whittier Ropewalk. I haven't a sixpence to scratch with and will be needing employment. Do you think I could sell rope to Yankees?"

Blessing stood on tiptoe and kissed his cheek.

"I think thee could sell lions to Christians, Lord Thomas!"

He winked at her but shook his head. "No, Blessing, it's just plain 'Tom Waggoner' now. Isn't there something in your Constitution about no titles?" He pulled her closer to his side. "I wonder, does the Society of Friends ever admit new Friends?"

"Those who truly believe, Tom Waggoner," she replied, her voice soft.

He smiled back and turned around for one last look at Portsmouth before it disappeared behind Harbor Island. His eyes clouded for an instant and he took a deep breath. Still looking at the receding shore, he raised her hand to his lips.

"Then let us voyage, my dear," he said. His eyes grew merry again as he turned to the windward side. "Does thee know, I was thinking on the mail coach, what does thee think about calling it 'The New England Ropewalk'? I mean, if it's as good as you . . . thee . . . says, then Whittier Ropewalk should cover the region."

She laughed out loud. He pulled her closer to him, even as the deck began to heave.

"I love thy laugh, Blessing," he said. "I hope to hear it for years and years to come." He leaned closer, his tone more confidential. "Does thee ever get seasick?"

"Not after the first day," she said, wishing that all the ship's hands weren't on deck, and the captain himself watching them.

He frowned. "Well, I will be. That was my last good suggestion for several weeks." He looked around, and kissed her again, to the cheers of the sailors clinging to the rigging. "I trust it will be enough to get me a job." He touched his forehead to hers. "I am planning to marry me a wife in Nantucket and should be gainfully employed."

A HASTY MARRIAGE

THE MARRIAGE OF ANN UTLEY, SPINSTER, from an excellent Derbyshire family, to Capt. Hiram Titus, widower, of the *Hasty* sailing from Boston, came about because of an international abduction. Or so the matter was reported to Miss Utley's mother, who shrieked upon hearing the news and prepared herself for a faint that never came, because the woman delivering the tidings seemed unappreciative of upper-class melancholia. In fact, Aggie Glossop, former governess to the said Miss Utley, appeared to be delighted by the whole turn of events. She even shook her finger at Mrs. Utley. "And don't say anything about marrying so fast. Ann has been waiting for this man all her life."

It came about this way . . .

* * *

No matter how many times he made the Atlantic crossing, Hiram Titus, captain and owner of the *Hasty*, always felt a little easier when his merchant vessel had wallowed past the sleek frigates in Portsmouth Harbor and his papers were safely in the hands of the harbormaster. In this Year of Our Lord 1807, with American distress with England, he knew that the master would give his ship's lading a good scrutiny. He was ready; he was also prepared with a notarized crew roster, which listed all his boys as loyal sons of New England, conceived and born on American shores. Not for him the danger of an undercrewed warship hauling off his men because they were Britishers who had declared for American citizenship. Curse England anyway, a country that didn't recognize that a man could change his allegiance. Because that was how matters stood, Captain Titus knew he had to dot every *i* and cross every *t* every time any of his merchant fleet left American waters. If Titus was anything, he was careful. He couldn't think of a time in his life when he had ever rushed into anything.

It helped to know the harbormaster too. An exchange of pleasantries, an offer of Madeira, and then both men were comfortably seated in the office that overlooked the scruffy town.

"We haven't seen you in ages, Captain," the harbormaster said after his first appreciative sip. "You've not been shipping to France on the sly?"

"I would rather drink Boney's bathwater than do that," Titus replied promptly, because he knew it was what the master wanted to hear. He leaned forward in his chair, remembering how easy it was to take the man's mind off trade. No need for him to know that a ship or two of Titus Maritime occasionally wandered profitably into French Caribbean waters. "As a rule, I don't conn my own ships anymore." He was not the man to play a sympathy card, but the way things stood in the world, one never knew. "My dear wife died six years ago, and since then I have remained at home. Our oldest boy follows the sea, one twin is at Harvard, and the other works for Astor's fur company, but I still have a young daughter at home who needs me."

"Admirable of you," the master replied. He poured himself another drink, not even observing that Titus hadn't drunk more than the obligatory first sip. "You have relatives watching her now?"

"She came with me, sir. She is ten and old enough. Besides, it is summer, and what is better than the ocean in summer?" *Even coming to Britain's cloudy, foggy shores,* he thought but didn't add. Too bad that England was not blessed with American weather. "I lay the principal reason before you, sir: The captain of the *Hasty* came down with the shingles suddenly, so I took his place."

The harbormaster poured himself another glass. "I thought it must be something dramatic, Captain Titus. You never were one to rush precipitately into a situation."

No, I never was, Captain Titus thought as he left the office, still quite sober, and full of information about the political situation that the master probably never would have divulged had he been more upwind of all that Madeira. So change was in the offing? He would be long on his way before that happened.

He stood outside the harbormaster's office, admiring the glint of the afternoon sun on the dark water of Portsmouth's excellent harbor. For one moment he felt a great longing to be sailing into Boston's own inimitable harbor. Despite all his years at sea, he was not a man to roam. Although he never would have wished sweet Tamsin's death, never in a million years, he was honest enough to admit that her untimely passing gave him every excuse to remain in port with their young children. He could hire others to sail his ships, and he did. So it went, and so it would go this time. Glossop's Nautical Emporium would have his return cargo in their warehouse already, of that he was certain: lace from Nottingham, knives and cutlery from Sheffield, woolens from Manchester's mills, straw-filled barrels of pottery, and tea from India. In the morning, dockyard workers would be off-loading pitch, rum, lumber, fur, and tallow from the *Hasty*. He would revictual promptly, and be gone in a week or so with a good tide. He would like to have taken Charity to London, but with the way events stood, it was probably best to stay close to Portsmouth. London would keep until more settled times. A week in port, another eight at sea, and he would be home in Boston.

It was a longish walk from the harbormaster's to the Nautical Emporium, but he relished every rolling step of it, secure in the knowledge that his sea legs would be gone by the time he crossed Ned Glossop's doorstep. Six years! He had been thirty-four on his last voyage. Now his sons were grown. Soon there would be wives and babies as another generation rolled around. The deuce of it: He was young yet, even though his shaving mirror told him middle age had approached, or was at least nigh. He smiled to himself; Tamsin would have laughed at his whining and told him to get another mirror.

Well, no matter; here he was at Glossop's Nautical Emporium. He stood there in the wagon yard a moment, looking around. *Interesting*, he thought. He knew it had been six years, but things were tidier. There would always be a certain amount of clutter in a wagon yard, but the trash was stowed, the kegs lined up neat against the wall like good soldiers, and coiled rope obviously had a place to call its own. Titus could credit only one event with this unexpected order: Ned Glossop must have gotten leg-shackled, no easy feat when one limb was wooden. He smiled to himself, guessing that the old rogue probably couldn't run fast enough.

"As I live. It can't be! Captain Titus himself?"

The smile still on his face, Titus looked up to an open hatch on the second floor of the warehouse. "The very same, Ned! I can't believe the merchant marines haven't hanged you for one keg of squealing beef too many!" he called.

Glossop laughed. True to his naval roots, he wrapped his legs—one real, one not—around a rope and handed himself down to the ground. By the time he got there, Titus was across the yard to shake his hand.

"Didn't think we'd see you again, Captain," Glossop said, shaking his hand vigorously. "Captain Peabody told us of your wife's death, and we are sorry." He looked around. "But where's Peabody? The lading bill did say to expect the *Hasty*."

"And she is here. Peabody's laid up in Boston with shingles." Titus looked around the yard. "I've never seen this place so tidy. What's happened to you in the past six years?"

"A wife, sir, a wife," Glossop told him. He leaned closer, as though he expected her to leap out from some corner. "She was a governess to gentry, so I hop to when she barks."

The glint in the merchant's eyes assured Titus that Glossop suffered no ill-usage. So did the extra roll of flesh around the man's middle.

Glossop followed the captain's glance and nodded. "I haven't suffered overmuch." He patted Titus's flat stomach. "That and a wrinkled neck cloth tells me that you haven't fared as well, laddie." His voice was kind.

"I have been over seven weeks at sea," Titus reminded him. "'Tis hard to get a laundress to come aboard. Did you ever try to put a flatiron on gimbals?"

The two men laughed over the nautical joke. Titus handed Glossop his stamped papers from the harbormaster. "What with the national climate, my friend, perhaps we'd better start swinging out my cargo tomorrow morning."

"Nothing simpler, Captain. Come on in now and meet Aggie Glossop." He tapped his wooden leg. "She keeps me on my toes! All five of 'em."

In less than a minute he was bowing to a dignified

woman with impeccable posture on the downward slope of fifty. "Mrs. Glossop, I must commend you for the way you've cleaned up old Ned here. I never thought a warehouse could be tidy."

The look she flashed her husband was a fond one, even if her words were a trifle starchy. "Captain Titus, anyone can be neat if he puts his mind to it."

All of a sudden Hiram Titus wished he had found a way to smooth out his neck cloth, or at least brush seven weeks of stains from his coat. Time to change the subject and fast. "Ned tells me that you were a governess for gentry."

It was a topic that must have suited her, because she seemed to relax. "Ah, yes, the Utleys of Derbyshire, for nearly twenty years," she said, and the starch was gone from her words. "An excellent family of quality, Captain. You won't find better-behaved young ladies anywhere."

* * *

Not until Ann Utley was sitting on her rump with her skirts up around her knees did it occur to her that perhaps she had just committed a rash act. She tugged down her skirts and looked around quickly for Papa's grip that he had taken with him on the Grand Tour years ago, when people could still visit France. It was lodged by Mama's roses, having missed the rain barrel by a few inches.

She stood up and wiped the dew off the back of her dress, grateful that she had earlier thrown down her cloak. It was draped sedately over the lowest tree limb, quite within reach. With that subdued garment—sober enough for an old maid—around her against the morning chill, no one would see the grass stains on her kerseymere. She put on the cloak and retrieved the grip, then waited, wondering if she wanted to be found or wanted to escape.

Standing by the oak tree, she wavered. No one

appeared to be about except the goose girl, who sat by the pond with her charges. Ann knew her mother never left her chamber before eleven o'clock, and the servants were still at breakfast. Her sister Clotilde—their brother in Spain called her Cloth Head—wasn't expected back from her fiancé's estate until later in the day. Ann looked at the timepiece in her reticule. She had at least until early afternoon, when Sir Barnaby Phillips would be toddling over for a serious conversation.

At least, so he had informed her with arch looks and a giggle over whist at Lord and Lady Stouffer's last night. "My dear Miss Utley, it is high time I spoke to your mother about a matter of the heart," he had whispered, while Lord Stouffer was noisily shuffling the deck. She had almost burst into nervous giggles of her own when he thumped his ample chest and started to cough from the exertion. Lady Stouffer had only given him a squinty-eyed glance. "Raise your arms, you twerp," she commanded of her nephew, and he had meekly obeyed.

Ann had seen him ridiculous before, but there was something about watching a grown man with his arms in the air in the middle of a drawing room that made her decide that it was time to run away and avoid the proposal she knew was coming the next day. Never mind that she had promised her mother that she would accept whatever proposal she got, since it would be the fourth or fifth since her come-out years ago. Even if she had promised, no amount of cajoling would convince her that a man in subjection to his aunt was the husband for her.

She did not expect another proposal. True, she was a trifle tall, but never considered that a deficit, especially after her brother, in a sodden condition, had informed her that men liked women with long legs. She never had the nerve to ask why, but some innate delicacy told her that it was probably something ladies found out after the nuptials. She had a nice face, having been informed of such on several occasions by men who weren't even fortune hunters. Ann thought she was too bosomy; at least, Dame Fashion had decreed that bosoms were not à la mode this year. Even Clotilde, who understood almost no jokes, had to smile when Ann announced that she had no idea where to stash her bosoms until they became stylish again.

Her mother blamed her eldest daughter's lack of success on the independent income Papa had left her. "If you had a little less money, you'd be inclined to look harder," Mama had told her once in a rare burst of candor. "Young ladies with incomes can be notoriously picky."

As she continued to stand under the tree and stare up at the room she had quitted so impulsively, Ann did not doubt the truth of her mother's words. "Mama, I do not have to choose just anybody," she had announced several years ago, after Lord de la Ware—too old, too prosy, too *satisfied*—had slammed the door of their town house so hard that a Ming vase crashed to the parquet.

And so she had chosen nobody, not so difficult an enterprise when one was nineteen, or even twenty-one. In sad fact, it had become easier as the years passed. *Ah, well.* Ann brushed the dirt off her dress. While she had felt smug and wise at twenty-two, now that she was facing thirty-two, she admitted to some distress. No panic, though—panic was only for the desperate.

She stared up at her window again. *Did I just crawl down the tree?* she asked herself with amazement. *Does the thought of Sir Barnaby terrify me that much?* When she realized that it did, she picked up Papa's valise and started across the field to Stover Green and the Speckled Hound, where she knew the mail coach always stopped. She had left a detailed note on her pillow for her mother, telling her precisely where she was going and assuring her that she would be home for Clotilde's August nuptials. *Don't be upset, Mama*, she had written. *I just cannot marry a man I see no hope of ever loving.*

Her long legs ate up the two miles to the village quickly, but not so quickly that she did not have time to admit that only a desperate woman would let herself out of a second-story window and run away like a child. She knew it was not a matter of disliking men; men were fine and had their place in the world, same as she. Ann Utley was just audacious enough to hope that somewhere in the world—certainly not in Derbyshire—there must be a man who wouldn't incline her to flight.

The mail coach was a new experience. She hadn't even been sure how one went about procuring a seat, but it had been a simple matter to stand in the line at the Speckled Hound and eavesdrop shamelessly on the comments of potential riders in front of her. By the time she got to the agent selling tickets, she knew to state Portsmouth as her destination and ask for an inside seat.

"Portsmouth, miss?"

"Yes, please." Thank goodness Papa had always advised her to keep money on hand. She had generally used it to bail out Clotilde when she overspent her quarterly allowance and didn't wish Mama to know.

"You'll go as far as London and purchase the rest of your route there."

"London? Yes, certainly." In the city she would send a letter by express to Mrs. Glossop and visit her banker. If she had lost her nerve by then, she could return to Derbyshire and Sir Barnaby's sweaty, predictable embrace. What a pity that ladies could not purchase commissions in the army, or take Orders!

* * *

In his hurry to be away from England, Captain Titus knew that he had miles to go before he could ever hope to achieve his own father's legendary patience. What should have taken only one long day, to swing his cargo on deck and off-load it to a little fleet of lighters that would ferry it to shore, had stretched into three days. Ned Glossop had been apologetic; he had no more patience than Titus over the delays.

"I blame the French, Captain," the man had said two nights later over dinner with Titus and Aggie. "What with more and more warships sailing with each tide and that blockade, the navy's sent out the press gangs until hardly any blokes dare show their faces on the docks."

Although Titus knew that his daughter, Charity, didn't understand, she still pressed closer to him. She would have questions for him as they were rowed back to the *Hasty*, and he wasn't sure how to explain war to a ten-year-old. He could only reassure her that they would be on their way soon and back on the open sea again, even as the days stretched longer in port.

"You can't get even a quorum of longshoremen?"

Ned shook his head. "Captain, I haven't managed that in over six months." He glanced at Mrs. Glossop. "Aw, Aggie, we've been through worse stretches, haven't we?"

"Indeed we have, Mr. Glossop," the woman said. She smiled at Charity. "In a few years things will look better, my dear Charity. You can come back here and your papa will take you to London." She leaned closer with an air of conspiracy that Titus figured had endeared her to many little girls. "I can tell him all the best shops when you come back again."

Charity nodded and relaxed against him. Titus tightened his grip on her shoulder. "Depend upon it, Chary," he told her. "I'll take you to emporiums and entertainments, and maybe even a play." He sighed. "But as for now . . ."

"I don't mind, Papa," she assured him. She looked at

their hostess. "Papa says you were a governess. Do we have those in Boston, Papa?"

"You don't!" He took another sip of wine. "You have an Aunt Mercy, who has consented to let you out of her sight for this voyage only."

Charity made a face. "Mrs. Glossop, does a governess make people mind, and keep their aprons clean, and insist upon clean stockings and soap behind the ears, even though it's only been two days since the last time?"

"That is *precisely* what governesses do, Charity," Aggie Glossop said as she rose to clear the table. "I also administered the rudiments of reading, spelling, arithmetical configurations, and provided heavy doses of good manners." She sat down again, and her eyes were kind. "Is that what your Aunt Mercy does?"

"All the time." Charity sighed and glanced at her father. "She tells me I am her sole occupation."

Ned Glossop laughed, and handed her a bowl of nut meats. "My dear, do you know that Mrs. Glossop received a letter yesterday from her last pupil? She told us she has run away from home."

"I tried that once," Charity said, "and Aunt Mercy helped me pack! She took all the fun out of leaving, so I decided to stay." The adults at the table laughed. "How old is she, Mrs. Glossop? Maybe she got tired of too much porridge, or . . . or brushing her hair one hundred strokes every morning and night."

"I rather think it was something else," the woman replied, and Captain Titus could not overlook the worry etched into her forehead. "Charity, she is thirty-two years old."

Charity gasped, then looked at her father with considerable alarm. "Papa, tell me that Aunt Mercy will not be looking out for me when I am so old! I could not endure that much porridge."

"I promise, Chary," he told her.

"I think it's a beau that won't step up to the mark," Glossop said. He popped a handful of nut meats into his mouth. "Right, Aggie?"

Titus tried not to smile, not with Mrs. Glossop looking so serious. Thirty-two and not married? Likely she was desperate because there was no beau in sight. For all the good breeding and manners that Mrs. Glossop insisted upon, this charge of hers must be a Gorgon.

The worry on Mrs. Glossop's face was genuine. "Maybe she just needs a change of scenery, Ned."

The merchant snorted. "Then she should be drinking the water at Bath, or taking a walking tour in the Lake District. Young ladies don't come running to their governesses in Portsmouth warehouses."

Thirty-two is hardly a young lady, Titus thought. *We call them antique virgins at home.* "Ned, perhaps you can put her to work in the warehouse," he said. "I notice you're shorthanded at the clerk's bench too."

Ned slapped a meaty hand on the table and chortled as though the captain had told the funniest stretcher in years. "What will folks think of us, Aggie? Imagine asking Quality to sit on a clerk's stool and copy bills of lading!"

"I think that might be an excellent proposition to put forward to Miss Utley when she arrives," was Aggie Glossop's surprising answer. "If she is going to run away, she can at least be useful."

After Aggie Glossop had fussed sufficiently over Charity, advising her to bundle up against the dockside chill and vague disorders and diseases, Ned Glossop walked them down to the wharf. "Mind you, Captain Titus, I do not think that navy press gangs would waylay you"—he lowered his voice so not to alarm Charity—"but do warn your crew."

"I have, Ned, and thank you for your concern."

Ned saw them into the waterman's ferry. "Come back tomorrow or the day after, and perhaps you will see Miss Ann Utley sitting on that clerk's stool!"

Titus laughed and then nodded to the waterman to take them into the channel. "Not if your good wife fears that her former charge will blind us with her beauty!"

"Aye, she could do that," Ned replied as he waved them off. "She could."

I will believe that when pigs fly, Titus thought as he wrapped his own boat cloak around his daughter, who was shivering. Obviously the Glossops had blinkers on regarding the runaway Miss Utley. No thirty-two-year-old spinster of his acquaintance was easy on the eyes.

* * *

After two restless nights at the Claridge, and a lengthy, somewhat argumentative visit to her solicitor, Ann Utley was completely convinced that it was against man's nature to be anything but duplicitous. Even when she stood on the pavement again outside of the firm of Rindge and Rumble, her reticule heavy with coins and paper, it did not seem fair to her that it should be so *difficult* to accomplish what men of business did every day. She doubted that anyone ever argued with her brother when he came by for funds, and she was certainly his equal in prudence and sound management.

She sighed. By the time the young Mr. Rindge had shown her to the door, his lips were set in a firm, disapproving line. At least he had not tut-tutted like his father and assured her that her mother knew best. "Marriage will settle you down, my dear Miss Utley," the old man had said, as though she were a wild creature and not a lady of mature years who was—until this regrettable incident—a nonpareil of decorum. "Go home and marry Sir Barnaby," he had said, when she had poured out her distress to him, a family friend who also knew Sir Barnaby.

When she had asked him point blank if he would wish such a silly man on his own daughters, he had at least possessed the honesty to look away before he recovered with the argument that—little did he know—sealed his future career as her solicitor: "My dear, look at it in this light: He has his own family money, so he will never trouble you much, and you will eventually have children to occupy your time."

Her face went red as she stood there on the street. *And what happens when the children are grown and we are back staring at each other over the breakfast table?* she asked herself. *Is my next consolation the grave?*

She knew she was being overly dramatic, but her sense of misuse persisted all the way to Portsmouth. The only balm to her wounded heart was her dear Aggie standing there with arms wide open when Ned carried her bandbox upstairs above the merchant office and stood back, carefully out of the way of two women with a long history between them. The tears came then. She let her old governess lead her to the settee, where she sobbed her misery onto the generous woman's shoulder.

"Aggie, *why* must I live my life to suit others? Have I truly become too discerning for my own good?"

From long acquaintance—although not recently—Ann knew that Aggie would answer neither question, but just hold her and let her sob; any homilies and advice would come later, when she was more of a mind to listen. Beef stew followed the tears, and then a comfortable bed with a warming pan followed the beef stew. The last thing she remembered was Aggie pulling the blanket up to her shoulders, touching a hand to her cheek, and saying something about "putting you to work to take your mind off your troubles."

Ann was in far better spirits when she woke. She put her hands behind her head and settled more comfortably into the mattress. *I really am too old to be so indecisive about Sir Barnaby,* she thought. *I have been completely aware of his interest for these three years and more, so I should not run away when he finally does what I had thought he would do all long. Is he really too silly, or am I too critical?*

No, he was too silly, she decided as she dressed and made her bed. It was up to her now to weigh his faults against the growing probability that no one else would ever offer for her. What a shame that the world was so imperfect.

She had not misheard her old governess. Aggie Glossop announced over tea and toast that she was putting her to work in the warehouse.

"Well, my dear, Mr. Glossop instructed me to ask you, and I assured him that you would be delighted to be of assistance."

Ann laughed and set down her teacup. "This is a novel experience!" She leaned toward her former governess. "My solicitors will be relieved to know that I can earn a living, considering my advanced years. That is, if you intend to pay me!"

"Not a penny," Aggie replied, and both women laughed. "This is for your room and board." She frowned then. "I do not know how well insulated you are against world currents, my dear, but we are nearly at war with the Americans, France is a nuisance, our navy is desperate for seamen, and dockworkers are in short supply because the press gangs nab them. It has become nigh impossible for us to hang on to our workers. Would you clerk for us?"

"I will, indeed," Ann said quietly, and then her merry heart revived. "Obviously a spinster will be in no danger from press gangs!"

And so she found herself in the warehouse in a sober gown belonging to Mrs. Glossop (they were much the same size), sitting on a high stool and copying lading bills.

Aggie herself walked the aisles of the warehouse, reconciling the invoices to the merchandise, within easy distance for help. So far Mrs. Glossop had patiently explained that *three cases of fried rod, exalted*, really meant *three cases of dried cod, salted*.

"What dreadful handwriting," Ann murmured, as she dipped the pen in the well.

Mrs. Glossop nodded to her when the door opened.

"There is the author of that wicked list, Ann. You can call him to account."

* * *

Titus was wrong. He was so wrong that he could only stand in the warehouse doorway and gawk like the greenest, most callow young man who ever shipped to a foreign port and ogled the local females. He resisted the urge to stuff his eyeballs back into his head.

The loveliest woman he had ever clapped eyes on sat at the clerk's desk, dangling one shoe off a foot that possessed—even at the distance of his perusal—a completely trim ankle. She looked at him in a quizzical way, then turned back to the document in front of her. He felt his heart almost thud to a halt in his chest.

She had taken little or no time with her hair, so he assumed that Aggie Glossop had snatched her directly from the breakfast table to the warehouse like the press gangs she abhorred. The lady—she could only be a lady—had wound her hair into a funny topknot, but most of the curls had already escaped. He didn't see many women in England with black hair, and none at home in New England, except among Indians. Her skin was radiant with health, her cheeks tinged with the delicate pink that a gentle, cool climate allowed. She frowned and pursed full lips as she stared at the paper in front of her. He wanted to act like the worst of seamen and plant a smacking great kiss on her.

He brought himself up short then, embarrassed at his untoward flight of male fancy, and reminded himself that he was forty years old, sober, and the father of sons old enough to marry and make him a grandfather. Still, just gaping at that vision of loveliness in a Portsmouth warehouse was probably going to require a cold sea bath tomorrow morning.

And here was Mrs. Glossop now, talking to him, but it might have been Swahili or Urdu, for all that he was paying attention. He forced himself to listen to her.

". . . and she has consented to help me here in the warehouse."

"What? Who?" he asked, embarrassed when his voice cracked like a fourteen-year-old's. Charity, standing beside him, giggled.

Mrs. Glossop began again, and he could not overlook the humor in her eyes. "Captain Titus, I want to introduce you to Miss Ann Utley of Derbyshire."

"Papa, you're supposed to move forward and bow, I think," Charity whispered. That was all it took. Chary was but ten, and he couldn't have her thinking her father was a complete nincompoop. That would come later, when she was fourteen or so. "Oh. Right," he said and crossed the warehouse, hoping that he would not trip over a dust mote, and wishing he were handsome and a wee bit younger.

It was gauche, but he held out his hand to her. Miss Utley's hand was cool and firm. "Delighted to meet you," she informed him, and weirdly, he hoped she meant it. "And this is your daughter?"

"Charity," he said. His heart lifted when his daughter made a pretty curtsy. "She is ten and making her first voyage to England."

Miss Utley smiled at his daughter. "You are probably wondering if the sun ever shines here, my dear."

"It *is* a little gloomy," Chary said.

Oh, my word, not to me, Titus thought. All the angels of social grace were urging him to stop staring, but he could not help himself. "We do get more sunshine in Boston," he informed her, then winced at the astringent Yankee-ness of his twangy voice. *You dolt, she does not need a weather report,* he told himself.

"And so do we get more sun in Derbyshire," she told him. Her eyes were the blue-green of the ocean in mid-Atlantic. She was looking at his daughter again. "But I am a runaway, Charity, and we must lump the good with the bad!"

Charity laughed, and he could not help smiling at the incongruity of Miss Utley's words. "Ladies who are your age do not run away," Charity said.

"They don't? Oh, dear me."

Charity looked at Miss Utley thoughtfully and came closer. The lovely lady on the stool twitched at his daughter's collar, smoothing it flat in an unconscious gesture.

"Well, I did." She took a deep breath, and Titus could tell it was a touchy subject. "But enough of that. My dear, can you decipher your father's handwriting?"

Charity came even closer and leaned against Miss Utley. She had never taken so quickly to a stranger, but watching them both, Hiram Titus had to agree that there was something about Miss Utley that welcomed children. And him, too. Heaven knows *he* wanted to lean against Miss Utley.

"I can read it mostly."

The lady looked at him again, the smile in her eyes unmistakable. "Then let us ask your father to find us another stool. You can sit by me and translate."

Surprisingly, Mrs. Glossop held out her hand to his daughter. "Come with me a moment, Charity. I can find a stool and you can carry it back." She clapped her hands and glared at Miss Utley. "And *you* can get back to work!"

Miss Utley only laughed and blew a kiss at her former governess. *My word.* He was alone now with her. If he hadn't already taken Mrs. Glossop's stern measure, he would have suspected her of doing that deliberately. Titus felt his collar growing tighter. It was as though he had never spoken to a woman in his life. He thought miserably that Tamsin must be sitting on some celestial cloud and chuckling over his dilemma. It was something she would do, bless her generous nature. And then, suddenly, he knew all was well.

"I can't have you getting crosswise with your employer," he joked.

"More like my slave master," she replied. "She's not paying me a penny for my labors. I must work for my room and board. Did you ever?"

Her easy wit pleased him. "At least she has not sent you to a workhouse, or to the law, wherever it is runaways go in England."

"Oh, no." She hesitated, and he thought she wanted to tell him why she had run away. She did not but turned back to his infamous lading bill and frowned at it. "I know Aggie introduced you as Captain Titus, but I really cannot decipher your first name."

"Hiram."

She dipped the pen in the well and wrote it with a neat hand. "Hiram Titus it is." She blew gently on the page, and he wanted to sigh with the pleasure of it all. "That is a . . . a formidable name. Are all Yankees so very biblical?"

"A good many."

"No one is tempted to call you Hi?"

It was his turn to relax then. "Not if your last name is Titus, Miss Utley. Wouldn't you agree that Hi Titus sounds like a disease?"

They laughed together, and Titus had never felt finer. As much as she had loved him, Tamsin had always seemed to stand a little in awe of him. Not so Miss Utley.

Charity emerged from one of the warehouse aisles, struggling under the awkward bulk of a stool. He hurried to help her, positioning it beside Miss Utley, then gave his daughter a hand up. He looked at his own bill of lading, almost but not quite leaning closer to Miss Utley, mainly because she smelled so delightfully of lavender and that indefinable odor of the female that registered so pleasantly in his brain. He pointed at the next entry. "Mind that you record that as 'a hundred beaver pelts,' rather than 'a hundred feverish Celts,'" he teased. "I doubt we'd have survived an Atlantic crossing with raving Scots in the hold."

"Oh, Papa," Charity said. She glanced at the lady beside her. "He does that, and I don't know why."

Ann Utley twinkled her eyes at him over his daughter's head and picked up her pen. "I cannot allow Captain Titus to be a distraction to my new assistant! Sir, you have our leave to go about your business." She put down the pen again. "Oh, have I nabbed her when you had something else planned? I wouldn't for the world disrupt your intentions."

If only she knew his intentions just then. His face reddened with the thought of them. "No, no, you're quite at liberty to snatch my youngest child and bend her to your will," he joked. "Mrs. Glossop had said something last night about helping her start a sampler this day, that is all. I am returning to the *Hasty* to swing some more cargo."

"Very well, then, sir, we will set you at liberty." She looked back at the lading bill, then at his daughter. "Charity, that cannot possibly be 'fifty cats.'"

"Fifty casks," he murmured, then bowed to them both, a gesture that made Charity's eyes widen in surprise.

In the yard, Ned was ready with the horses and wagon. Titus hauled himself aboard for a return to the harbor. He turned to Glossop, unable to restrain himself. "Ned, that is without question the most beautiful lady I have ever clapped my eyes on."

"She's a looker." Ned spoke to his horses and they crossed the yard. "I knew you were seeming a bit skeptical-like the other night, but now you know what I mean."

"Oh, do I! Why on earth did she run away from Derbyshire?"

Ned motioned for him to get down and open the gate. He drove the wagon through and Titus closed the gate and climbed up again.

"Captain, Aggie says she was afeared that some silly little prig was about to propose, and it put wings to her heels."

"That can't have been her only proposal."

Ned shook his head, then moved his wagon into Portsmouth traffic. "Aggie declares there have been many, but Miss Utley just hasn't found the right bloke yet to warm her cold feet on winter nights." Glossop looked sidewise at him. "How long'd it take you to decide?"

About ten seconds, maximum, he thought. "Oh! Tamsin?" He thought a moment, hoping that the warehouseman wouldn't notice that lapse. "I'd known her all my life, and it just seemed like the right thing to do." No quarrel there. It had been the right thing, but Tamsin had never poleaxed him as had one glance at Ann Utley.

"P'raps Miss Utley is pickier than most of us." Ned nudged him in the ribs. "It took me twenty-five years to convince Aggie that I was the man for her! Miss Utley's a late bloomer too, I suppose."

* * *

To her personal amusement or chagrin (she wasn't sure which), it took Ann several moments to stop breathing at an elevated rate after Captain Titus had closed the warehouse door behind him. Although she could not recall when she had seen a more remarkable-looking man, Ann was hard put to explain to herself just what it was that attracted her. He was a tall man, which never failed to arouse some level of interest. It may have been the web of lines around his eyes that crinkled so readily when he smiled. As she considered the matter, she doubted that she had ever known a man with such wrinkles around his eyes. The men she knew were gentlemen, not sea captains who worked to earn their bread by suffering exposure to raw wind and salt water.

And here was his delightful little daughter, eager to help, and quite unaware that the lovely lady beside her was deliberately plying her for information. By the time noon came, Ann knew that Charity had three older brothers. One twin was an agent for John Jacob Astor and the American Fur Company; the other was at Harvard trying to decide on a course of law. The eldest sailed regularly to the Orient with furs for emperors in exchange for porcelain and spice. So much commerce and activity seemed almost exotic to Ann, while to Charity, it was just the way the Titus family lived.

She also learned that Hiram Titus was forty years old, a native of Boston, fond of squash pie (whatever that was), and prone to snoring when he slept on his back. Ann hadn't the slightest idea what to do with all this refreshing knowledge, except enjoy the slightly clandestine pleasure of eavesdropping on an interesting family.

The afternoon went much more slowly, because Aggie had sat Charity down in her parlor to instruct her in the fine art of samplers and sent Ann back to her clerk's desk to copy another lading bill, this one for a man-o'-war bound for the blockade.

As the hours passed, she found herself looking at the warehouse door, wishing for Captain Titus to materialize. She wondered at her interest, knowing herself fairly well, and knowing that if he did appear, she would probably be speechless. After a moment's reflection, and four more lines of hogsheads of salted beef, boxes of ships' crackers, and eggs packed in salt, she decided that she would have plenty to say to him, if he only asked the right questions.

He came into the warehouse again when afternoon shadows were making her look about for a candle and her back was starting to ache from bending forward on the stool. With a smile, but no words, he took in the fact that his daughter was elsewhere, pulled out her unoccupied stool, and sat upon it. She watched him up close now. His eyes were emphatically brown, and his hair brown with flecks of light in it, obviously from much exposure to sunlight. When he spoke at last, what he said startled her.

"Miss Utley, what do you think of Americans?"

In her surprise, it did occur to her that only an American would ask such a question. Her knowledge was limited to so few of that species, but it seemed a logical surmise. And he seemed to actually expect an answer from her.

"They are brash, forward, opinionated, stubborn, and probably loyal," she said, her answer coming from nowhere she had ever been before. "I expect they are fun to know, but I should sincerely dislike to cross one."

She decided right then that his laughter was probably his best feature: no drawing room titter, but a full-throated delight, head back, eyes half-closed.

"You have just described my favorite hound!"

Ann put her hand on his arm, something she hadn't done with a man in recent memory. "Well, sir, you should not have asked, had you not wished to know!" She leaned toward him a little. "And you, Captain, are a wonderful father with a daughter who adores you." She leaned back, triumph in her eyes. "So this tells me that Americans are fine folk. Children are never wrong in such matters."

There was such a look in his eyes then. She knew she had touched the right chord in him, and it humbled her to realize how close he must be to his children. Her hand was still on his arm; she increased its pressure. "They mean the world to you, don't they?" she murmured.

"Aye," he replied, his voice equally soft.

Ann remembered herself then and removed her hand from his arm. Embarrassed now, and not looking at him, she capped the inkwell and wiped off the pen. All the while, she was thinking of Sir Barnaby Phillips and wondering if a man so enamored of his own company, and cowed around his relatives, would ever consider children more than a necessary nuisance. She thought not, and dismissed the man without another qualm, thankful all over again that at her advanced age, she was still agile enough to shinny down a tree and escape.

"I hope that Aggie Glossop will not summon the beadle from the workhouse if I announce to her that I have copied enough questionable handwriting for the day," she said to the captain.

"Quite the contrary. In fact, my duty here is to summon you upstairs to supper, provided that you remember your manners and do not eat more than your employers."

"Aggie said that?" Ann asked with a grin.

"I admit to some embellishment," he confessed. "Chary says that is one of my more regrettable failings."

"You have others?" she teased.

"According to my daughter, I possess the distinct character flaw of being far too predictable," he said promptly. "Let this be a warning, Miss Utley. Should you marry and have a family someday, please note that your children will always keep you well-informed of your more glaring deficiencies."

She thought he would get down from the stool, but he sat where he was, close enough to her so that she could smell ship's odors of tar and hemp. His presence emboldened her enough to ask, "In light of your question to me, what do you think of the British, Captain?"

He didn't answer right away, but leaned closer momentarily to look at the bill of lading on the table in front of her. "So the HMS *Jasper* is headed out to sea soon. Will it be to the blockade, or will the *Jasper* search into American waters and meddle there?" He looked directly into her eyes, and she could see no apology. "Miss Utley, I do not trust your countrymen to do me no harm."

"But I would never," she said impulsively.

After a pause in which his eyes never wavered from her own, he said, "I do not doubt that, either. I have . . ." He paused again.

"A dilemma?" she prompted, amazed at her own temerity.

He got off the stool and held out his hand to help her down. "A burning urge to eat someone's cooking besides what comes from the *Hasty's* galley. Do hurry, Miss Utley! How would it appear to my hostess if I were to leave you behind in my headlong rush to the Glossops' dining room?"

She had not anticipated a moment alone with Aggie before supper, but there was time for a word while Captain Titus was sitting with his daughter and admiring the rudimentary beginnings of a first sampler, as only a father could. She watched them a moment from the doorway and was startled when Aggie Glossop put a hand on her shoulder.

"I hope you did not mind being herded into a clerk's work today," she began.

"I did not mind at all," Ann replied, as the other woman closed the door of the sitting room. They walked down the hall together, toward the dining room. "In fact . . ." She paused, uncertain of what she really wanted to say.

Aggie supplied the text with real aplomb. "He's a charming man, isn't he?"

"Oh, Aggie, I've never met anyone quite like him." The words tumbled out of her, and she felt like a schoolroom miss again. "But . . . but he's dreadfully common, isn't he?"

"I never noticed," was Aggie's quiet reply, her tone more tender than Ann could ever recall. This was not the starchy governess speaking to her charge, but woman to woman.

"I mean . . ." Ann stopped in confusion. She didn't know what to say, but to keep silent would be to deny the man's effect on her, and she had the strongest urge to share her feelings. "Aggie, I just wanted to look at him all afternoon, even as I kept telling myself that he isn't handsome at all." *What's the matter with me?* was her unvoiced plea. She trusted her governess, even after all these years, to hear that question. She also expected that proper and upright female to tell her to go home to Derbyshire and associate with those of her own sphere.

Aggie Glossop did neither thing. She opened the door to the kitchen, spoke to her cook, then looked at Ann. "You can direct the captain and Charity to the dining room, my dear."

"Aggie!" she whispered furiously. "What is happening to me?"

Aggie put her finger to her lips. "I knew Ned Glossop twenty-five years before I agreed to marry him. Do you know something? I always thought him extraordinarily handsome."

"Oh, but Aggie, he is . . ." She stopped, embarrassed.

"Not?" Aggie grinned at her with mischief in her eyes, something Ann never expected to see. "He is to me, my dear. Now go and be the perfect hostess, or Captain Titus will think I never taught you any manners."

*   *   *

She was quiet during dinner; indeed, she could not help herself. *You would think I have been living in a house with no doors and windows,* she thought. In her worry in recent months over her own puny state of affairs, she had paid little attention to any news beyond Derbyshire's borders. Listening to Captain Titus's sensible comments on recent Orders in Council, and Napoleon's latest Milan Decrees, she felt uncomfortable of her own ignorance. Somewhere between the soup and the sweets, she became aware that there was a wider world of working people trying to carry on in the face of war. She did not know why she had not realized this sooner, then comforted herself with the thought that many of her sphere never did experience such an epiphany.

She even began to suspect that these working people lived lives far more interesting than her own. She had only to look at how animated Captain Titus became when talking about a good wind and the mew of seabirds that meant the coast was near, if not yet in sight. Ned Glossop shared his favorite moment, that time when all the stores in the warehouse were on hand, ample proof that no tar in the king's navy would be shortchanged in his victuals. "It's a pledge I make every day, Aggie," he told his wife simply. "I was one of those tars some years ago; I know what it's like to go hungry." He leaned toward his wife and patted her hand. "Makes me proud to be called Honest Ned."

Aggie smiled at him and gazed with such pride and love on that unlovely man that Ann had to clench her jaw tight to keep from tears. It was absurdly simple chatter that someone like Sir Barnaby would ignore and avoid, but Ann found her throat constricting with the honor of it all. Before she had so uncharacteristically escaped from her bedroom window, the most serious decision of that week had been whether to choose bread and butter or cake at the tea table. These people knew more about the rich texture of life because they lived it.

The only one quieter at the table than Ann was Charity, seated on her left. She thought at first that the little girl was tired, but when she noticed red patches blooming in her cheeks, she gently put her hand against the child's face. Her hand came away warm. When Aggie got up to clear the table, Ann joined her, something she had never done before. She could see that Aggie was startled, but her former governess recovered quickly, nodding and asking Ann to remove the platter and bowls.

"Aggie, I think Charity is ill," she whispered in the kitchen.

"I did wonder," the woman said. "She sneezed a number of times this afternoon, and she has been so quiet. I fear our wonderful English climate is not agreeable to her."

Ann set down the platter for the scullery maid to scrape. "Should we ask Captain Titus if she can stay with us tonight? I have no doubt that he is an excellent father, but he might not know what to do for her."

She watched Aggie hesitate, but to her surprise, she shook her head. "I think not, Ann. We would be meddling."

"Oh, I hardly think this—"

"No, Ann," Aggie interrupted, her voice quiet. "They should both return to the *Hasty*."

She remembered that tone from the years when Aggie was her governess. "Very well. Let's at least suggest that she bundle up well against the night air."

"Certainly, my dear. Certainly."

By the time she returned to the dining room, the Tituses were preparing to depart. Charity carried the sampler she had begun that afternoon. Ann tied her bonnet on securely and stood back while the captain slung a cloak about his daughter's shoulders.

Aggie Glossop watched the proceedings a moment, then touched her husband's arm. "Ned, do go along with them and tell Charity about the time you were nearly shipwrecked on that cannibal island."

Titus laughed. "What, and give her nightmares?"

"Papa, you know it will not be any more fearful than the tales David tells about fur trading in Canada," Charity said, anticipation in her eyes.

He nodded. "And probably not any worse than Charles's adventures at Harvard, minus—hopefully—the cannibals! Do come, Ned, and enliven the walk."

"Ann, after a day in the warehouse, the bloom is quite gone from your face," Aggie said. "Go along and escort Ned back so a press gang does not apprehend him."

"Aggie, what would they want with a broken down old tar?" he asked affectionately, even as he held his arm out for Ann.

To Ann's delight, the captain held out his arm for Ann too. "That's my office, Glossop," he told the man. "You're telling Charity a tale, and I can be the escort." He nodded to Ann. "Provided you approve, of course."

"Oh, I do," she said promptly and felt her face go red. *Could I be more eager?* she asked herself. "Let me get my cloak."

By the time she returned with it, Ned and Charity were at the end of the road. Captain Titus waited for her. They started off together, but the captain was in no hurry to catch up to the old man and little girl ahead of them. She, who was renowned in some circles for her innocuous drawing room patter, could think of absolutely nothing to say. *Ask him about his sons,* she thought desperately. *Is there something about Boston you have been yearning to find out?* "Who is president of the United States?" she blurted out finally, when the silence was too great.

"Tom Jefferson," he said promptly. He stopped. "Miss Utley, what do you *really* want to ask me?"

She laughed out loud. "I can't for the life of me think of anything," she replied frankly. "I just feel a little shy, for no particular reason, and it seemed too quiet."

He resumed his stroll and she walked alongside again. "Miss Utley, what a pleasure it is to walk beside a female who can match me stride for stride." He tucked her arm through his. "Usually I try to be accommodating, but I forget, with the consequence that short females have to trot and turn red-faced."

That was humorous and harmless enough. "Consequently they avoid you?" she teased.

"Alas, no, Miss Utley. In American circles I am considered quite a catch."

I don't doubt that for a moment, she thought, at a loss again for any response.

But it was his turn. "Ned tells me that you fled Derbyshire to avoid a proposal, Miss Utley. Isn't that a bit extreme?"

"It was the basest sort of impulse," she replied. "One moment I was stalking around my room, ready to throw things, and the next thing I knew, I was headed down the oak tree."

He laughed that full-throated laugh that she found so charming. "One proposal too many, or not the one you wanted?"

She considered the matter. "Probably a bit of both. I had all but promised Mama that I would accept the next offer that came my way, but why did it have to be some-one with pop eyes who is intimidated by his aunt?"

"Daunting, indeed," Titus murmured. "Was he too old, too?"

"Oh, not as old as you," she said without thinking, then clapped her hand over her mouth. "Do excuse that!"

"Nope," he said, but his tone was charitable. "I consider myself well seasoned."

"Well, Mama declares that I am too . . . too discerning. Perhaps that is my frustration, sir. I would like to please my mother and assure my brother that I will not be a spinster aunt to blight his sitting room in years to come. But . . ." She paused, not sure how to finish the thought.

"But the selection in Derbyshire is limited?" he suggested.

"Not to hear my mother tell it," she declared. "And so I ran away."

They walked slowly. She couldn't see why Ned Glossop had not chosen a better road to the dock, considering how littered with rubble this one was. She made no objection when Captain Titus took her hand to help her around the broken cobblestones. She also made no objection when he continued to hold her hand, beyond the reflection that Aggie Glossop had told her years ago to beware of seafaring men. His hand was warm, and she wanted to hold it. What was even stranger, she felt that she should have been holding it for years.

But he does not trust the English, she reminded herself as they ambled along the dark street. *And we certainly do not dabble in the same social brook. My income is probably greater than his. This is folly, and so I shall remind Aggie. If only he were not so handsome.* She tightened her grip on his hand instead of turning him loose. "Captain, I'm thirty-two," she said, her voice soft. "I suppose that is what frightens me the most. I mean, I . . ."

She had no idea what she wanted to say, and no idea why she was trying to say it to someone she had met only that morning. But it didn't really matter, because he stopped walking, pulled her close, and kissed her.

She had been kissed before on several auspicious occasions by men who also knew what they were doing, but never before by someone who was precisely the right height and heft. Mama would probably have said he was holding her indecently close, but Mama wasn't there. Those other gentlemen—probably all of them long married by now—had smelled of eau de cologne or wood smoke, but she decided that tar and hemp were quite to her liking. His lips were warm, and she didn't want him to stop. For one moment she hoped she was not pulling in closer to him, and in the next, she didn't particularly care.

He stopped then, stepping back with a stunned look on his face, his eyes as wide as a child's. "My apologies, Miss Utley," he said, and he sounded far less confident than only a moment ago. "You . . . you . . . you have every right to haul off and slap me! I was only intending to give you a little kiss on the forehead to assure you that there was nothing wrong with being thirty-two . . . my stars, I wish I were thirty-two again! And now I am babbling, which is something I do not ordinarily do. I—"

Amused now, Ann put her fingers to his lips to stop the stream of apology. She had no intention of slapping a man who had made an honest mistake. He startled her further by kissing her fingers. As amazed as she was, she could also tell that it was a natural reaction. When he started to apologize again, she stepped back and put her hands behind her back, but knew she could not disguise the twinkle she knew was in her eyes.

"Captain Titus, I simply will not have you apologizing! It is perfectly obvious to me that you are a man who has been away from the society of women too long."

He stopped and stared at her, then smiled and shook his head. In a more normal voice, he said, "I was going to babble something about being too long at sea, but you are right, Miss Utley. The voyage was only seven weeks, but Tamsin has been gone six years. I miss the ladies."

He said it so simply and with such frankness that her embarrassment died before it had a chance to raise the color in her cheeks. Plainly put, he was a man who liked women; not a rake, not a rascal, but a rudderless former husband with considerable goodwill toward the fair sex. She could no more understand why he had not been led away into marriage years ago than he could probably understand why she avoided proposals. She credited the whole matter to one of life's little mysteries and decided to be flattered rather than offended. Not another man of her acquaintance would ever have said anything so honest.

"Captain Titus, you have quite cured me of my melancholy. Indeed, no one could have done it better!"

Ned Glossop had engaged a waterman before they arrived at the dock. With a smile and a bow, Captain Titus gave them both his good night and helped Charity into the small boat. "Miss Utley, if you need help with more words tomorrow, I am sure Mrs. Glossop will let me take time out from my sampler," Charity called, and the waterman put his hands to the oars.

"Not the Aggie I remember!" she joked. "Keep Charity bundled up, Captain." Soon they were dark shapes on the darker water. Standing there watching the small craft, Ann knew that when the *Hasty* spread her sails and lifted anchor, she didn't want to be there to watch. Absurd tears tickled her eyes and she blinked them back, prepared to tell herself, as often as she needed to that no one fell in love in less than twenty-four fours.

* * *

She never knew that a one-legged man could move so slowly. To her excruciating frustration, Ned Glossop was content, on that pleasant June evening, to amble slowly back to his Nautical Emporium. It was all she could do to walk quietly beside him, nodding where appropriate, and letting him continue a spate of sea stories that his conversation with Charity had begun. She wanted to grab up her skirts and hoof it back to the emporium, where she could pour her extreme distress onto Aggie's shoulder. To her dismay, she wasn't even sure if the first emotion was distress.

They arrived at last, and Ned offered some apology about having to go to the warehouse to make sure of a shipment for tomorrow. When he turned his back, she hoisted her skirts and took the stairs two at a time. She threw open the door to the sitting room and announced, "Aggie, he kissed me! What am I supposed to do now?"

To her credit, Aggie Glossop didn't even drop a stitch from the hose she was knitting. Beyond a slight start when the door banged open, that redoubtable female smiled and patted a spot on the sofa beside her. "Do sit down, my dear."

Shocked at her governess's calm demeanor, Ann did as she was told. She took a deep breath and then another. "Aggie, men aren't supposed to do things like that."

"Perhaps not British men, my dear," Aggie suggested. "I have been around a few Americans in the twelve years I have been married to Mr. Glossop, and I have noticed a difference in them." She beamed at Ann. "Perhaps you have discovered what it is?"

"Aggie! He didn't ask my permission, or . . . or even stop to consider that I move in a vastly different sphere, or . . . or probably have pots more money than he does! What is the matter with him?"

Aggie put down her knitting and turned slightly to

face Ann. "You aren't listening to me, my dear," she began calmly. "Let me say it more plainly. For all that they speak English, and heaven knows we share a common heritage, I do not believe that Americans think the way we do."

Ann gasped and put her hand to her mouth. "Do you mean . . . can you mean . . . that proprieties don't matter?"

"Not precisely, although his actions this evening may confirm that suspicion for some." Aggie patted Ann's hand. "It's something else. I'm not sure I can even define it."

Ann leaped to her feet and took a rapid turn about the room. "What on earth should I do?" She plopped down on the sofa, then got up quickly, as though the fabric burned her. "Aggie, he is so common!"

Her governess pursed her lips into a tight line that Ann recognized from years earlier. "You're still not listening, my dear. Americans don't care about formalities. If you told him he was common, I think he would only stare at you and laugh. Ann, they are Americans. If the thought of that frightens you, then by all means get on the mail coach tomorrow morning and go back to Derbyshire, where you are safe."

Ann sank onto the sofa again and leaned her head against her governess. "I am not looking at this in precisely the right way, am I?"

"I fear not."

"I think he is a lonely man."

Aggie laughed and hugged her. "Perhaps not anymore, my dear."

She sat up, agitated again. "But, Aggie, he's had time to find another American! Surely I am not the only woman on earth who has looked at him with admiration? He is so handsome, and kindness itself." She stopped. "Oh, dear, what am I saying?"

Aggie's voice was quiet. "And you have had years to find an Englishman. I do not pretend to understand any of this, but I also do not disregard it." She looked at her charge, her expression puzzled. "There is something else. He appears to like the ladies, but it is so much more." She sighed and stood up. "I do not know. Go to bed, Ann, and try to sleep. If it's to be the mail coach tomorrow morning, Mr. Glossop will take you there."

* * *

Hiram never usually had trouble sleeping in a sheltered harbor, where his ship bobbed gently on the more mannerly swells than those found in the middle of the Atlantic, but tonight was an exception. He lay in his berth, hands behind his head, stared up at the compass, and tried to think of anything but Ann Utley. He succeeded for a while, thinking about the talk his first mate had overheard in a grogshop about the odds of England being at war with the United States within the month. He knew he could be at sea in less than a week, now that the *Hasty*'s hold was filling up with English goods bound for Boston. He resolved to prod Ned Glossop to revictual his ship at the same time he was loading the cargo.

"Blame it and blast, he's shorthanded," Titus muttered out loud, turning over his pillow to find a cooler spot. If he could get some sort of guarantee from the harbormaster, perhaps he could use his own crew to go into the emporium and help. He would ask in the morning. And if the man said no, Titus would break out his special store of Jamaican rum and bribe him.

Eventually, even these larger worries paled before the fact that he had made a complete idiot of himself tonight by kissing Ann Utley. He closed his eyes in the dark and felt the shame of it wash over him again. It was only going to be a harmless peck on the forehead, something he might do for Charity, instead of a kiss of breathtaking proportions. He groaned and rolled over. He was forty, but blast it again if his thoughts weren't awfully young.

And yet there he was, practically tingling at the thought of Ann Utley, like a man with nothing on his mind but women. He was the kind of sailor he would warn Chary about when she was older and ripe for the Talk. Too bad there was not someone to sit *him* down for the lecture on propriety, and how to treat females properly and earn their respect. He would be lucky if the lady said two words to him tomorrow when he returned to the Nautical Emporium. *She will say precisely two words, you chufflehead,* he thought sourly. *"Go away!"*

Sitting up, his head in his hands, he asked himself why, out of all the ladies in Boston and contiguous towns, none had kept him awake as Ann was keeping him awake now. He had eaten many a meal in hopeful widows' houses and danced a jig with younger women who made no attempt to hide their admiration. He had even walked a few home from church and sat on front porches for afternoons of tea and biscuits. In every instance he had paid his respects and gone about his business, content of a good night's sleep.

This is a weird set of circumstances. I walk into a warehouse in a seedy British port, and I am in love, he thought, more in awe than misery. *I haven't seen a prettier face in years, and I think she is even sensible. My sons will probably be bringing home wives soon enough, which means grandchildren for me. And here I am, ready to clamber into the marriage bed again myself. If I do that, my grandchildren will probably have uncles and aunts younger than they are!*

He chuckled at that and felt the mantle of unease fall away from his shoulders. He was making mountains out of molehills; in a few more minutes he could sensibly convince himself that he was just lonely and far from home. His longing for that woman would pass, and he would return to being the sensible, sober Captain Titus, responsible man of business and the father of three grown sons and a daughter. He lay down again and rolled onto his side.

He was startled awake an hour or two later. Someone was standing right beside his berth. For one wild, irrational moment, he wanted it to be Ann Utley, even though he knew that was utter folly. *We're at war*, was his next thought, and then he heard the muffled sob of someone crying into her sleeve.

"Chary?" he asked gently, reaching out to his daughter. "Are you not well?"

Her response was to sob out loud now. He sat up quickly and pulled her onto his lap, holding her close. She was warm, almost hot to the touch, and there was that smell of fever about her. He wouldn't have known that odor with his three boys, because it was always Tamsin who hurried out of bed to tend them in the middle of the night. But his wife had died when Charity was only four, so he knew many hours with a sick child. She sneezed several times. He found a handkerchief from somewhere, and she dutifully blew her nose.

He gathered her close and lay down with her. With a thankful sigh, she burrowed in close to him. "I'm sorry, Papa," she murmured. "Maybe England does not agree with me."

He chuckled. "Go to sleep, honey. John Cook will make a poultice for your chest tomorrow."

"Miss Utley will help me," she said.

He smoothed the damp hair back from her face.

"What makes you so confident of that?"

"I just know it," Charity replied with the logic of childhood. "Now go to sleep, Papa."

And he did.

* * *

After half a night's tossing and turning, thoroughly dissatisfied with herself, Ann resolved to petition Ned

Glossop to take her to the mail coach stop in the morning. In the other half of the night, she changed her mind. After all, Aggie needed her help at the clerk's desk. If Captain Titus should come into the warehouse, she would look at him with equanimity, because hadn't he told her that the kiss was really a mistake? Surely she was enough of an adult to overlook a mere misdemeanor. Besides, she had no longing to return to Derbyshire, where nothing was resolved. She sighed and stared at the ceiling, knowing that she would eventually return to find Sir Barnaby Phillips as silly as ever.

Before she dozed off, Ann reminded herself that the captain had made some remark about hurrying to revictual the *Hasty* and be on his way before war was declared. "See there, Ann," she said out loud, her voice drowsy. "He will be gone in a matter of days and you will never see him again."

And why should that make her cry?

Knowing that she looked every one of her years, Ann avoided the mirror while she dressed, avoided her former governess's eyes over a hasty breakfast, and slunk off to the warehouse to complete the manifest for the HMS *Jasper*, interrupted last night when Captain Titus took her off to dinner. She hauled herself onto the stool, uncapped the inkwell, pushed a fresh steel tip onto her pen holder, and stared down at the manifest.

She sucked in her breath, wondering what had ever possessed her to write so plainly and carefully, *six barrels of Hiram Titus*. Aghast, she stared at the original, which read, *six barrels of salt beef.* Her face hot, her heart beating, she carefully scratched through her mistake, then looked back at what she had transcribed earlier. Oh, mercy, there it was again: *Hiram Titus packed in straw*, instead of *marmalades and jellies*. Scratch went her pen again. Panic in her heart now, she ruffled through the other pages, only to find *Hiram* where sticking plasters, ship's bread, and rice should have been. Perspiration beaded her forehead as she corrected her mistakes and prayed to the Almighty that Aggie Glossop had not checked her work that morning and found it seriously wanting. Surely not, she convinced herself, when her heartbeat slowed to its usual rhythm. Aggie would have made some comment over breakfast.

She had finished correcting the manifest when the warehouse door opened. Her small sigh of relief to see only Aggie quickly evaporated when Captain Titus came in right behind her. She looked down at the manifest again, hoping that his name would not come popping through her careful corrections like a fishing bob.

It did not, and she glanced up again. The captain looked so serious this morning, almost, to her way of thinking, like someone who had slept as little as she.

Aggie spoke to her. "Ann, I . . . we . . . have a great favor to ask you."

"Ask away, my dear," she replied. "You know you can have anything up to half my kingdom." *That's right, Ann*, she told herself. *Keep a light touch.*

Captain Titus smiled at her feeble witticism, but his eyes were still full of concern. "Miss Utley, my daughter is ill and she needs someone besides a ham-handed father to look after her."

"I thought she felt warm last night," Ann replied, getting off the stool. "Of course I will tend her. Is she upstairs?"

"She's still on the *Hasty*. My cook has made a wondrously odorous poultice of sage and oil of eucalyptus, and Charity declares that no one will apply it but you." His eyes were both tired and full of apology. "She is only contrary when she is ill."

"And quite entitled, I imagine," Ann murmured. "Of course I will go, Captain."

"That's my girl," Aggie said. "I assured him that you would not shrink."

She felt her good humor returning. "Certainly not! Let me only get my cloak and—"

"Uh, there is a little more to it than that," the captain said, and it was Aggie's turn to smile. He held out a pair of trousers. "Getting onto the *Hasty* in a dress would prove a challenge, Miss Utley, as there is a rope ladder."

"But how does Charity do it?" she asked, trying not to stare like a wild woman at the trousers over his arm.

"She wraps her legs around my waist and I carry her up and down the ladder on my back," he said, his face quite red.

"Oh." Ann took the trousers and looked at them dubiously.

"I think we are much the same length in the legs, Miss Utley, if you will pardon the observation," he told her as he held out a thin rope. "I know your waist is not as wide around as mine, so this should keep 'em up." He looked at Aggie. "Mrs. Glossop says she can find a proper canvas shirt in the warehouse. Something for cabin boys."

"Very well," Ann replied, wishing that her voice were not so faint.

"I'll find that shirt right now," Aggie said. "Ann, go upstairs and pack your clothing in a bundle. I'm certain you will want to put your dress on again when you reach the *Hasty*."

"Indeed I will," Ann assured them both.

The captain managed a bow that stuck Ann as quite elegant. "You're relieving this father's heart," he said to her, then nodded to Aggie. "I'm going to find Ned and urge him to revictual us as soon as possible." Again she saw the doubt in his face. "Aggie, I don't know. There's more talk on the wharf."

"You've heard nothing from an official source?" her governess asked.

His smile was wry. "If war is declared, Aggie, the only official source we will get is an officer of the Royal Navy climbing aboard to declare me a prisoner and the *Hasty* contraband!"

She stood there holding the trousers and rope as he loped off to the wagon yard again. "What on earth have I just agreed to, Aggie?" she asked.

"Something rather more exciting than transcribing manifests or boring yourself to death listening to prosy old Barnaby Phillips!" Aggie said tartly. "Hurry up now. I'm preparing a basket of lemons and lozenges you can take. I might even find one or two of those books I used to read to you when you were about that age, my dear." She squeezed her arm. "Oh, Ann! It will just be for a day or so."

They started for the stairs to the quarters above. "You should have listened to me last night when I suggested we keep Charity here," Ann reminded her.

"I know," Aggie replied, but to Ann's ears she sounded almost too contrite. It was on the tip of her tongue to accuse her governess of engineering this whole turn of events, but she reconsidered. Aggie Glossop was many things, but she was no manipulator.

In the privacy of her room, Ann removed her dress and pulled on the trousers. Captain Titus was right, which gave her another pause. To her knowledge, no man of her acquaintance had taken such a measure of her legs before. *Perhaps that is what Americans do*, she thought sourly. Aggie was right; they truly were a species apart.

Aggie brought her a canvas shirt that fit well enough without being oceans too long. She carefully tucked it into the waistband of the trousers and cinched the rope tight. "Well?" she asked.

"You'll do," Aggie said. She took Ann's bundle of cloth-ing from the bed. "I've made another bundle of things for Charity. It will be an easy matter to tie a rope to them both and sling them up to the deck of the *Hasty*."

Captain Titus waited for her in the wagon yard. As silly as she felt, she was pleased a little to see the way the lines around his eyes crinkled up with good humor, light-ening the soberness of his expression. "I was close," he said. "Just took one turn of the cuffs, eh?"

"Both my parents were tall, Captain," she replied, for want of anything better to say.

"Well, you look finer than frog's hair, Miss Utley."

"What?" she exclaimed, then laughed. "I pray *that* is an Americanism!"

"Probably." He winked at her. "Think of this as something to tell your friends next winter when con-versation lags."

Ned insisted upon driving them to the dock, and even handed Ann up onto the wagon seat with all the grace of a coachman. The captain clambered into the back, con-tent to sit upon a hogshead of salted beef, one long leg negligently propped up on the wagon side. He leaned down to take the basket meant for Charity from Aggie and listen to her last-minute advice. Ann watched him over her shoulder, and found herself admiring his easy grace all over again. She knew a few sea captains, even an admiral or two, and she could not fathom even one of them sitting so casually among ship's cargo.

And here I am in long pants, she thought, as Ned spoke to the horses and they rumbled slowly off. *At least my hair is not braided into a tarry queue and I do not brandish a cutlass in my teeth.* She smiled at the thought and resolved to ask Captain Titus how on earth pirates managed it.

Before the gate closed behind them, she looked back at Aggie and waved. To her surprise, her old governess was dabbing at her eyes. Ann half rose in the seat and cupped her hand to her mouth. "Aggie, dearest," she called, "it is only for a day or two!"

That mild joke seemed to make Aggie cry harder. She was sobbing quite earnestly into her apron now. *This will never do*, Ann thought. "Aggie, I promise to write from America and send home my wages!" she teased and sat down again.

She heard a mighty sniff beside her and glanced in surprise at Ned, who was wiping his face with his sleeve. "Oh, for heaven's sake, what is the matter with you Glossops?" she scolded. "You would think I was bound for foreign lands, and not just Portsmouth harbor!"

For all that she could swear she saw tears in his eyes, Ned gave her a stern look. "I just got a cinder in me eye, you silly widgeon," he said with some dignity. "Now behave yourself, or I'll turn ye over to the press gang meself. They'd like a Long Meg who could climb a ratline."

Captain Titus laughed and reached over to prod Ned. "I'd fight you for her, Ned, 'cause I need a nursemaid now." He stood up and propped his elbows on the back of the wagon seat. "This is what you get for climbing down a tree, Miss Utley."

His arm was pressing against her shoulder, but she leaned toward him anyway, simply unable to help herself. "You, sir, are a rascal. I am surprised that any American entrepreneur trusts you with a ship."

To her further surprise, he and Ned exchanged glances, and both men started to laugh. Ned chirruped to his horses. "Sit down, Captain, before I bump you out. Miss Ann, I know you'll never believe this, but the captain here owns a whole fleet of ships." He made a face at the captain. " 'E's a regular Yankee-Doodle nabob!"

"I never would have reckoned," Ann said, unable to

keep the surprise from her voice. "Captain Titus, are all, uh . . . Yankee nabobs so casual?"

He made no pretense at dignity, but she watched the wrinkles around his eyes deepen. "Miss Utley, you would be amazed at me in my office, with my charts and graphs, and world map with colored pins."

"Maybe I would not," she said slowly. "I'm beginning to think that nothing would surprise me."

She considered the matter all the way to the docks, while Ned and Titus kept up a running commentary about the business of preparing the *Hasty* for sea. "How many ships do you own?" she asked as Ned stopped his team at the dock and waved his arms to summon a waterman.

"Ten merchant vessels, and I have half interest in four whaling ships out of Nantucket." He hopped down and held up his arms for her. "I like the ocean, Miss Utley, for all that I have not been to sea lately."

"Because of Charity?" she asked, and let him help her to the ground.

"Aye. She needed me at home." He looked toward the harbor. "And I wish we were there now."

She felt a little ripple down her spine. "You think war's coming any day now, don't you?"

He nodded, then ushered her forward to the dock as Ned hailed a waterman. "What will happen to Charity if I am incarcerated?"

"I would take care of her," she murmured.

He inclined his head toward hers. "I rather believe you would, Miss Utley. Mind your step now."

Her bundles around her, they sat close together in the stem of the boat as the waterman rowed toward the only tall-masted ship in the harbor flying American colors. The rain began when they were less than halfway across the choppy water. Titus pulled his boat cloak around both of them, tugging her close. "Your cloak's not waterproof," he offered for explanation.

Oddly enough, she wasn't sure she even needed an explanation. The rain pelted down, and she was comfortable and safe, pressed close to his chest. *I am far safer than he is,* she thought. *Why on earth should my government penalize this good man for trying to earn a living? Has the world gone mad?* Sitting there in a little boat, suddenly it mattered to her, and she knew why: She loved him. In fact, she would probably never love another. If she possessed any courage at all, or maybe just a little less dignity, she would have turned his face toward her own—they were so much the same height that scarcely any effort would be involved—and kiss him. He was even looking at her, and she almost didn't need to know what he was thinking. This could be the easiest thing she ever did.

"*Hasty*, Captain," the waterman said then and backed the boat with his oars until they bobbed alongside the tall ship. She stared at the dangling rope ladder.

Titus tossed him a coin and unlimbered himself from beside her. He stood up carefully and whistled. In another moment, a sailor was grinning down at them from the deck above that looked amazingly far away to Ann. "Send 'er up, sir," he hollered down in the same sharp, spare-toned twang as his captain. She forced herself to look at the ladder and gulped.

"Stand up slowly, Ann, and grab hold of the rope," the captain said. "I'll give you a boost up on the next swell."

"I don't know," she said. The ladder looked so tiny as the boat rose and fell.

"Ah, now, any woman who can climb down a tree can shinny up a rope ladder," he assured her. He put his hand on her rump and grinned at her. "Didn't Aggie ever warn you about sailors? Now!"

Too terrified to do anything else, she did as he said

as he boosted her to the ladder. She clutched it as the little boat dropped away and the *Hasty* rolled. She took a deep breath and started to climb. *You daren't look down,* she told herself as she climbed steadily. In a few moments she felt pressure below her that told her Titus was right behind. And then two hands from the deck above reached down, grabbed her under her armpits, and swung her quite handily onto the ship.

Titus came up quickly, and then the sailor sent down a line for the bundle and basket. Ann went to the rail and looked down—way down—at the small launch that was pulling away, and the still-dangling rope ladder. "I don't even want to contemplate climbing back down that thing," she murmured.

"Then don't," he told her. "Didn't Aggie ever make you embroider a sampler that said, 'Sufficient unto the day is the evil thereof'?"

She grinned at him, her equilibrium on even keel again. "I already told you what a mess I made of my first sampler." She stood still while the captain settled her cloak straight around her again. "Now where is my charge?"

"This way." He handed her the bundle and took Aggie's basket on his arm. "Mind that you duck your head below deck. You have the same problem I have."

She was careful to avoid the overhead beam as she followed him down the companionway on the steep treads and felt her hair just brushing the ceiling. "One would think that since you own this fleet, you could make the ceilings taller," she told him.

"Wasted space, Annie Utley," he said, and she smiled again at his free use of her first name. There was no denying that now he was back in his own domain, he seemed more cheerful. She would overlook his social blunder.

He led her down the narrow passageway to a chamber with many small-paned windows across the stern of the ship. "These are my quarters," he told her. "I put Chary in my berth and made up this cot for you, if you have to stay tonight." He glanced behind him. "I took her cabin out there."

Charity sat up when she saw Ann, her eyes wide. "Oh, Papa, you did get her," she said and lay down again. "Miss Utley, thank goodness you have come."

"Such drama worthy of Siddons!" Ann exclaimed. She came close to the berth and touched the child's head. "Do call me Ann, my dear," she said, then glanced over her shoulder. "Everyone else seems to be doing that." She set down her bundle and turned around, quite firm in her resolution. "All right, Hiram, go fetch that poultice and close the door after you. I'll put on my dress again, so you had better knock."

He grinned and knuckled his forehead at her, but did as she said. She heard him whistling down the passageway in a moment. "Your father is considerably happier on his own ship," she told Charity. She let fall her cloak and undid the rope knotted about her waist. "Let me dress, and then I'll see what I can do for you."

By the time he returned bearing a small poultice, she had settled her cap about her head and was tying on her apron. "Just set it on the table," she told him as she hitched herself up into his berth. "I am going to comb Chary's hair first. Ladies always feel better when they look neat."

He stood there watching them both as she combed the child's hair. Charity leaned against her with her eyes closed. "Excellent," he said quietly. "I am just not proficient at hair."

"Nor did I expect you to be." She lifted Chary's dark hair with the comb. "This is a beautiful color."

"Aye, like her mother's."

His voice was tender, and Ann felt the oddest moment of jealousy, which passed quickly, to her relief.

He came closer and touched Ann's shoulder. "I am supervising the last of the cargo this morning. This afternoon Ned's going to begin the revictualing. Water kegs come on board last, probably around noon tomorrow."

And then you will be under way, Ann thought, and felt that tickling sensation behind her eyes. *I should treasure this moment, I suppose.* She enjoyed the firm pressure of his hand much as Chary appeared to find pleasure in the combing of her hair. "We'll manage quite well, Captain."

"I like Hiram better."

"Actually, so do I," she said promptly, a little surprised at herself.

The pressure increased for a moment; then he went to the door. "Do take those lemons to your cook," she asked. "If he will make some hot lemonade for Charity, and bring it here, along with some clear soup, I believe we will rub along pretty well . . . Hiram."

"Consider it done, Ann."

She wished he could have stayed, not that she needed help with the poultice—which was certainly odorous enough to be medicinal—but because she relished his company. She had known much wittier men, elegant fellows who could keep her in stitches for hours. She had danced many evenings with lords and officers who made her look far more graceful than she knew she was. But when all was said, they had not touched her heart. They had not even come close. But there was Hiram Titus, tall and genially commanding, with wrinkles around his eyes from too much sun and wind, and hands grown hard with work. He had that amusing Yankee twang that would have made him the laughingstock of many a refined salon. He was the kind of fellow that men of her social circle would have laughed about after dinner. If he ever came up in conversation, it would be with condescension.

She loved him, for all that their acquaintance was

brief. If she had not taken momentary leave of her senses and climbed down that blessed tree, she never would have met him. How odd were the workings of fate! But swift on the heels of her joy was the reality that he was probably sailing in another day to prevent his capture in port if war broke out. There would never be an opportunity for courtship. Not that there ever was, she told herself bleakly, and a little ruthlessly. When would such a man ever be invited to her mother's estate? What circles could they possibly move in together? She sat quietly beside Charity's berth, nearly astounded at her rare good fortune, and her utter despair because of it.

The cook came with soup and lemonade; Charity dutifully ate, then promptly slumbered. Ann roamed around the small space allotted to the captain and his daughter. She could hear cargo being thumped deep into the hold. A glance out the small windows showed many boats plying to and from the shore laden with boxes and barrels. She turned away from that glaring evidence of a hasty departure.

Ann looked at what he read on the small table beside the berth, smiling to see a well-thumbed Bible and a book on navigation, equally used. There was also a letter half-written, perhaps to one of his sons.

She picked up a miniature on the table and contemplated the lovely lady within it, a woman with dark hair and blue eyes and a smile most serene. She seemed to be looking beyond the painter as she smiled, and Ann wondered if the captain had been sitting there, and perhaps smiling back at her. She set down the miniature and looked away. Tamsin Titus was probably small and dainty too, someone who would never climb a ship's ladder in men's trousers.

Oh, I am making mountains out of molehills, she thought, as she felt Charity's forehead, then resumed her traverse of the cabin. *He sails tomorrow probably, and I will never see him again. Life is not fair, Ann Utley, but you already knew that. Even if he does feel for you even a fraction of what you feel for him, these things take time, and the time of our few moments breathing the same air is about to run out.*

"This will never do," she whispered. "You have to get a grip on yourself, Ann." She sat very still then, knowing from experience that she could will any tears away, if she had the mind to. She did not and cried quietly instead, distressed to think that by tomorrow morning she would be back at the Glossops'. Nothing would keep her there for long; in fact, she doubted that she would ever visit them again. The memories would be too great. Better to stifle in Derbyshire than pine in Portsmouth.

* * *

Captain Titus was tired right down to his bones when he rowed with his silent crew back to the *Hasty*. Night was coming. He hoped Ann would not mind staying the night aboard ship, but a press gang was already prowling the docks, and he did not feel inclined to chance the matter. He had rounded up all his crew that he could and left a message at their favorite public house for the others to meet him on the dock at first light, without fail.

His last meeting with Ned Glossop had been disturbing. Looking around to make sure that no agents lurked in his wagon yard, the old fellow had told him that the skipper of the HMS *Corinthian*, waiting to be revictualed, had let drop that he expected orders tomorrow to American waters. "I'll know something by two, at least," he had said as he pressed his bill into Titus's hand. "The tide'll be in your favor too."

To his fear that they wouldn't have time for all the water barrels, Ned only shrugged. "If you're first off the block, laddie, you'll likely beat anything to the Azores. Plenty of water there."

After finding his crew and promising to pay Ned's bill first thing in the morning, they rowed in three boats back to the *Hasty*, no one talking, but everyone taking a measure of the warships in the harbor. What they saw relieved them somewhat: the *Jasper* was stepping a mast, another ship had no sails, and a third was revictualing, as he was. Only the *Corinthian* made him pause. Trust the captain of such a renowned warship to leap for the gate like a greyhound, food or not.

He felt a measure of relief on his own deck and quietly went to his cabin, where the door was ajar. The sight before him seemed to roll a weight off his shoulders, which, in itself, was a sensation he had not experienced since Tamsin's death. How many times, after fractious wranglings with victualers, or news of ill winds, had he come home to their house on Ousley Street, bearing the burdens of Sisyphus, only to be lifted by that welcome face? Tamsin could make him feel that the worst ailment was no heavier to bear than a sack of feathers.

Admiring Ann Utley, he felt that way again. She was not mindful that he stood in the doorway, and he relished the moment. She was leaning back negligently in his favorite chair, her long legs crossed at the knees in a distinctly unladylike way that suited her. As much as he wanted to admire the shape of her legs under that dark dress, he was more captured by the way her hand rested along Charity's arm. His daughter's eyes were closed, but Ann was reading out loud to her in a low voice. Everything about her showed how much Ann cared for his beloved daughter.

His father had told him years ago that it was the ladies who made life bearable. He had known this to be true with Tamsin, but until now it never occurred to him that he might be lucky twice. No, he should amend that; it would have been true, if he hadn't been in a pelter to be safely out of English waters, or maybe even if he had the tiniest notion how to court a woman. Tamsin had his heart from childhood and had required no pursuit. Ann would require some time invested, and he had no time at all.

So he just stood there admiring her a moment longer, knowing that when he rowed her to shore tomorrow morning, he would be the unhappiest man in the universe.

* * *

He spent the next few hours with them. Charity was infinitely better, the feverish color of her cheeks fainter now. She ate a little, but cautiously, and kept everything in her stomach, which was another relief. Ann was subdued, answering his questions in that serene manner of hers but offering few observations of her own. Something told him that if he were not in the room, she would be pacing up and down. She sat still enough, but her energy appeared to be restrained on a tight leash. Perhaps she did not care much for the ocean.

As Charity talked to her, Titus tried to consider Ann Utley dispassionately. Certainly she was too tall for fashion, but he could find no fault with that, or with her womanly shape, quite unlike Tamsin's lifetime slimness. He itched to touch her. He decided that her creamy complexion was not something that could be duplicated in the United States. Maybe it was the result of life in a cool, misty climate. By the end of the evening, when he reluctantly bowed himself out and into his own chaste and narrow berth a door away, he dreaded his expected dreams.

He should not have troubled himself; nothing could have been farther from him than sleep that last night in Portsmouth Harbor. He worried about everything he could think of: Charity's health, the oncoming war, a chance that the *Hasty* might spring a leak mid ocean, that little bare but growing bald patch on his head where his part originated, the safety of his dear sons in their various locales, a certain but discernible weakness in his stomach muscles, the price of goods in Boston—anything to keep from thinking of the lady who slept so close to him in the next cabin, but so eternally far away.

He got up once; perhaps he shouldn't have. He heard her moving around in the cabin sometime between one and two o'clock, in response to what sounded like a question from Charity. Worried suddenly for his daughter, he wrapped a blanket around him and knocked softly on the door.

He had to smile. By the light of the full moon outside, he could see both Charity and Ann in the same berth now. He came close and touched Ann's shoulder. "All's well?" he asked.

"Aye," she said, and he laughed softly, because she was trying to imitate his own speech.

"Aye, is it? You're starting to sound like a Back Bay woman," he joked, "except that it's 'aye-yah,' not just 'aye.'"

He could see her smile, and also the way she held Charity—asleep again—so close to her body. He rested the back of his hand against his daughter's forehead, relieved to find it cool. To his infinite pleasure, Ann wrapped her fingers around his wrist.

"You needn't worry, Hiram," she whispered. "I think I have an inkling what she means to you."

She released him too soon for his own satisfaction, and there was nothing he could do about it. In perfect misery, he leaned forward and kissed Charity's cheek. Then he couldn't help himself, because Ann lay so close. He kissed her forehead, then rested his cheek briefly against hers, which was the wrong thing to do, because it put him in amazing proximity to her. It was late and he was tired, but he couldn't be totally sure that he didn't plant another kiss on that stretch of warm skin where her neck became her shoulder.

She murmured something deep in her throat that he could feel with his lips. It took a supreme force of will to leave the room, but doomed him to stare at the overhead deck, wide-awake, for the rest of the night.

At first light he was on deck, dousing himself under the pump, letting the shock of cold seawater put him back into a businesslike state of mind. His Congregational minister in Boston was never so right as when he spoke about the flesh being weak. Another pull from the pump sparked a small revolt. "And what business is that of the Lord Almighty?" he growled under the water. His own Puritan guilt made him stop short and endure another unnecessary few minutes under the cold water as penance.

He stood on the deck, a towel around his middle, and watched the activity of the other ships in the harbor, the HMS *Corinthian* in particular. He could see no movement above decks yet, no signal flags, no small boats clustered about like iron filings to a magnet. He looked to the docks, where Ned Glossop's lighter was already setting out. Shivering now, he watched as the lighter came closer, and the cargo was water kegs. Now it was time for his own sigh of relief. By the end of the day he would have enough stored for a comfortable cruise, but by noon there would be enough to endure short rations to the Azores, if worse came to worst.

He dressed and knocked on his cabin door by seven o'clock. Ann answered it. He could tell by the blush on her cheek that he hadn't invented that early-morning kiss, but she kept her counsel—*drat her*—the lady that she was.

"The lighters are coming now with water," he told her.

He was sure he saw dismay on her face, followed by

that cool, bland, calmness that could mean anything. "I'm not ready to go yet," she told him. "Charity has eaten, but I want to help her with her bath."

"And you may," he replied. "I'm going on deck to watch them start down the water kegs, and then I'll go in to settle my account with Ned. Can you be ready by noon?"

"Most certainly," she said.

He wished mightily that he knew her better, that he could get some hint more of her feelings for him, beyond her fingers on his wrist this morning, or the way she had half turned her head to accommodate his lips on her neck. Or maybe it was all in his imagination. He didn't know what to think and felt more like the most callow youth who ever flirted with the young ladies.

By the middle of the morning, the lighters had gone ashore and returned with another cargo of water. He assigned two of his crew to row him to the dock, where he sent them in search of the few remaining crewmen, and took himself to Glossop's Nautical Emporium.

He thought he saw Ned at the window, but suddenly the door banged open and Aggie Glossop ran out. His nerves instantly on edge, he just stood there in the wagon yard, looking wildly around him for British marines with muskets held at port arms. To his surprise, Aggie grabbed him by the hand and pulled him toward the warehouse door, which Ned was even now holding open.

"Heaven help me, has it happened?" he asked.

Ned nodded, his eyes on Titus's face. "We just heard from the number one on the *Corinthian*, who is probably eyeing your ship, even now!"

Without a word, Titus slammed down the money he owed the Glossops and bolted for the door, his heart somewhere up around his ears. "I haven't a moment to waste," he shouted over his shoulder.

"One moment, Captain," Aggie said, and handed him an envelope. "This can wait until after you are at sea. Hurry now!"

He stuffed the letter into his shirt front, blew Aggie a kiss, and ran for the dock. Luckily, his crew had found their remaining comrades. When they saw him coming at a run, they hurried into the dinghy and sat ready with the oars. He loosed the rope from the hawser and stepped into the boat a split second before his sailors pushed away from the dock. "Fast as you can, lads," he urged, his eyes on the big warship riding at anchor too close to his vessel. "War's been declared and the hounds are loose."

No one said anything as they crossed the harbor. He stood up carefully to test the wind on his face and knew that he had a chance. He was scrambling up the ladder to the *Hasty* before he remembered Ann Utley. *I hope she relishes an ocean voyage*, he thought grimly. *There's not time to send her back.*

* * *

Ann was pulling on her trousers when she heard kegs rolling across the deck above, then men running. She buttoned her pants and rolled the cuffs, listening. She glanced over at Charity, who was sitting up now, her face intent. "What are they doing?" she asked.

The little girl shrugged. "I don't know. This is my first voyage."

Ann hurried to button up her shirt and tuck it into the trousers. She was knotting the cord around her waist when the sails dropped with a whoosh that must have sounded all over the harbor. *My stars*, she thought, *this ship can't be under way.*

But it was. She ran to the windows and stared out to see empty lighters pulling away quickly from the ship, the men rowing for all they were worth. The dinghy that she knew was to take her back to the dock was tied aft and bobbing just under the windows, quite empty. "We're moving. My goodness, Charity, do you suppose he forgot I was on board?"

Charity climbed out of the berth, tugging at her nightgown. "I don't think he's that absentminded."

Has war been declared? Ann asked herself as she smoothed back her hair with hands that trembled and tied it with a cord. Perhaps if she hurried she could convince him to at least summon a waterman to row her back to shore. She looked around the cabin quickly and saw nothing of hers that she would take the time to bundle up. "I must hurry," she said and opened the door.

Charity followed her into the narrow companionway. The ship was definitely picking up speed. Ann kissed Charity quickly and gave her a hug, feeling all out of sorts with herself: unhappy to leave, and yet in a pelter to get away. Clotilde was getting married in August, and she had promised to serve punch on the lawn.

She ran for the ladder, intent upon gaining the deck. *Oh, you will get such a scold from me, Hiram Titus*, she thought as she picked up speed. *It doesn't do to kidnap Englishwomen, you dear, misguided man.*

It was her last thought. "Miss Utley, mind your head!" she heard Charity shriek, but it was too late. She slammed into the overhead beam and fell flat on her back without so much as a groan.

* * *

"Ann. Ann. Come now, Ann."

The voice sounded faraway and tinny, and someone was gently patting her cheeks. She opened her eyes, but everything was black. *Good heavens, I'm blind*, she thought in a panic, until she realized that there was a cool cloth on her forehead that covered her eyes too. Her head definitely rested in a man's lap. She knew that etiquette dictated she should sit up immediately, but the matter seemed quite impossible. She couldn't even raise her hand to move the cloth, much less lift her head. *I will just stay here*, she thought. *It's improper, but I don't care.*

The deck gave a mighty heave and then pitched forward. *I am going to die*, she thought, and didn't even try to stifle her groan. The hand stopped pummeling her face. He folded back the cloth, and she blinked in the half-light of the companionway, where she lay in Hiram's lap at the foot of the ladder.

"You hit just above the bridge of your nose," Hiram told her. "I think one of your eyes is going black."

She looked up at him. At first he looked like someone viewed from the bottom of a pond; then he quit shimmering as her brain stopped bobbing about inside her skull. She closed her eyes—or rather, her eye; the other one was already shut and swelling—and murmured, "I am supposed to serve punch on the lawn in August. Now what are you going to do about that?"

It seemed perfectly rational to her, and she couldn't imagine why his stomach began to shake. "It's not funny," she told him quite seriously.

He let out a sigh then and carefully pulled her into his arms and close to his chest. "Ann, it's war, and I had to get across the bar before the tide turned."

If this was sailing, she wanted no part of it. She held her breath as the ship rose and rose, and then dropped into a trough. "I'm going to be sick," she said in a strangled voice.

He must have been prepared for that eventuality, because he pulled a bucket close and turned her face toward it. She obliged him by vomiting up everything she had eaten in recent memory. She didn't want to look in the bucket when she finished, because she knew her toenails were probably floating on top.

Hiram sat her up carefully and wiped her mouth with

his shirttail. She tensed when the ship rose again on a swell. He tightened his grip on her, pressing his hand firmly against her rib cage. She closed her eyes and moaned when the *Hasty* plummeted down the chute again.

"It's going to do this all the way to Boston?" she asked, her voice faint. Her gorge rose again, which surprised her, because she knew there was nothing left in her entire insides. "Six weeks?"

"Uh, more like eight on the return trip, Ann," he replied.

"That's Miss Utley to you," she snapped, but the effect was dulled by another humiliating perusal of the bucket. As angry as she was, she leaned back against him when she finished, exhausted. "If a man-'o-war finds us, I'll turn you over myself."

He only chuckled. "You and who else, Miss Utley? Come on, now, let me help you up."

She hadn't realized the extent of the appreciative audience until two crew members hurried to prop up her other side and help her to her feet. The bucket looked far away, which alarmed her, because she felt a huge urge to hug it again. "If I die, will you bury me at sea?" she managed to gasp. "Tie a cord around my knees when you pitch me over, so I'm decent?"

Titus laughed. "You'll feel better in a few days. Everyone does."

* * *

He was right, of course, drat him. She didn't remember much of the next few days, except that he kindly unbuttoned her trousers, peeled off her shirt, and helped her into her nightdress without comment. As she gagged and retched, he bound her hair into pigtails—"To keep your hair out of the bucket, Miss Utley"—and kept a flannel-wrapped cask of hot water at her feet. ("I don't know why it helps, missy, but it does.")

She shook her head at his offer of broth and prepared for death. It would have been an easy death and much more pleasant than "kissing the wooden goddess," as Titus so aptly expressed it when she rolled from his berth and threw herself on her knees by the bucket. It was his continual good cheer that drove her to distraction until she wanted to throw a spike in his general direction.

The low point came toward the end of the interminable week, when she uttered a two-word sentence she had heard from her brother once when he had been unseated from a horse. Hiram looked at her, eyes wide, brows raised, and then that smile came again, even as she was preparing to cover her face with the sheet in embarrassment.

He had sat down beside her in the berth and rested his elbow on her upraised knee as casually as though she had murmured something nonsensical and affectionate. He compounded her misery by smiling at her in that peculiarly disturbing way that must have been the reason she sprinkled his name so liberally through the *Jasper*'s lading bill. "I could be wrong, Miss Utley," he said, "but I think there is something special about a man who'll hold a lady's head steady over a bucket."

He patted her knee then in a most proprietary manner and left her to stew in her own juices. The door hadn't even shut before she realized that he was absolutely right. When he came back later that afternoon with broth, she was dressed—thanks to Charity's assistance—and sitting, if a trifle unsteadily, in the chair by the windows. She knew she should apologize to him and opened her mouth to do so, but he was reaching for a hairbrush and telling her to lean forward.

When he finished unplaiting her hair and brushing out her snarls, she said simply, "I'm glad you do not hold grudges, Hiram."

"Wouldn't dream of it, Ann," he replied. He stood up

and nodded to Charity. "Make sure she eats all that broth, dear. She's looking a little wan, and that won't do." He pointed upward. "My watch now. Maybe if you feel good enough tomorrow morning, you can join me on deck."

Humor seemed the best recourse. "That might put me too far from my bucket."

He laughed. "We have a lengthy railing to lean over and a whole ocean to puke in, Annie Utley." He came back to the berth then, and his face was serious as he put his hand gently on the bump on her forehead. "You'll be all right now. I know it."

And she was. Next morning when Ann came unsteadily up the ladder, practically hand over hand, Charity was already standing next to her father on the poop deck, her arm around his waist. Ann watched her, envying her casual stance, even as the *Hasty* continued its dip through the troughs of the waves. *The sea is in your blood, child*, she thought. She didn't think she could manage more steps, but he was there at her side to help.

Charity clapped her hands. "I knew you could, Miss Utley."

She let them lead her to a wooden spool and sit her down. Hiram handed her his own cup of coffee. "Hope you like it black."

"I prefer tea, sir."

"You're in the American merchant fleet now, m'dear," he told her. "Coffee it is." She smiled and took a sip, glad to be in the open air again, pleased that she had abandoned the idea of death. Hiram handed his spyglass to Charity, who hurried with it to the railing; he sat down beside Ann.

"I'm sorry it came to this," he told her. "You know I didn't mean to kidnap you, but I had to beat the warships out of the harbor."

"Any sign of them?" she asked, handing back the cup.

He shook his head. "Can't figure it. The *Hasty* is small potatoes, but we are a prize ship, if captured." He touched her shoulder with his. "But I'm not one to borrow trouble from tomorrow." He took a sip and handed back the cup.

She took another sip. "What are my chances of getting some fresh water to wash my hair? I did my best to keep it out of the bucket but wasn't entirely successful."

He shook his head and accepted the cup. "Can't spare it. We don't even have enough water to get us halfway across the ocean." He looked at the cup. "Wonder if I can mix half fresh and half salt water for coffee?"

"What will you do?"

He finished the coffee. "I'll gamble that no warship is ahead of us to the Azores, and take on water there." He hesitated, as though he didn't want to continue his thought. He looked out at the ocean and was a long time in speaking. "I can leave you in Terceira. There's a British consulate who will see that you get home."

"Oh." She couldn't think of anything else to say.

* * *

There followed the strangest three weeks of Ann's life. She settled into the ship's routine as surely as if she had been born to it. She and Charity continued to share her father's larger berth, the two of them staying awake late to talk. It became sweet second nature to hold Charity close, enjoy her warmth, and hear about her brothers and what little she remembered of her mother.

Even sweeter was her time with Hiram Titus. He seemed to have included her in his life as though she had always been there, even if he did say he was going to leave her in the Azores. She wondered at first why he continued to share his coffee with her every morning, until it dawned on her that the homey habit must have been something he did with Tamsin. She even wondered if he was aware of it, or if his husbandly kindness—she couldn't think of a better thing to call it—was just an extension of his generous nature. It was as though something monumental had been decided in his mind, but nothing said.

She plucked up her courage one day and asked the cook about the matter. She had developed a certain rapport with him during Charity's brief illness and his poultices for her own black eye—an interesting lime green now—and wounded forehead. Hiram had told her that John Cook had been with his fleet, in one capacity or another, since, the days of the colonial revolt, when Titus was a pup of ten—Charity's age—and his own father's cabin boy. Cook seemed a logical vessel for the kind of information she sought.

She sat on an empty water keg in the galley, watching him stir up a barley soup that was more stew than soup because water was so scarce. "John, tell me," she asked. "Did Captain Titus and his wife marry young?"

The cook reached into the saltcellar. He raised his hand to sprinkle some salt in the pot, then must have thought better of it. "Best we don't have too much salt, Miss Utley," he told her. "Makes a body thirsty." He settled for a tiny pinch. "Aye, they were young. I think he was seventeen and just back from a voyage and she was the same."

"They couldn't have had much of a courtship," Ann suggested.

"Nay, none at all," he told her and settled himself on a corner of the table. "His father told me once that he thinks Tamsin and his boy just happened to find themselves in the church one day when the minister was in a splicing mood." He leaned forward, as if relishing the little confidence. "Some wager he never even proposed."

"Surely he must have!" Ann said, unable to keep the surprise from her voice.

John Cook shrugged. "He has a way of just assuming things."

She couldn't deny that. "That's no way to court the ladies," she persisted. "No wonder he hasn't remarried."

"No wonder," he agreed, the soul of amiability. "I reckon this, miss: The lady who wants him this time around will have to speak up. Ladies like Tamsin don't appear much."

Well, I want him, she decided, as John turned back to his stew. *But I wonder if I am any braver, particularly since he is another species altogether*, she thought, as she climbed to the quarterdeck. *I wish I knew, really knew, if he felt a tenth for me what I feel for him. I mean, is he just a man who loves women, or a man who loves me?* She knew her own nature well enough, she who had survived a number of proposals with her heart quite untouched but her mind wary. If he chose to let her remain in the Azores, then so be it. He would have to speak first; her character and pride required it.

It was a dismal consideration. She stood on the quarterdeck and looked at the sky. And looked again. Her heart thumped in her breast. Land birds wheeled and mewed overhead. She walked to the railing and looked out at the same time the man in the crow's nest called, "Land ho!" She heard the captain on the poop deck slam his spyglass inside itself. Seeing her there, he motioned to her.

He aims to show me the Azores, she thought, and shook her head at him. Charity called to her too, but she quietly went belowdeck, crawled into her berth, and pulled a blanket over her head. She lay there until she began to sweat, then threw back the covers, angry with the lady who was too proud to march up the steps, declare that she loved him, and refuse to leave the ship, and sad for the lady who knew—really knew for the first time—what it felt like to love someone. There wasn't a thing she wouldn't do for Captain Hiram Titus, and at the same time, she wanted to box his ears.

Trapped between indecision, despair, and a lurking humor over the absurdity of it all, she suddenly understood him. She stared at the compass overhead and then began to relax. He was forty, some fifteen years married and then widowed, with no idea how to court a lady. All he knew was how to be a husband. She had better swallow her pride and speak before the love of her life sailed away with the morning tide.

She got out of the berth, brushed her hair with his brush, wished for the hundredth time that voyage that she had another dress, then went on the quarterdeck. She stood there watching the captain, who had trained his glass on the harbor. She looked up at the crow's nest, where a sailor was doing the same thing. She quietly climbed the steps to the poop deck and stood beside Charity. Already the water just inside the harbor was calmer, more serene. The air was redolent with what smelled like jasmine and orange blossom, and heavy with humidity. The buildings gleamed white, with red roofs, and smoke spiraled from chimneys.

As she watched the beauty before her, a bell began to toll. At home in England it would be evening. She felt a sudden pang, a physical pain. *It may be that I never see my home again*, she thought. She closed her eyes, thought of everything lovely she would miss, and opened her eyes. *We make our choices,* she told herself. *I have made mine, even if the captain doesn't know it yet.*

Suddenly he was too far away. She hurried to his side just as he put down the glass and nodded to his helmsman. "We're going in, laddie," he said. "Not a warship in sight."

If I just stand here, he will drape his arm around my waist and haul me up next to his hip, she thought. He did precisely that, and she took Charity's hand and pulled her in front of them both. Ann rested her hands gently on her shoulders and enjoyed the feeling of the captain's long fingers on her waist. To her amusement, they strayed down to her hip, and he patted her in such a proprietary way that she knew she was right; this man was not one to court, but he was already the best husband she could ever hope for.

"It appears we beat the bad news, Annie," he told her. Only a deaf person would not have heard the relief in his voice.

"We can get water, Papa?"

"Most certainly."

"I have a favor then," Ann began, after directing his fingers back to her waist. "Since we are soon to have ample water, I would like to wash my hair."

"I'll have a water keg sent to the cabin right away. There are one or two left." He looked at Charity. "Isn't there some Spanish soap in that cabinet by my berth?"

He seemed to recall everything he had to do then, now that they were sailing into a safe harbor, and turned away to bellow orders that sent sailors climbing nimbly up the ratlines to trim the sails. The water made a different sound against the ship as it slowed. He stood by the rail a minute more, a solitary figure, and her heart went out to him. *How difficult it must be to hold so many lives in your hands, my dear,* she thought. *You have my utmost admiration.* Impulsively, she went up behind him then at the rail, wrapped her arms around his waist, and kissed that spot just below his ear that she had been admiring for three weeks at least. How nice to be tall and able to reach it so easily, without jumping up and down, or standing on boxes.

"Annie, you're compromising me," he joked, his Yankee twang unmistakable. She laughed and kissed him again, then left him there to stare out at the harbor and figure out what to do. The helmsman grinned at her as she walked by, and she smiled back. *I believe I will be a very good American,* she thought.

Charity didn't remain below deck except to take a long drink of water from the fresh cask. She looked at the glass and then drained the last of the water. "Ann, why is it that when I knew I couldn't have much water, it was all I wanted, all the time?"

"I don't know why that is, either, my dear." She paused, struck by the thought that she had felt the same way in the warehouse the afternoon she inadvertently wrote Hiram Titus's name all through the *Jasper*'s invoice. *I knew he would be leaving then, and all I wanted was for him to stay and stay,* she thought. "Maybe shortages are good for us, now and then. They remind us of what we have."

"They do."

When she heard Charity's feet on the deck overhead, she closed the door, sighed, and took off her dress that John Cook had so obligingly washed for her in salt water a couple of times while she had huddled in a sheet in the cabin. *I wonder if there is a ready-made dress in Terceira I could buy,* she thought, *or a generous woman of my height who would relinquish a dress of her own. I'm willing to wager that I'll be getting married tomorrow, and I'd rather not look like a penniless ragbag.*

With a sigh of satisfaction to be free of the dress, she dipped water from the keg into the washbowl and went in search of the Spanish soap. It was where he had said it would be, and there was also a letter wedged between the cabinet and the berth. She picked it up and recognized the handwriting. "Well, Aggie, what did you write to the captain about?" she asked out loud and set it on the pillow.

She turned back to the basin and peeled down her chemise. It was only a moment's work to run a cloth with Spanish soap over her torso, but oh, the pleasure of at least moderate cleanliness without salt. She dried herself and pulled up her chemise again. She dabbed the soap on her hair and began to work her fingers through the suds, humming to herself, enjoying the moment.

Then other hands were in her hair. She started in surprise, then couldn't help smiling underneath her mane of wet hair. "Captain, you have far trumped any possible compromise of mine," she told him, amazed at how matter-of-fact she could sound, when her heart was practically pounding through her rib cage.

"Oh, I don't care," he said mildly. His fingers massaged her scalp. "We'll take the dinghy into Terceira tomorrow morning."

"If you still think you're going to turn me over to the British consulate, you're mistaken."

"I thought we'd report to the harbormaster—I'm careful about these things, Annie—and then see if the consulate knows of a parson, or a minister, or whatever you call them."

She could hear him dipping clean water into a pitcher. He poured it carefully on her head, already the husband, or perhaps still the husband. She closed her eyes against the soap, and also against the thought that made her knees weak: *Thank heavens I climbed down that tree.*

"Is this a proposal?" she asked, knowing that her voice must be muffled under the weight of her hair and the water.

"Annie, I believe it is. Since the war is on, and I know none of my ships will be sailing from port until it ends, I need a rich wife."

She laughed, knowing that she could point out the obvious to him, that her money would be embargoed in its London bank as long as that same war lasted. "Then you should have found an . . . an . . . American nabobess with ready funds," she told him.

He squeezed the water from her hair and turned her

around to face him. "I wanted you," he said, and there was nothing of teasing in that tone. "I love you, Ann Utley. For the past three weeks I have been wondering how to tell you I'm crazy for you, and then how to ask you to marry me. Thank heavens for war."

She threw her arms around him and clung to him, even though she knew she was soaking him. He kissed her quite soundly, held her off and took a good look, rolled his eyes (which made her laugh), and kissed her again.

She just stood there, unembarrassed and calm. "I was resolved to wash my hair, go on deck again, and propose to you, my love," she told him simply. "You weren't going to leave me here in Terceira. I love you."

He just looked at her for the longest moment. "Dear Annie," was all he said.

She was drying her hair when he noticed the letter on the pillow. "It was on the floor . . ." she said, following his glance.

"Deck," he corrected automatically.

"On the deck by the berth. I'm certain that is Aggie Glossop's writing." Feeling a little shy, she buttoned her dress and sat by him. "What can it be?"

He looked at it a moment, then tapped the letter on his forehead. "She practically threw it at me as I ran out of the warehouse and told me to open it after we made open water. I completely forgot." He opened the letter with his thumbnail. "I recall stuffing it inside my shirt. I guess it fell out when I took off my shirt, and I didn't notice. Maybe I owe them more than the first bill."

He took off his shoes, then lay down on the berth.

"Lie down, Annie," he said.

"What if Charity comes in?" she asked.

"She can lie down too," he said affably, patting the spot beside him. "There's room." He pillowed her wet head on his arm and took out the sheets of close-printed paper with his free hand. She shut her eyes, content to lie there and bask in her good fortune.

"Well, I'll be . . . ," he said, and then burst out laughing.

Ann opened her eyes and sat up. His eyes merry, he handed her one of those infamous manifests from the HMS *Jasper*. "It says, 'Hiram Titus in oil,'" he pointed out, when he could speak. "And look there, 'Hiram Titus in cotton wadding.'"

She flopped down again beside him. "I thought I caught all those," she said in a faint voice.

But he was reading the letter now and shaking his head. When he finished, he rose up on his elbow to look at her. "Ann, we've been diddled by champions."

"What can you mean?"

He lay down again, pulling her close, even though he was as wet now as she was. "There's no war, Annie! She and that rascal Ned said that just to get me out to sea with you on the *Hasty*."

She opened her mouth, too astounded to speak, as he said, "Listen, my dear. 'Ann is far too proud and set in her ways to make a decision, so I am making it for her. Do take good care of her, Captain, and bring her back for a visit now and then.'"

Ann wasn't sure whether to laugh or to cry, so she did both. She took the soggy handkerchief that the captain gave her and wiped her wet face. She rose up to face him. "I was all prepared to take the mail coach back to Derbyshire when you rowed me ashore that noon, Hiram," she told him.

He kissed her. "And I probably would have let you go, my love," he said softly. "I'm no expert at this love business. I couldn't woo a lady if my life depended on it."

"That is as bold a lie as I have ever heard," she replied as he kissed her eyelids and then worked his way down to her throat.

"It's true, Annie," he said. "But I am one fine husband."

* * *

There was no international incident over the kidnapping and subsequent marriage of Miss Ann Utley, British subject, to Captain Hiram Titus, American. The British consulate had grown lethargic and indolent from his years in the sultry climate of the Azores and didn't want to face the paperwork involved in a major event. Better to let it slide, especially since the bride—dressed in a hideous gown, but Quality nonetheless—clung to the Yankee like a barnacle. There was a vicar on Terceira who tended to the spiritual needs of the small British colony there, and he married them, even without banns or a special license.

Hiram had his own doubts that the marriage was strictly legal, but he knew he could make things right or righter, anyway when they fetched Boston and were able to make a binding civil arrangement. Besides, his legs were long and he wanted his own berth back. And truth to tell, the sight of Annie in a wet chemise and petticoat had taken a few years off his life. Waiting another five weeks for a parson to mumble over them seemed like a study in stupidity to someone who would be forty-one in November.

Charity was happy enough to return to her own cabin. Her father and new mother assured her that she could pop in every morning, but only after she knocked first and waited for a reply.

Not too far into the voyage from Terceira, Ann Titus decided that honeymooning on a seagoing vessel was quite to her liking. Thank goodness she had a well-seasoned husband. Someone else could pour punch in August for Clotilde's wedding.

Writer's note: That same summer of 1807 when the *Hasty* was returning from England, the HMS *Leopard* pounced upon the USS *Chesapeake* outside of Norfolk, killing three, wounding eighteen, and impressing four. President Jefferson's countermeasure, Embargo Act of December 1807, nearly destroyed New England shipping. War didn't come until 1812.

Something New

"There is no new thing under the sun."
ECCLESIASTES

*T*HERE IS NO PLEASURE QUITE LIKE THE *pleasure of sitting in a hot bath, secure in the knowledge that I will not be summoned to fire a round at anyone or anything*, thought Major John Redpath of the Royal Horse Artillery. He carefully sank lower in the tub and contemplated his bare knees. *I will lie here up to my neck in hot water, and if anyone knocks, I will say fearful things such as—*

Knock.

"Come in," the major said with a sigh, quite unable to break six years of habit. "This had better be very good," he added, before the door opened. "Oh, it is you. Parkhill, go . . . go . . . far away from me."

The lieutenant grinned and leaned against the door-jamb. "Yes, sir! But only after my wedding, sir, and that is what I have come to see you about."

"Not interested," the major said, looking for something to throw. "Not even if your fiancée were to come in here and scrub my back."

"She would never!" said Lieutenant Sir Edmund

Parkhill, shocked. "Not Emmeline! I'll be dashed lucky if she scrubs mine!"

What is it about me that no one thinks I mean what I say? the major asked himself, as he regarded his most junior lieutenant. *When we are serving the guns, no one questions me. But put me in a tub, or a bed, or a bordello, or a church, or even a necessary, and I am fair game to all my officers. I am entirely too accessible,* he decided as he stood up to soap himself, then sat down quickly when Lt. Parkhill was followed into the room by one of the laundresses. The water sloshed from the tub and he sighed again.

"Sir, I have a matter to discuss with you that can't wait," she said, glaring at the lieutenant, who knew when he was outranked and took up a defensive position in the window. "It is about Marie Deux."

"Mrs. Hurley, could you not wait until I at least cover my privates?" he grumbled, reaching for a washcloth.

"And about your privates," she began.

Ed Parkhill started to laugh as the major looked down into the water, then up at the laundress, who probably outweighed him, particularly in her current condition.

"Major Redpath, the ones outside! The ones who are getting drunker and more disorderly by the minute."

"I didn't think you meant the ones in the water, Mrs. Hurley," the major said, smiling in spite of himself. "Leave them alone—the ones outside—and let them celebrate Boney's abdication, please. Marie Deux? What is that little puss up to?"

The laundress looked less sure of herself as she came farther into the room. She rubbed her belly, big with another of Sergeant Hurley's botherations. "Sir, I just can't take her along to Belgium. I didn't win in the lottery so I have to travel overland, and it's too much, Major Redpath."

"I expect it is," he agreed. "I'll see what I can do, Mrs. Hurley," he said, absently scratching himself.

"I knew you would, sir," she said as she left the room. The major looked at the lieutenant balancing in the window. "There she goes, certain that I will solve her problem," he complained. "Why do people do that around me?"

"Because they know that once you are acquainted with their problem, you will solve it for them," the lieutenant said promptly. "There is something about you that inspires complete confidence. It is a knack you have. Now, sir, about my wedding . . ."

"Aye, the answer is aye," Major Redpath sighed, fishing for the washcloth. "Since I am so obliging, I will oblige." He stood again to soap himself, after a wary glance at the door. "Now tell me what I have agreed to."

"A simple matter."

"It always is," the major said wearily.

"You and I are going on furlough to England at the same time, sir. I wish you to accompany me to Kent and be my best man," Parkhill said. "That's all."

The major soaped himself thoughtfully and motioned for his lieutenant to hand him the bucket. He poured the cold water over himself. "If that's all there is to it, Ed, I'll do it."

I wish everything were that easy, he thought, as he shaved, dressed, and kept an eye on the clock. Beau Wellington was particular about his officers arriving on time for functions. Redpath leaned his cheek on his hand, stared at the heaping mound of unfinished paperwork in front of him, and said a monumentally dirty word in French. He got up and went to the window.

The church bells in Toulouse had not ceased to ring since announcement of Napoleon's abdication had reached the town from Bordeaux. He could not begin to describe the gratitude that welled in his heart. He was alive, he was healthy, with furlough home in Scotland coming up, following a wedding in Bath. He looked out the window again. "Marie Deux, what am I to do with you now, lass?" he asked.

As it happened, she was seated in the courtyard below with the other laundresses' children. Hands folded, feet together, back straight, she watched the Hurley's toddler fall and rise and try to join the others in their chase after a ball. Patiently she retrieved the squalling child, wiped his face like the little mother she was, and resumed her watch.

He smiled as he observed her. "Marie Deux," he murmured, "were you ever young?"

He knew she couldn't be much more than four, herself. Ed Parkhill had told him how they had found her among the French guns after the third siege of Badajoz, too starved to cry as they approached to look at the French battery, English artillerymen on a coachman's holiday. "She was all eyes on a scrawny neck," Ed had told him several months later, when he joined the Second Battery. "She just sat there and watched us." Then Ed shook his head, amazed all over again at the perspicacity of little girls. "And then she held out her arms to us. Dash it all, but that's how it is: I suppose daughters of the guns know sons of guns, eh, sir?"

Poor Marie Deux, he thought, watching her, *you were flotsam in the sea of war*. Parkhill admitted to him later that his first inclination was to pass her by. "She would have been dead in a day, Major," he remembered in the telling. "But we couldn't. Call it artillerymen's courtesy."

Major Redpath understood. It was the same humanity that always compelled him to tour the remains of all French batteries following a battle. He had dispatched more than one horse struggling against death, or French *bombardier* ghastly with wounds, begging and pleading for a quick end. Artillery was unforgiving and cruel to victim and server, he knew. He found a perverse fascination in sitting on a French limber and looking across the field, wondering about that point of view.

"We artillerists are always concerned about point of view, Marie Deux, for it is our business," he said, looking out of the window. "What would be best for you, now that your country is ours, and Boney is gone?"

It was a question he carried with him to the town hall, where Wellington had ordered dinner for his officers and allies. He had to watch his steps in the streets of Toulouse. Everywhere enterprising Gallic merchants were busy discarding any signs of Bonaparte from shop windows and facades, and throwing the remnants into the street. He stood a moment to watch masons chipping the carved N and B from the front of the town hall. Everywhere bells tolled.

He joined the dinner guests, quickly locating Sir Thomas Picton, his division commander, all hearty and foul of mouth, and wearing his top hat even indoors. *I wonder what the gentry at home would think if they knew we would and did follow that smelly lump of leadership all over Spain, and gladly, too?* he thought.

"Sir, I need your advice," he asked, before the dinner began in lengthy earnest.

"Well, John, speak up. Don't know why you artillerists are so soft-spoken."

Standing with his commander in an alcove off the dining hall, he told him about Mrs. Hurley and Marie Deux. "She's been mothering Marie since her husband found her on the field at Badajoz, sir. Now she wishes to be released from the obligation, and I, for one, think she deserves to be heard."

To Redpath's relief, Picton listened with interest. The general himself had proved vulnerable to Marie's considerable charms, as he lay recuperating from wounds of Badajoz, so Parkhill had told him. Mrs. Hurley had been pressed into service as a nurse, and she made the rounds of the makeshift ward within the breached walls of Badajoz, towing little Marie after her, nursing her too, with an open-bloused generosity that saw no enemy in a hungry child.

"Is she still a pretty minx, John?" the general asked.

"Aye," Redpath said, thinking of the times he had been very nearly skewered by her dark eyes and way of watching him so carefully, as though she knew he commanded and must be cajoled, and perhaps obeyed. "Aye," he said again. "She has her French ways of getting to us all."

The general leaned against the wall. "Have you thought of a Spanish orphanage?"

Redpath had, and the idea found no favor with him. Marie was French from her name to her accent, and he feared her treatment in an orphanage in Spain. "It doesn't seem wise, sir," he said. He shrugged. "Neither does a French orphanage. She has been with the Second Battery for so long now, that I do not know how happy the Frogs will be about her, either. It's a dilemma."

Both men were silent, letting the continuing toasts to Wellington and euphoria of victory swirl around them. "I don't know why it's your problem," Picton said at last.

"It's my battery, sir," Redpath responded quietly. "I may not have been there to approve or disapprove the whole thing in the first place, but when I assumed command from poor Williams, I took on all the Second, not just the guns."

General Picton nodded. "So you did; so we all do. Well, sir, are you married? Maybe your wife would like a remembrance of Spain besides your sorry self."

Redpath laughed and shook his head. "No to both

charges, sir! Even if I were leg shackled, I can't fathom springing a four-year-old on an unsuspecting wife."

"Nor I, John." He leaned against the wall, his hand raised as if painting a picture. "There is your loving wife, hands on her corset strings, dying to see you after . . ." He looked at Redpath.

"Six years . . ."

". . . six years, and you walk in with a child and say 'Surprise!'"

"I can't imagine it," John said. He was silent, waiting for Picton to continue.

"Very well, blast your eyes, Redpath, I'll see what I can do," the general said at last, and then managed a rueful laugh. "Now it's my problem?"

John Redpath grinned and stepped aside for a waiter staggering under a tray of bottles. "That's what Horse Guards pays you so much for, General. Cheers now." He snagged a bottle from the tray as the waiter struggled past. *Ah me, champagne in dusty bottles*, he thought, as he nodded to his general and went to take his seat. *It's about time we took France.*

After the dinner—all toasts and well-deserved applause for Beau Wellington—John Redpath strolled back to his quarters. The bells were silent now, but men who had found dusty bottles of their own leaned against each other or slumped in corners. All the stars were out, and probably even more than usual, considering the victory celebration, and he walked slowly, savoring the idea of peace and a return home, if only for a brief furlough.

Not for the first time, he wished there were a wife waiting for him, hands on corset strings, as Picton so baldly put it. He had been at war almost twenty of his thirty-six years, serving the guns all over India, and then Portugal and Spain. He couldn't complain, really. The time had passed quickly, and beyond a little deafness in one ear—an occupational hazard—he was healthy and the possessor of all his parts, no mean achievement for a gunner. Of course, there had been scant opportunity to seek out a wife. In the rush and fervor of war, he had not minded, really. For some reason, the ladies liked gunners. He hadn't suffered in the romance department.

He sat down on the steps of the cathedral to enjoy the champagne buzz that filled his head, even as he scrutinized his solitary life, and found it wanting. *I am tired of one-night women*, he thought, *and different cots in different bivouacs, and food served in a mess hall or on a stick over a campfire, and washing myself in a gun bucket, and drinking out of empty shell casings.* Chin in hand, he sat on the steps and wondered what it would be like to read the morning paper seated across the breakfast table from someone who smelled good, or wake up to children running into his room and jumping on the bed, as he used to do as a small boy.

He wasn't too drunk to realize that he didn't have the slightest idea how to go about the getting of a wife. It was knowledge ungleaned in all those years of war. He considered asking Ed Parkhill, who seemed to have navigated those shoals successfully, then discarded the idea. *No, no, he thinks I know everything*, the major reflected sourly. "I do know a lot, but somehow I do not think elevations, azimuths, and apogees will get me a wife," he told the drunk soldier snoring nearby. "I wonder what will?" he asked as he got up and headed in a more or less straight line toward his bed.

* * *

General Picton was as good as his word. Two weeks later, he skirted around the battery as the men of the Second discharged their final rounds, preparatory to swabbing out the guns thoroughly and readying them for transport to Belgium. Redpath, his interest trained on his lovely six-pounders, was startled out of his black-powder reverie by Picton's hand on his shoulder.

"Yes, sir," he said, removing the cork plugs from his ears and leaning close to his commander.

"I've found the place for your Marie Deux," Picton shouted over the guns. "My family donates a cartload of money each year to St. Pancras Orphanage at Austell. I've already sent a letter, and they will be expecting our French minx."

Redpath nodded, his attention on his guns again as one of the gunners spilled a casing of powder. "Sergeant Mathey," he shouted, leaping to his feet from his perch on a caisson. "On report! It's a wonder Soult didn't mash you in the last engagement!" He returned half of his attention to General Picton. "Excuse me, sir? St. Austell's out of St. Pancras?"

"No! The other way around! Austell!" The general grabbed Redpath by the neck and towed him away from the guns. "St. Pancras out of Austell. You know, near Land's End. Redpath, pay attention!" He shrugged, his irritation momentary. "At any rate, my ADC is drawing up a letter of introduction for you."

"Have him give it to Lt. Parkhill, sir," Redpath said, replacing his cork plugs. "Better yet, Parkhill is already packed and his case is in the courtyard. Have him put it inside, if you please, sir."

Picton nodded, grinned, and gave Redpath a shove back toward the battery. "Letter to Parkhill, it will be. And I am interested in a report on this." He held out his hand and Redpath removed one plug. "Let us clap hands, Major. I've never thanked you for six years of the best."

Redpath shook his commander's hand, felt himself amply repaid, wondered why his eyes were brimming over—particularly since he was used to all that smoke—and returned to his guns. It was late that night before he reluctantly left the loading area, feeling out of sorts and melancholy as he always did, when he was going one way, and his guns another. Toulouse was quieter now, settling into the routine of peace. He passed the ambulance trains taking wounded back to the convalescent hospital at Fontarabia. He, Parkhill, and Marie Deux would ride with them tomorrow, leaving for home from the port in Spain. He looked up from his contemplation of the cobblestones to see Mrs. Hurley waiting for him outside his quarters, bundle in one hand, and Marie Deux in the other.

"Here she is, Major," the woman said, bending down to straighten the cotton fichu on Marie's tidy bodice, and give her skirt a twitch. "Now, do as you're told, miss, and I'm sure you'll find a good family in England."

You might as well tell her she's going to the moon, Redpath thought, as he watched Marie's eyes well up with tears. His heart did a little flop as he saw her sniff them back, shudder, and then grab Mrs. Hurley in a tight embrace. Awkward in her pregnancy, the sergeant's wife knelt on the cobblestones, her own grip strong. "I wish it could be different, dearie," she murmured into Marie's ear as the child clung to her. She looked up at the major, her eyes appealing for help. "Gor, Major, it's hard to leave, but I don't know what else to do."

She wrenched herself away finally, handed the bundle to the major, and put Marie's hand in his. *What small fingers*, he thought, as he nodded to Mrs. Hurley, wished her the best of luck, and stood with the child until the woman had turned the corner. He winced inside, waiting for Marie to cry, but she only took a tighter grip on his hand and leaned against his leg.

"Where is this England?" she asked suddenly. "Can I ride there on the caissons with the other children?"

He knelt beside her in the courtyard, amazed at the impact of her words on his heart, as he saw in his mind's eye the children, dusty but uncomplaining, riding the caissons or balancing on the limbers as the Second Battery, Picton's Third Division, wound its way the length of the Peninsula. That and walking was all she knew of transportation.

"Lass, you will be two weeks traveling by ship, and then you will be in England," he explained, knowing that his words meant nothing to someone who had never seen more water than the often-stingy rivers of Spain. He ignored the familiar catcalls and comments of his fellow officers returning to their quarters, surprised that it should matter so much to him that Marie Deux understand what was happening to her. He could tell she did not; she sighed heavily .

Two weeks and six years has been this journey, he amended to himself as he lay in his cot later that night. He had made a pallet for Marie Deux out of his discarded clothes, patting it smooth for her and giving her his pillow. She was asleep now, breathing quietly and evenly in the little room, and he smiled that her evening's work to organize him had worn her into solid slumber.

"I am now going to pack six years of Spain," he had announced to her as she perched on his hat case, eating the mush and milk he had cajoled from the mess hall. "Of course, I should have done this much sooner—you may only consider Lt. Parkhill's much better example—but dash it all, Marie, I am a busy man. *Muy ocupado.*"

He had held up one of his powder-burned shirts and was vastly amused when Marie set down her bowl, shook her head, and declared, "*Mais non, monsieur*," in the firm tone of one who knows, counseling one who doesn't.

"Oh, you are my fashion arbiter?" he murmured as he discarded the shirt. "How French of you!"

She did not understand sarcasm any better than any other four-year-old, but she was obviously waiting for him to hold up another shirt. He did, and she rejected it too, and the next one, and the next.

"Marie, I will go to England naked!" he protested.

"You can have more shirts made, monsieur," was her imperturbable reply as she returned to her mush and milk, all the while keeping him under close observation, lest he should sneak in a shirt she did not approve.

She shook her head over his trousers too, restoring his good humor by her Gallic contempt of his wardrobe. "Monsieur does not for one moment think he should take holes to this England?" was how she phrased it, with an expressive cut of her hand that made him turn away and cough, so she would not think he was laughing at her.

"I wouldn't dare," he replied promptly, and his beloved campaigning trousers, powder burns, holes and all, ended up on the growing discard pile. "I know, I know: I can have more made in this England!"

To his huge amusement, she nodded seriously, as though relieved he was finally showing a lick of sense. "You should know these things, monsieur," she commented as he coughed some more. "Mrs. Hurley claims that you lead the Second," she added, great doubt in her voice.

He couldn't help himself then, laughing out loud and wondering why on earth he had never considered the splendor of his raiment before as he and the Second had blasted their way through Spain. He sat on his packing case, contemplating Marie and trying to imagine himself through her eyes:

"I was pretty shabby, wasn't I?" he asked her finally.

She nodded. "I will overlook it," she said generously. "Maybe you were *trés ocupado,*" She declared in her combined French, English, and Spanish that Redpath had dubbed Franglish.

Maybe I was "trés ocupado," he thought later as he

watched her sleep. She had been properly impressed with his dress uniform that he carefully put last into the packing case. She had even hopped off the hat case to finger the epaulets and rows of gold braid, her eyes wide. Then she looked at him, mystified, as though she wanted to ask why on earth he didn't wear this instead of his usual campaigning rags. She must have thought better of it, because she confined her remarks to a whispered *"C'est bon,"* that got him back into her sartorial good graces.

He watched as she smoothed down the deep blue fabric, her fingers light on the gold trim. To his amusement, she rearranged the two tassels on the front in a more pleasing design. "There," she said, like God resting on the seventh day. "It will do."

Ah, there is a lucky family in England that doesn't even have any idea of the good fortune shortly to come its way, he thought as his eyes began to close. St. Pancras or St. Austell's or whatever that place was called will have no difficulty placing this charmer. She will go to an unsuspecting family, place herself in charge, and organize them beyond their wildest dreams.

* * *

It was a short crossing from Irun to Portsmouth, rendered palatable by Marie Deux. Impervious, apparently, to seasickness, she had calmly wetted a cloth and wiped his face after his bouts at the bucket, and he was reminded of the care she took of the Hurley's children younger than she. It gave him some perverse satisfaction that she ignored Ed Parkhill, moaning and groaning in the other berth. *I have a devoted and efficient handler*, Redpath realized, as Spain receded from his vision and his heart, and he allowed himself to think of Scotland, and home.

When he could function, he rewarded Marie by taking her on deck frequently, where she stood like a little admiral, admiring the view from the poop deck, and capturing the loyalty of most of the watch. "Your daughter?" the captain had asked him, and it almost gave him a pang to say no, and explain Marie Deux's origins. "We keep cats," was the captain's only comment, and he realized how extraordinary had been the Second Battery's salvage of a dying child from a French battery. His appreciation for his mush-hearted gun crew welled up all over again, and he longed to see them, and his guns, in Belgium. He frowned. *It will not be the same without Marie Deux there*, he thought.

Portsmouth was no more than a welcome spot to feel the ground again, engage a post chaise, allow Lt. Parkhill time to dash off a brief missive to his fiancée in Bath, and start for St. Pancras, near Land's End. "At least, I am almost certain the village was St. Pancras," he said, as he and Lt. Parkhill sat in the post chaise and waited for the postboys to stow the luggage.

"Major Redpath!" Parkhill burst out. "You're not sure? I mean, sir"—he gulped—"I mean, I just wrote my fiancée that we would be in Bath in three days, sir!"

Redpath frowned. "I think it was St. Pancras. Yes, I am certain. Well"—he paused, looking at Marie Deux, who leaned against his sleeve, asleep—"it's a simple matter, Ed! I told General Picton to have his ADC put the letter of introduction in your packing case. Just get it out and look at it."

Parkhill nodded. "A simple matter." He stuck his head out of the window. "Boy, there, boy? Bring down that packing case, there's a good lad." He started from the vehicle, then gasped and sat down suddenly on the top step as though someone had yanked his legs from under him.

"An old wound, Ed?" Redpath sympathized, his eyes full of concern. "It won't do to go bum butt a week before your wedding."

His lieutenant was silent for a long moment. "The packing case in the courtyard," he said, striving to keep his tone conversational, to the major's ears, but unable to keep the rising panic from his voice. "My packing case."

"Well, yes. You were already packed," Redpath explained.

Parkhill turned around slowly to look at him, his face as pale as though he still pitched and tossed in the transport. "Major, I gave my packing case to Jack Beresford in exchange for his, which was larger. You see, I had presents for Emmeline and her sister and needed more space, and Major Beresford had lost most of his personal effects in that fire. We traded."

The two men stared at each other. "I am almost certain it was St. Pancras," Major Redpath said slowly. "Of course, I had those cork plugs in my ear, and the guns were going off . . ."

". . . and they've always claimed your full attention, sir," the lieutenant concluded, shaking his head mournfully. "Oh, Major Redpath."

"St. Pancras," Redpath said decisively. "I'm sure of it." He ran a finger around the inside of his collar, surprised suddenly how warm it was for May in England. "Well, maybe I'm not so sure."

* * *

There, now, thought Audrey Winkle as she folded the last of Emmeline's trousseau petticoats and stuck her needle back in the pincushion. *I have hemmed everything in this house except the butler's trousers. Every frock and walking dress and ball gown has been oohed and ahhed over, tried on and ironed. Mama has given Emmeline "The Lecture" and scared her to death. The mints and marzipan are cooling in the milk house. Cook and housekeeper are still speaking to each other. It only remains for Ed Parkhill to get here and marry my wretched sister before she turns into an ogre fit only to frighten bad children into good behavior.*

Audrey laughed out loud at the image of Emmeline, all blonde, pink, and sweet-smelling being used as a disciplinary object lesson. She went to the window, pulled back the drapes—newly cleaned and restored—to look out on the gathering darkness of late spring. *I wonder if I was so terrible before Captain Winkle so kindly married me?* she thought, wondering why, after all these years, she still thought of him as captain and seldom as Matthew.

She leaned against the drapes, sniffing the sunshine still held in them, even as the moon rose like a benediction over the newly planted fields. *If I had known him better, perhaps I would think of him today as Matthew,* she considered. *As it is, I do not remember what color his eyes were, but then, eight years is a long time to recall so brief a husband and lover.*

She knew from time-honored experience that she could still close her eyes and see him as though screened through her wedding veil, handsome, confident in his naval uniform, hand resting self-consciously on his sword. But his eyes? Were they gray or blue? Not that it mattered. The next time she saw him, they were closed in death. He wore the same uniform, the peaked hat tucked at his side, all cozy and big shouldered in a coffin that seemed too narrow to contain the life that had been his. Admiral Lord Kitchen of the Blue Fleet had presented her with his sword, which now hung over the fireplace in her room, looking supremely silly with its background of pale green walls, white-trimmed mantel, and china doodads. She wanted to put it away in the closet, but Mama would have been aghast. As it was, she would go days and days now without even a glance at the miniature of him that rested on her bedside table.

She never told Mama, of course, any more than she

would have admitted to her or even Emmeline how it set her teeth on edge when they looked at her with profound sympathy still, even after eight years. They didn't need to know how she resented the lingering, loving way they spoke his name occasionally, as though Captain Winkle of His Majesty's Royal Navy was someone soft and effete to be remembered in hushed tones. She closed the drapes. They never understood how robust he was, how fun, how lovely, how blasphemous, how naughty.

"Ah, well," she said out loud. "I wonder that anyone knows how to mourn." She had grieved and suffered and buried her husband of two months, replacing the highest joys with the deepest pain, enduring it and willing it to take her too. And when she could finally stare down death and not shudder at the remembrance of its cold pall on the one she loved, she knew that she was through mourning. When she could remember the joy without the sorrow and feel something close kin to peace, it was over. She knew she had been ready for some years now to find another husband. She had thought at first to never marry another military man, but Audrey Winkle was open to suggestion.

And now the world was at peace again, and Napoleon on Elba. The gentry of her circle would return to the concerns of business and land, and if an older widow of twenty-eight years held some attraction over the young sprites who dressed in light muslin and practiced dance steps and how to pour tea, her prospects were at least sanguine.

She knew she had a pretty face; that sort of thing ran in the Caldwell family. True, not everyone could be blonde like Emmeline, but there was room in the world for brunettes with brown eyes and graceful carriage. It gave her a little perverse pleasure to note that her own figure was neater than Emmeline's, even at her advanced age. Several respectable widowers had come to call and gaze down at her fine bosom when they thought she wasn't aware, but Audrey Winkle smiled, flirted gently, and knew that somewhere in the world, there had to be younger men still. They weren't all dead on battlefields, or drowned in the sea, or victims of sudden illness like Matthew.

Of course, the reality that one of these paragons with ginger in his step and a twinkle in his eye would ever appear on her doorstep was unlikely in the extreme. *This will be the difficult part,* she considered, as she gathered the last of the petticoats and folded them. *I must eventually convince Mama that I am quite able to set up my own establishment, and in a livelier locale than a house on the outskirts of Bath, where gouty old men come to drink the waters, belch, and complain about the government.*

She had the income from her dear dead Papa, and all of Captain Winkle's prize money too, so the issue was not financial. She needed her own place, and soon, what with Emmeline already chattering on about how wonderful it would be to have Aunt Audrey close by to help with new babies. *A pox on Aunt Audrey,* she thought, as she took a deep breath and prepared to venture into the rest of the house with its visiting relatives and wedding plans. Aunt Audrey would rather have babies of her own, and they didn't grow in succession houses under strawberry leaves. *A husband was essential for that,* she thought, *and fun in the bargain.*

Petticoats draped over her arm, she stepped in the hall and discovered too late that tactical error as her mother bore down upon her. *Too bad that one cannot press a hand against a door to detect heat and looming mothers of brides,* she thought with resignation as she smiled at her mother.

"Where have you been hiding?" her mother demanded,

taking her by the arm and hurrying her toward the dining room.

"Mama, I was not hiding," she protested gently, knowing the truth of that question and owning to a touch of guilt. "I was finishing the last of Emmeline's petticoats. Mama, where are you taking me?"

Tight of lip and pale of face, Mrs. Caldwell's fragile appearance was belied by the strength of her grip on her elder daughter. Amused, Audrey hurried to keep up, wondering what Dr. Welch would say if he could see his most constant patient practically trot down the corridor without even breathing heavily.

Mrs. Caldwell stopped in front of the dining room doors and flung them open with the strength of ten. "There!" she exclaimed, her voice filled with ill usage. "Can you imagine?"

Audrey couldn't, particularly since she could see nothing out of place in the impeccable room, set with several smaller tables for the bridal dinner. "Mama, perhaps it's a little early to set the tables for . . ." she hedged.

"Audrey, you are so dense at times that I could scream!" Mama said. "I had the servants set it up to see the effect." She paused dramatically. "How can we face all our relatives and friends?"

"Mama, there is nothing wrong!" Audrey said.

Mrs. Caldwell burst into noisy tears, turning to sob on her elder daughter's shoulder while Audrey looked closer.

"My dear, you can't be concerned because the tablecloths are just slightly yellow?" she asked at last.

Mama sobbed louder. "And the goblets!" She raised her hand helplessly and let it fall.

"Oh, Mama, the patterns are so close no one will notice," Audrey assured her. She tried to make a joke of it. "I will be amazed if Ed notices anything but Emmeline."

It was a foolish effort, and she should have known better. Mrs. Caldwell gasped and heaved herself off her daughter's shoulder as though it burned. "Sir Edmund! Sir Edmund! Not Ed! Audrey, where are your manners?"

Audrey looked behind her. "I thought I brought them into the room with me. Mama! Don't be silly! It's been Ed for years." *Years, indeed*, she thought, trying not to smile at her mother. They had all watched Ed Parkhill grow from a skinny lad with a stutter, into a firm of jaw, clear of eye young man whose title had always sat lightly on him. Orphaned young and living on the nearby estate of a now dead uncle, Ed Parkhill had spent more time at their place, keeping company with the Caldwell brothers and worshipping the ground Emmeline glided over. "Mama, Ed doesn't give a rap about tablecloths or goblets," she soothed. "I doubt he's even seen anything so refined in the last few years. It doesn't matter!"

Mrs. Caldwell dried her eyes and glared at her daughter. "It matters a great deal, Audrey! We have a certain standing to maintain in Bath, I will remind you." She stared at the offending tablecloths and goblets as though willing them to shrivel away, then turned her displeasure on her daughter. "I am determined to have a wedding that no one ever forgets. You will find new tablecloths in the morning in Bath and check every china shop in town for that pattern." She jabbed her finger at the goblet closest to her. "A rose etched on the side."

Audrey gritted her teeth and kissed her mother's cheek. "Certainly, dearest! I will not rest until everything matches. Oh, dear! Whatever will we do about Uncle Eustace and his eye patch?"

Mama was still in no mood for frivolity. "Don't try me!" she exclaimed. "You and Matthew may have settled for something a bit more jolly—oh, those Winkles were a trial at times—but I intend for my only daughter marrying into the ranks of the nobility to have a memorable wedding, one unequaled in the annals of Bath. That is all."

Audrey knew this was no time to mention to Mama that a baronet was hardly coin of the realm. *Oh, when did Ed go from being just old Ed to Sir Edmund?* she wondered. *And why is this wedding starting to turn into a monster? And where is Ed?*

* * *

The whereabouts of her fiancée was certainly on Emmeline's mind in the morning. The two of them teetered and balanced on stools in Mama's sewing rooms while the seamstresses crawled the floor and measured hems. (*The only hems I have not finished,* Audrey thought with amusement.)

"You don't think he has cried off," Emmeline asked, as the seamstresses released them from tyranny and they removed their wedding finery.

"No!" Audrey declared. "We know Ed better than that, Emmy. At least, I do."

"I still wonder where he is," she said while Audrey buttoned up her work dress. She frowned. "He scribbled something about 'a little business to take care of,' and then he would be here. That should have been yesterday."

"Wasn't he traveling with his commanding officer?" Audrey asked, turning around for Emmeline to button her now. "Major Redpath must be an older man; perhaps he took sick."

"Perhaps," Emmeline said slowly. "Still, I think it is rude and inconsiderate of him and so I shall tell him."

Audrey shook her head. "Don't waste your time on things that don't matter, Emmy. Trust me on this one."

Emmeline rested her cheek on her sister's shoulder. "But it does matter to me! What will people think if the groom is late?"

What, indeed? Audrey thought later as she sat in the kitchen mulling over the week's menu. *Sometimes I wonder if Emmeline really loves Ed, or if she just likes the idea of a wedding.* She owned to a twinge of guilt. *I suppose if Captain Winkle and I hadn't hurried to Portsmouth for a quick wedding before he prepared to embark for the West Indies, Mama and Emmeline would not feel the need so much for an elaborate affair that no one will ever forget.* She smiled to herself and looked at the menus again. *As it is, Emmeline will probably not remember anything of the day anyway, and Mama will have spent a lot of guineas solely for the entertainment of relatives and friends who will only talk and gossip about us.* She grinned. *As we gossip and talk about them. Oh merciful heaven, spare me from this small society!*

They were still waiting and wondering after dinner, and long after the lamps had been lit. Emmeline stalked back and forth in front of the window while Mama languished on the sofa and Audrey pretended to read. Emmeline's mood changed with the minute, from "He is dead in a ditch and I have wasted the best years of my life writing to him!" to "Mama, why must men be such a trial? Do you suppose he became lost and didn't want to ask directions? Men are like that, you know." Audrey kept her eyes on the book and tried not to laugh out loud, considering that her stock was low enough anyway with Mama.

"Audrey, you will go into town tomorrow and match the goblets and find new tablecloths," came Mama's firm voice from the depths of the sofa. "And if you see Dr. Welch, tell him my heart is palpitating all over my chest."

"Yes, Mama."

They were beginning to think of bed when Emmeline halted her forced march in front of the window, threw up the glass—which brought faint cries of anguish from

Mama—and leaned out. "I know I see a vehicle," she said. "Oh, Audrey, come look."

Audrey looked and felt a measure of relief. No question there was something coming. Carriage lights glittered through the newly leafed trees, and soon they could hear the horses.

"If it is horrid Uncle Eustace and Aunt Agatha come early, I will scream," Emmeline declared. She grabbed her, sister's hand. "Audrey, do you think he will have changed? It's been two years."

Audrey took her sister by the shoulders and gave her a gentle shake. "I know he will have changed, my dear." She put her forehead against her sister's. "That's one thing else we need to talk about. It's been a long war, and war does things to men."

And women, she thought as she watched the vehicle turn into a post chaise much muddied from travel. *War has robbed me of a husband, and babies, and old age with someone I loved. I do hope Napoleon is vastly uncomfortable on Elba.*

The post chaise stopped in the driveway. Audrey waited for Emmeline to fling the door open and run outside and into her fiancé's arms, but she did not. *Oh, I would,* thought Audrey, feeling anguish wash over her as though Captain Winkle were but newly dead. *I would throw myself into his arms and have to be pried out for meals and baths.* "Go to him, Emmy," she whispered, when she could get her lips to move.

Emmeline shook her head. "No. I am angry at him for being late."

And so it was the butler who welcomed Lieutenant Sir Edmund Parkhill into his love's home. Audrey steeled herself for the pain she knew would come when Ed gathered her sister into his arms and forgot the war. *If I dig down deep enough, I can stand this too,* she thought as she moved slowly toward the sitting-room door to greet her future brother-in-law.

What happened next wiped out any pain she anticipated. With an expression more unreadable than usual, the butler opened the door, and in walked Ed Parkhill, carrying a sleeping child in his arms. He was followed by another man as shabbily dressed as himself, but with more gilt on his uniform. Audrey knew she would remember forever the light in Ed's eyes, which changed to open-mouthed astonishment as Emmeline gasped and staggered toward him, jabbing her finger in his direction.

"Edmund! A child! How could you!" she shrieked in dying tones that would have done Mama proud, except that Mama had already lapsed into a quiet faint. Before Audrey could move, her sister pressed her hands to her temples, uttered an unladylike noise, and sank gracefully toward the floor.

That Emmeline did not land on the parquet and do herself an injury, she owed entirely to the other officer, who stepped quickly forward and snagged her on the way down. To Audrey's further astonishment, he grinned at Ed. "I told you to let me carry Marie Deux, you simple Simon."

"But . . . but . . . ," the dumbfounded lieutenant began, then stared at his love lolling in his commanding officer's arms.

"Where should I put this darling lass?" the man asked. He settled Emmeline more comfortably in his arms and looked toward the sofa, then at Audrey. "It appears your mother has jumped to conclusions too. Goodness, what a fainting family. Ed, close your mouth. You'll catch flies, you know you will."

It was all so artless and spoken in the most wonderful brogue that Audrey had ever heard. It had heather, and sheep, and bracken and burn, and short days and long nights in it, brisk, bracing, and cheery and totally in command, no matter how softly spoken the words.

"Over here, sir," she said, collecting her wits one by one, which seemed to have rolled out of her ears and onto the carpet. "Goodness, indeed! I don't think we quite expected to see Ed with child so soon."

The officer grinned at her choice of words. "I warned him, but 'pon my word, he's a naïve soul, isn't he? Even after two years in Spain. Ah me. Ed, put Marie down somewhere and come here and prepare a mighty explanation for your . . . sister-in-law, is it?"

Audrey nodded, suddenly and surprisingly shy. She held out her hand. "Mrs. Winkle."

He set down Emmeline and took her hand in his. "Charmed, indeed."

She couldn't think of anything to do with her hand at the moment, so she kept it in his. He was a man of some height, and up close, even shabbier. What distinguished him in the quiet room was the uniformity of his coloring, which was the light mahogany of a warmer climate. It matched almost perfectly the red of his hair, and blended with a fair sprinkling of freckles. *I am looking at a Celt cast ashore from some tropic location where surely nature never intended him,* she thought with amusement, her hand still in his.

His eyes were a brilliant green, a delightful contrast to his hair and complexion. She thought him handsome beyond words. "Major Redpath?" she asked, even though she knew it could be no one else. No Englishman ever looked so much like the soil he sprang from; nature designed Scots to be permanently marked with their homeland, she decided, as she observed him and forgot her swooning relatives.

"John Redpath," he replied, his voice cheerful, and so soft she had to lean closer. He still didn't seem inclined to release her hand, and she couldn't understand why that didn't bother her. "Sorry, Mrs. Winkle. We gunners tend to speak softly. I think it's a consequence of all that shouting to be heard over loud noises."

His reply was so ingenuous and his accent so charming that she wanted to hear it all over again, from the top. And did she step closer to him, or was it the other way around? She couldn't be sure. *Well,* she excused herself, as she released his hand, *if he wouldn't speak so softly, I would not need to tromp on his boots to hear him.* He smelled of wool and travel, and John Redpath.

Ed deposited the sleeping child on the carpet and Audrey came closer to look at her. *What a pretty child,* she thought, as she hurried to Ed and grasped him in her arms. She stood on tiptoe to give him a loud smack on the cheek.

"Oh, Audrey. Should we revive them or should I offer a brief explanation to you first so you won't think me a complete rake?"

"Explain, you rascal." Audrey separated herself from Ed's returning embrace and looked at the butler, who stood like Lot's wife in the doorway. "Ames, bring some wet cloths and some whiskey, please." She twinkled her eyes at Ed. "This is not a sherry occasion. Tell all now."

"I should, for it's my doing, considering that I command," the major said, stepping over Marie to stand beside her. "Members of the Second found Marie Deux after Badajoz and raised her in the battery. I command a softhearted gun crew, Mrs. Winkle. Now that the war's over, I'm on furlough, and General Sir Thomas Picton told me of an orphanage." He looked at Ed and shook his head. "I'm the guilty one; I misplaced the directions to the orphanage."

"And we've been traveling all over Land's End looking for a St. Pancras, or St. Austell, or St. Anybody, until we are sainted out," Ed continued, picking up the story.

"No luck?" Audrey said.

Ed shook his head. "I knew Emmeline would be wondering where we were, so we came here. Major Redpath said he'd take up the hunt after the wedding." Ed took Audrey's hand again and kissed her fingers. "And that's the truth of it, my dear."

Audrey grinned. "I never doubted for a moment. Here now, have some refreshment while I revive my family. Major, take off your cloak and make yourself comfortable, please!"

* * *

She had to hand it to the artillery, which moved in promptly with explanations, blandishments, and apologies enough to remove the suspicion from Emmeline's eyes, when they opened again. Mama was a more difficult subject, to Audrey's embarrassment.

"This won't do, Major," she told Redpath as she leaned against Audrey, sniffing at her vinaigrette. "I can't imagine what our friends and relatives will think when they hear of this. You must find that orphanage at once, sir, or keep that . . . that . . ."

"Wee lassie?" the major suggested.

"French camp follower trash is more what I think," Mama said roundly. "At any rate, I'll not have such leavings strewn about to wreck a most perfect wedding, Major!"

"Of course not, Mrs. Caldwell," the major said, as Audrey burned with humiliation. "I don't know what got into my lads, to save a two-year-old from a bombed-out French battery, but there you are. Marie Deux and I will keep ourselves scarce."

Mama nodded. She looked at Audrey. "I don't know where we'll put her. All the relatives will be arriving tomorrow." She began to pick at the handkerchief in her lap, as the tears welled in her eyes. "This is so upsetting!"

"Oh, Mama, we'll manage." Audrey swallowed her shame and looked at the major. "She can sleep with me tonight."

"Audrey! Suppose she has fleas or some disease."

"Mama, this is a little girl and she must go somewhere," Audrey said, her voice firm. "Major, tomorrow I can get a cot for her in my dressing room, but I am certain we will be fine tonight."

"Mr. Winkle won't mind?" the major asked as he carried the sleeping child upstairs.

"Captain Winkle is dead these eight years, sir," Audrey replied, holding her candle so he could see the steps over his burden.

"I'm sorry," he replied. "Was he Army?"

"Navy, sir. Here's my room."

The child woke when he set her on the bed. *How pretty you are,* Audrey thought, as the captain removed her little traveling cloak, obviously cut down from an army coat. She reached out to finger the child's curls. "Hello, Marie Deux," she said, her voice soft so as not to startle her. "I always wanted curls."

The major sat beside her on the bed. "You don't need them," he said, and turned slightly to look at her. "Everything works as it is."

It was an ingenuous statement, but somehow it did not startle her. *Sir, our acquaintance is too brief for such a compliment,* she thought. *But say on, anytime you choose, and let me soak in your marvelous accent.* "Well, I thought I wanted curls," she amended.

"You'll sleep here tonight, Marie," the major said as he helped the little girl from her dress. The child only nodded, accepting her, the room, and the arrangement with a matter-of-factness that touched Audrey. *Here is a little one who is used to anything life throws at her,* she thought, as she took the dress from the major and draped it over a chair. *My family should study this instead of reject it.*

The major got up then. "Well, I'll leave the rest to you ladies," he said. He bent down to touch Marie's cheek. "All right, Petty Chew, don't snore."

The child smiled at him. "You snore, Major, not me."

The major laughed. "So I do, lass!" He looked at Audrey. "We've been making a pallet for her on the floor in too many inns, Mrs. Winkle."

She nodded. "One does what one must." She glanced at Marie, whose eyes were closing already. "'Petty Chew'?"

It was the major's turn to blush. "I started calling her '*mon petit chou*' and that was more than the gunners could handle," he murmured, and she could almost feel his embarrassment at such a homely, intimate nickname. "'Petty Chew' she is." He patted Marie again, then to Audrey's surprise, picked up the miniature of Captain Winkle on the bedside table. "A handsome man."

"I thought so too."

His eyes went to the sword over the mantelpiece. "It doesn't really fit in here, do you think?" His voice was soft, but full of that same confidence of command that she remembered vaguely from Captain Winkle.

"No, it doesn't," she agreed, surprising herself in an evening of surprises. "I've been meaning to take it down for a year or more now, but I'm not tall enough to reach that last bracket."

"I am," he said as he put the miniature facedown, went to the fireplace, reached up, and removed the sword. He leaned it in the corner. "Good night, lassies. You say I'm two doors down?"

She nodded, wondering at all the feelings playing tag in her head. She thought she should be offended but couldn't imagine why. *He comes in my bedroom, turns down Matthew's miniature, takes his sword from the wall,*

changes everything, and I let him. I have known him less
than an hour, and I am in the middle of something. I wonder
what it is?

Puzzled with herself, she gently shook Marie awake
and helped her from her petticoat, smoothing down her
wrinkled chemise. "I'm sure I can find you a nightgown
that fits in the morning," she said. "Mama never threw
out anything." She readied herself for bed, tying on her
cap, her eyes on the miniature still lying facedown. She
righted it, then picked it up, took a long look, and put it
in her drawer under her handkerchiefs and stockings.

As Audrey blew out the lamp and lay down, Marie
moved close to her with a sigh. It was an easy matter to
put her arms around the child and enjoy her warmth.
She looked at the bare spot on the wall over the fireplace,
thinking that one of her watercolors would look fine
there. *I hope Major Redpath is comfortable in that bed,* she
thought, as she rested her head against Marie's curls and
listened to her even breathing. She closed her eyes, wondered outrageously if he had freckles everywhere, and was
glad the room was dark.

* * *

He woke early, as he always did, startled awake by the
silence of the room, and wondering briefly where Marie
Deux was. He relaxed against the pillow, remembering
that she was two doors down, where he wanted to be.
Lucky Petty Chew, he thought, as he got up, washed, and
shaved himself, gazing into the mirror with some dissatisfaction that he was not as handsome as Captain Winkle.
As he dressed, he toyed briefly with the idea of tiptoeing
back into Mrs. Winkle's bedroom and repositioning the
sword on her wall. He could throw himself on her mercy
and apologize for his presumptuous behavior in removing
it last night. He had the good sense to reject such a stupid
idea. *I am sure she would love to see a strange man walking*

about in her room, benevolently and contritely rehanging her husband's sword, he thought sourly.

As he sat on his bed to pull on his boots, he was struck by an odd idea. He had been twenty years at war, and deep into the routine of it all, knowing that nothing new would ever happen to him. War had robbed him of everything except more war, and it was all he knew. But something new had happened, and his logical, mathematical, practical artilleryman's mind could not begin to explain it. *I will not try*, he thought.

Emmeline and Ed sat in the breakfast room. Despite his own relative inexperience with women, he recognized tension without requiring a manual. He nodded and smiled to them both and hurried to the sideboard, wondering if the silly widgeon was going to continue to punish her love for bringing home a French waif from the wars.

Apparently she was. "Edmund, I wonder that you and Major Redpath didn't just leave that child."

"Marie Deux," Redpath said quickly, not meaning to interrupt what was certainly not his quarrel, but unable to stop himself. "She has a name." *And nicknames, and some of us are fond of her.*

". . . that child at any orphanage in Land's End!" she concluded. "Surely it would not matter to General Picton, even if he did take some interest."

He sat down at the table, struck by the good sense of what she said, and chilled by it at the same time. "Well, no," he agreed, looking to Ed for help. "I don't suppose we even thought of that."

Then you are an idiot, her expression told him, even if she said nothing.

The lieutenant gazed at his fiancée. "Maybe we weren't really taken with any of those institutions we saw, Emmeline, my love."

"I cannot feel that is important, Edmund," Emmeline replied. "Why am I thinking that Mama and I will have to explain that child—"

"Mary Deux," Redpath interrupted.

". . . over and over to everyone who shows up? It is too much to ask and will be hard for some to believe. You know how people like to think the worst and jump to conclusions."

You certainly did, he thought dryly.

She dabbed at her lips with her napkin. "I have to ask myself if you are determined to scotch—excuse me, Major—my plans."

The major watched her expressive face and was curious what trick of light had made her seem so attractive last night as she swooned in his arms. *I must have been overly tired,* he thought, as he held up his cup for tea from the footman.

Emmeline stopped her tongue until the footman closed the door quietly. "I think that the sooner you find a place for . . . for . . ."

"Marie Deux," the major filled in, his voice sounding dangerously patient to his own ears and obviously to Lieutenant Parkhill too. His subaltern shifted uneasily in his chair.

". . . that child, the more comfortable Mama and I will be," she finished, with just a trace of a pout in her voice that made him begin to pity Lieutenant Sir Edmund Parkhill.

The return of the footman with muffins and toast stifled the hot words that bubbled up in him, and then Mrs. Winkle and Marie Deux came to breakfast. He rose when they entered the room, happy to admire Mrs. Winkle in morning light. She nodded to him and blew her sister and Ed a kiss, then helped Marie at the sideboard, while he was content to regard her and let his breakfast get cold.

I have been missing English skin, he decided, as he watched the light play on Mrs. Winkle's marvelous rose complexion. She wore an attractive lace cap that covered her glorious dark hair but brought emphasis to her eyes, warm brown like Marie's. He noticed how she touched Marie's cheek and then rested her hand lightly on the child's shoulder. *I would like to be touched like that,* he decided, as he looked at his food again. *And return the favor. I would wager she is as soft to the touch as she is gentle on the eye.*

"Major Redpath."

He glanced up in surprise at the barely spoken words to see Emmeline watching him, her eyes full of amusement. "To spare you any possible disappointment," she confided, her voice low as she watched her sister across the room, "my dear Audrey said years ago that she would never marry a military man again."

"Emmy!" Lt. Parkhill hissed. "Mind your manners! This is my commanding officer."

"I know, my love, I know," she replied quietly, the soul of complacence. "It is merely that I do not wish to see Major Redpath unhappy."

I doubt you care at all, he thought, but he nodded, and returned his attention to food that held no attraction for him now. Her words were food for thought, however, and he chewed them along with the bacon. *Am I that interested,* he asked himself, *and so obvious?* He almost shivered with pleasure as Mrs. Winkle sat beside him. *You are too late, Emmeline,* he thought, as he smiled at Audrey Winkle. *I am already unhappy.*

Audrey turned her attention to Marie Deux, seated next to her, and saw her organized with napkin, spoon, and bowl before she looked at her own plate. She ate as a hungry woman ought to, pausing once to inquire if his food was not to his liking.

"Oh, it is fine," he hastened to assure her. "I suppose I am still used to weevily porridge, or fried hare, or whatever we scared up from the bushes in Spain."

I sound like an idiot, he thought desperately. Would anyone here mind if I suddenly let out a roar, grabbed Mrs. Winkle, and threw her over my shoulder? The prospect was so appealing that he could feel himself turning redder than his uniform collar. To his relief, Lt. Parkhill laughed and pushed back his chair.

"So am I, sir! Do you know I even had trouble sleeping in my bed last night?"

Oh, forgive me, so did I, he thought. *Please keep talking, Ed.*

His lieutenant did not fail him. "And when the maid came in with hot water and jerked the draperies open with that zipping sound, I nearly climbed under the carpet!" Parkhill toyed with his fiancée's loose hair around her neck. "Emmy dear, it takes a while to readjust, I am discovering. Things change."

"Do you change, Edmund?" she asked, brushing away his fingers impatiently. "I am sure I never do."

Parkhill said nothing, but he continued to watch her thoughtfully when she returned her attention to her toast.

"Well, my dear sister, I am going to gird my loins now," Mrs. Winkle said as she crossed her knife and fork on her plate. "Mama insists that I turn Bath inside out in my search for tablecloths white enough for the finest wedding ever seen in this shire, and goblets that match each other. Marie, will you accompany me?"

"I'll come too," Redpath offered.

"Excellent!" she said. "I am sure Mama and Emmeline cannot spare me a footman or a maid to give me countenance. You will do."

Oh, I would, he thought. *I would do most splendidly, Mrs. Winkle who-thinks-she-should-not-like-military-men.*

"While you are in town, stop at the Foundling Home on the High and the workhouse," Emmeline said, as calmly as though she suggested that Audrey pick up a new scent at the perfumers.

"I will not," Audrey said quickly, then blushed. "Excuse my presumption! Of course, I suppose, you are right. This *is* what you want, isn't it, gentlemen?"

The major looked at his lieutenant. "It must be what we want," he said finally. "That was the original plan, at any rate," he temporized.

"And nothing has changed, has it?" Emmeline asked so sweetly that he wanted to leap across the table and throttle her.

Everything has changed, he thought, *everything*. "No, nothing has changed," he mumbled. He sighed and glanced at Marie, who was watching him with an unreadable expression. "At your service, Mrs. Winkle."

* * *

Major Redpath decided by noon that if a bomb were to suddenly drop on him—an eventuality he had anticipated for years now—he would die a happy man. He had just spent the best morning of his life, going from shop to store to warehouse, looking for tablecloths and goblets. *If only Picton could see me now*, he thought, as he offered his opinion on the relative whiteness of damask that all looked the same to him.

He took wicked delight in the realization that Mrs. Winkle seemed to care as little about tablecloths as he did. Marie did the final selecting, to the amusement of the clerk. "Your daughter is remarkably perspicacious," the clerk told him as he bundled the tablecloths in brown paper and string.

"She is, isn't she?" he agreed without a qualm. "She takes after her mother," he added, his unholy glee increasing as Mrs. Winkle blushed and looked down at her shoes.

"I do not mind telling you, sir, that you are a rascal," she said as they left the shop, Marie skipping ahead.

"You could have denied it," he said reasonably.

"And create a scene in a shop?" She laughed then. "Well, is she your daughter? I've heard Ed's story."

"Then believe it," he said. "I came to the Second from the Torres Vedras lines after poor Captain Williams lost his neck at Badajoz. It had a terrible effect on his head."

She grimaced, and he had the good grace to blush in his turn. "Excuse an artilleryman's humor, Mrs. Winkle, but we've earned it," he apologized. "Sergeant Hurley found her. The men named her Marie Deux after the Second, and Mrs. Hurley let her suck." He shook his head. "I do remember that she was almost two then, we think, or maybe more, but so thin and scrawny. Mrs. Hurley thought it best."

"I wonder that she did not wish to keep her," Mrs. Winkle said. They were walking slower and slower now, but there seemed no need to hurry.

"It's a hard service, Mrs. Winkle," he explained. "Mrs. Hurley lost the lottery and has to travel overland to Ostend. The guns and her husband were going by sea, and she is not, and there are three bairn and another in the making."

When Marie came skipping back to tug on his sleeve, he realized that they were just standing there on the sidewalk. She stopped in front of him, her hands on her hips. "Major Redpath, we have work to do! Hurry along!"

Goblets were a problem. Mrs. Winkle would hold one after another up to the light for him to see the design, and he would stare at her instead. He couldn't help himself. She was the most beautiful woman he had ever seen, and she stirred him to the depth of his heart in a place he hadn't dreamed existed.

"I know why you are doing this," she said finally, after looking in another shop.

"Oh?" he asked, certain he was guilty with whatever she charged him.

"You want to make sure that I never trouble you with another shopping expedition during your stay," she accused.

And there they stood until Marie reminded him that the clerk was expecting some response. "We'll take the whole lot, pitcher, plate, and all," he said, drawing out his wallet. "It will be my wedding present to the happy couple." He directed the packing crates to the Caldwells' Bath address and offered his arm to Mrs. Winkle again.

After a jovial lunch where they all laughed too much and earned stares and whispered comments, they knew they could not avoid the next stop. "I'm sure I do not like this, but Emmeline is probably right," Mrs. Winkle said as she clutched his arm tight this time and directed him up the High Street beyond the shops to where the avenue turned into a narrow lane of overhanging houses and sewers smelling of centuries of use. "We can at least check it out," she concluded, doubt evident in her voice.

St. Elizabeth's Foundling Home was even more grim inside, low-ceilinged, cold, and dark, as though denying spring in bloom everywhere outside. While he spoke quietly to the matron, a cadaver of a woman dressed in unrelieved black, he noticed that Marie Deux had backed herself up against Mrs. Winkle until she could get no closer. Audrey's hands were laced strong across the child's chest, and her eyes filled with dread.

"Major, this child of yours . . . "

". . . not mine . . ."

"Whatever you say. This child is too old for our institution." With a flick of her hand, the matron motioned them after her down the cramped hallway, ill-lit and echoing with the cry of small children. "However, if she is capable, we could use her in here." She opened the door on a large room where cheap tallow candles smoked and burned and babies sobbed.

He forced himself after her into the room, grateful in his soul that Mrs. Winkle refused to enter with Marie but stood anchored in the doorway, the child tight in her grasp again, her face turned into the widow's skirts this time. *I can't do this,* he thought, as he watched with anguish as girls not much older than Marie tended the babies, their hair unvisited by a comb or brush and their eyes red-rimmed from the smoking candles. One or two of them looked at him with hope but the others didn't even glance up as they hurried to change babies and feed them.

The matron was looking at him expectantly, and he fought to subdue the disgust that rose in him and return some civilized comment. "I . . . uh . . . I wonder that you can remember all their names," he managed finally.

The matron gave a humorless laugh. "We do not name them, Major! They are numbered. If they live to a year old, then we pick Bible names for the wretched little sinners. It is our Christian duty."

He closed his eyes against loss of life and dignity worse than any battlefield, turned on his heel, and left the matron standing there, her mouth open. "See here, sir, we do the best we can!" she hurled after him.

"You'd be kinder to line them up and shoot them down," he shouted, setting off more babies crying. "Come on, Audrey, let's get out of here!"

He almost ran into the street, speechless with horror, striding rapidly along until Mrs. Winkle protested. "I'm sorry," he said then, slowing his pace and letting her tuck her arm through his. She leaned against his arm, and he touched her face, then quickly picked up Marie. The child burrowed her head into his shoulder, her grip so tight on his neck that he winced. "Don't worry, Marie Deux," he said into her ear. "That's not the place we had in mind." She said nothing but only clung tighter, her legs wrapped around him now.

It was a long, wordless walk home, but neither of them felt like hailing a hackney. Mrs. Winkle clutched his arm, her knuckles white on his sleeve, Marie dug into his neck, and he could think of nothing to do now except hold them both and wish, like a coward, for the simplicity of artillery.

Mrs. Winkle released him as they came up the front steps, looking around in surprise at the post chaises and carriages that lined the drive. She sighed. "The relatives have descended."

They entered the house quietly, Audrey tiptoeing down the hall, listening to the buzz through the sitting-room door, and motioning him down the hall to the servants' stairs. He followed her down to the kitchen, presided over by no one more intimidating than the cook.

"I cannot face any of them, even my brothers," Mrs. Winkle said as she removed her pelisse, took off her bonnet, and fluffed her hair. She sat down and Marie perched on her lap. "My dear, what would you think of some milk and biscuits?"

Marie did not answer for a long time. She leaned against Mrs. Winkle, who gathered her close. From the security of the widow's arms, Marie Deux looked at him. "Please, sir, you would not—"

He did not allow her to finish. "I would never, Marie Deux," he said, his voice so fervent that it shook. His heart cracked as she sighed and relaxed in Mrs. Winkle's strong embrace. "Then *oui*. I would like milk and biscuits." She smoothed down her worn dress with a womanly gesture that cracked his heart again and allowed Cook to pour her some milk.

He left her at the table cosseted by Cook and followed

Mrs. Winkle down the hall to a storage room, where she directed him to take down a dress box. She knelt by the box and opened it, smiling for the first time since luncheon and pulling back the tissue. "Mama kept all my clothes. Do you think this will fit Marie?"

He nodded, touched at her generosity of spirit. "She will be lovely."

Mrs. Winkle nodded, folded the dress, and put it aside. She tugged out several others, as well as petticoats, chemises, and a nightgown, which she held up and looked at for a long time. "Major Redpath, what are we going to do?" she asked out of the blue.

"Well, we know we are not going to throw her to the Christians at St. Elizabeth's! I can't imagine the workhouse would be much better." He sat down beside her on the floor and leaned against the wall. "I could kick myself for mislaying the address and location of that orphanage General Picton recommended!"

Her smile was strange and disquieting. She reached for his hand and he grasped hers gladly, partners in confusion. "You do not for a moment think that General Picton's choice would be any better than what we saw this afternoon, do you?"

He considered her question and could not look at that strange smile. "You are likely right, Audrey. If we are thinking to confine her to a British orphanage, then Sergeant Hurley and the others should just have passed her by and let her die in the French battery at Badajoz. It would have been more humane."

"Could you keep her?" she asked, releasing his hand.

He shook his head. "I'm not married, I am due in Belgium in a month, and I cannot see how I can manage it. What about you?"

"Mama would never permit it."

"Ed and Emmeline?"

"I think not," Audrey said quietly, the shame evident in her voice. "I fear my sister is not given much to charity, sir."

"And neither are we, if we don't think of something," he said frankly. She looked so young and small, sitting there on the floor cross-legged, with children's clothing around her. "You could marry, Audrey. In fact, I can't imagine why you are not married. Captain Winkle may have been a good man, but it's been eight years." *My, but that was personal and plain-spoken*, he thought. *I haven't even known this woman twenty-four hours, and already I am prying into intimate corners where no one invited me.*

"My offers have been from older men and widowers," she said simply. "They want companionship, someone to mind their children, or a woman to look pretty at social functions. I have become wary of men with a plan, sir." She hesitated. "I had something more in mind."

"Love again, lass?" he asked, his voice soft. "Some people want the moon and stars too."

She reddened. "Silly, isn't it?"

He couldn't think of anything else to do but kiss her then, lifting her onto his lap and kissing her so long that he had trouble breathing and finally had to stop before he really wanted to. *I'm not so good at this,* he thought, as he put his arms around her and let her rest her head against his shoulder as Marie Deux had done so recently. *This woman I want to kiss, and I'm not very good at it.*

But I could learn, he thought as Mrs. Winkle took his head in her hands and kissed him. He heard steps coming toward the storage room. "Cease firing," he murmured, and set Audrey Winkle off his lap. *I wonder if I look as disheveled as you do?* he thought, and decided that he did. He combed his hair with his fingers and hoped that whoever came through the door was blind.

* * *

Oh, dear, thought Audrey, trying to smooth her hair back under her cap again and calm the wrinkles in her dress at the same time. She glanced at the major and decided, with a blush, that perhaps she had better step into the hall and close the door after her. *Men are so inept at times like this*, she thought. To her relief, it was Uncle Eustace meandering down the hall, he of the eye patch earned forty years earlier in the retreat from Lexington. *Oh, the relatives*, she groaned inwardly as she came forward with her arms outstretched. Uncle Eustace seemed startled at her embrace, and she needed no more confirmation that his other eye was none too vigorous anymore.

"Audrey!" he exclaimed at last, holding her off for a better look. "My, how you've grown."

"I sincerely hope not," she said with a smile. "We only saw each other at Christmas!"

He had the good sense to laugh at himself, then inquired after the wine cellar again, holding out a battered tankard that he always traveled with, to Aunt Agatha's disgust. "I know it is here somewhere and there's rum in it. Your mother serves nothing but sherry, which gives me wind," he complained. He moved to the storage room, and she leaped in front of him.

"No, Uncle, not that door," she said hastily.

He grinned at her and pinched her cheek. "You act like you have a lover in there, missy!"

She joined in his laughter, hoping that he was overlooking the wild expression she knew was in her eyes. "My dear uncle, let me show you to the wine cellar," she said, taking him firmly by the arm and steering him past the storage room. She helped him down the short flight of stairs and saw him seated comfortably in front of a keg of rum before she hurried back to the storage room door.

She was debating whether to open it, when Major Redpath came out, looking more himself, except that his lovely red hair still stuck out in several directions. *I should not do this*, she thought, but she did it anyway, standing on tiptoe to smooth back the hair behind his ears. "There now, sir! Unless you and Marie Deux wish to meet my incredibly proper . . ."

Uncle Eustace was already singing something decidedly lusty in the wine cellar. The major let out a shout of laughter before he covered his mouth with his hand. She pushed him against the wall and giggled into his sleeve. "Stop it now!" she ordered, when she could talk. "Well, most of them are high sticklers. I recommend you and Marie make yourselves scarce until dinner."

"Very well, my dear," he said.

Oh, please don't kiss me again, she thought, already amply well-acquainted with that look in his eyes. "You realize of course, that we have to forget what just happened in the storage room, Major," she began, striving for a dignified tone.

He continued to regard her with that same disquieting expression she remembered from her few memorable nights with Captain Winkle. "I am not sure there is that much amnesia in the entire universe, Mrs. Winkle," he said. "I still think you should marry."

Marry you? she asked herself. *Well, propose, and let us see what I do, for even I am not sure.* "I've already told you I have no prospects right now," she found herself saying when he made no more comment.

"It shouldn't be hard," he said, and she knew from his expression that amnesia hadn't set in yet.

"Well it is," she assured him, sounding more tart than she wished. "Do I just go up to someone I hardly know, introduce myself, and say, 'Marry me?' I think not, Major."

That is precisely what I wish to do, she thought mournfully, after she left him and Marie Deux safely hidden in the kitchen. *I am certain men have proposed on less provocation than I offered in the storage room—heavens, did I do all that?—and yet he does not.* She went up the stairs, slowly. *True, I have only known him twenty-four hours, but my heart tells me that I know him well.*

Her attempt to escape upstairs to the solitude of her room was foiled by Mama, who bore down on her, wringing her hands and ripping at the little scrap that used to be a lace handkerchief.

"Drat Major Redpath and that child!" she stormed, stopping Audrey's route of escape.

"Mama, you are unfair!" she protested as she worked her way past her mother and started up the stairs.

Mama followed. "What I am is severely exercised! Half of our plaguey relatives are winking and nudging each other, sure that Edmund is the father, and the other half hold with Major Redpath and wonder why you, of all people, were hanging on his arm!"

"When did you . . . ?"

Mama sighed and dabbed at her eyes. "My wretched cousin Loisa peeked through the draperies and saw you in the driveway! Really, Audrey, I don't know what has gotten into you! It will not do. That child must go!" She began to sob. "I would send the major away if I could, but he is the dratted best man!"

She cried in earnest, a storm of tears that brought several heads popping out of open doors to gawk and stare. Mrs. Caldwell glared back and the doors closed. "And now the ladies' maids will spread tales all over Bath!" she whispered, almost stamping her foot in her rage.

Audrey took her mother in her arms and crooned to her like she would comfort a distressed child. "Mama, trust me. It will still be a fine wedding, one nobody forgets! In fact, if you wish, I will spend all day tomorrow getting the flowers ready in the church, so that is one less worry."

Mrs. Caldwell's sobs turned to sniffles and then stopped. She blew her nose hard on the handkerchief Audrey gave her. "And that child?"

"She will not go to St. Elizabeth's, Mama," Audrey said firmly. "But yes, something must be done, and we all know it."

Mrs. Caldwell was satisfied. "Soon, Audrey, soon. Surely there is one adult among you who can get a little girl into an orphanage! How difficult can this be?" Her attention was distracted by a relative calling to her from the first floor. "I don't know why all my plans are turning to mud, Audrey," she said mournfully, then turned a smiling face on the woman looking up at her on the landing. "Coming, dear Matilda, coming!"

* * *

Dinner was the unrelieved trial Audrey dreaded, and she had just cause to feel shame for her relatives. There was Mama, tight-lipped and white-faced, glaring at Major Redpath and Marie Deux; and Emmeline and Ed sitting close together like conspirators, far from the major. And there were the relatives, looking, tittering, and talking among themselves about how ill-bred a man could be to fling such a wartime souvenir in the faces of good women everywhere, and little realizing their own vulgarity. She knew what they were thinking, despite mounds of explanation—she was sure—from Mama and Emmeline, and it pained her.

After a day in her delightful presence, she knew Marie Deux was a child of considerable nuance, one who must be fully aware that she was an object of derision. She ate her dinner in silence, eyes on her plate, despite the remarks that Audrey directed at her in kindness. She inched herself closer and closer to the major until she was almost sharing his chair with him.

Audrey could hardly bring herself to look at the major.

She knew him well enough to know that he would never say anything untoward to her relatives and reinforce their rudeness with his own. She tried to see him as they were seeing him, someone shabby, silent, and dour. ("He has been at war, you idiots! There is no tailor on the front lines!" she wanted to shriek. "And if he seems dour, you have made him so!") They would never know the depth of him, and the huge kindness that refused to allow him to jettison his burden at the nearest foundling home or workhouse. They saw only a Scot to fit the stereotype, and missed the man of passion, honor, and rightness.

She was hardly surprised when Major Redpath and Marie disappeared upstairs after dinner, and she had to suffer alone through a long incarceration at the whist table, exchanging pleasantries with people she wanted to flay, and drinking tea when she wanted to grind her teeth. She tried to catch Ed's eye several times, but he avoided her glances, as though ashamed of the part he was playing.

It was easy, finally, to plead a genuine headache and drag herself upstairs. She went wearily into her room, kicking off her shoes and flinging away her cap. Her heart lifted momentarily at the watercolor of spring flowers she had hung over the fireplace, and then lifted still more when she heard Marie Deux singing in her dressing room.

She went in quietly, and Marie looked up and put her finger to her lips. Major Redpath lay there sound asleep, stretched out on the cot. Marie was curled up on the pillow beside him, her knees drawn up to her chest, taking up the little space he left her. "He was telling me a story to put me to sleep," she whispered to Audrey.

"I would say he was not successful," Audrey whispered back, her eyes lively with good humor again. "Your lullaby seems to be more effective." She held out her hand to Marie, who quietly left the cot, stood a moment over the major, then carefully unbuttoned his uniform jacket.

"Should we leave him there to sleep?" she asked Marie doubtfully as they stood in the dressing-room doorway, watching him.

Marie nodded. "He's grouchy if you wake him," she said.

I wonder if he would be grouchy if I woke him? Audrey thought, then made an unsuccessful attempt to coax her mind into other channels. Captain Winkle never complained when she woke him in the middle of the night.

This is not a profitable topic, she told herself, but she was content to watch him and see how the lines smoothed out in his face when he slept. She noted with quiet amusement that he tucked his thumbs inside his hands like a child, asleep in full confidence. *I wonder if you ever dream about battle?* she thought, and decided that he did not. A man who could relax that completely was someone who put his cares away when he closed his eyes and did not recruit them again until morning. *Well, sir, let us make you more comfortable*, she thought, as she gently reached for the side buttons on his trousers and undid them. *I can't have you thinking that all the dreadful Caldwells wish you ill. I know I do not.*

She helped Marie into the hand-me-down nightgown, touched to see how well it fit. The sleeping cap enchanted Marie, who looked at herself this way and that in the mirror, while Audrey undressed. *You're such a French-woman*, Audrey thought, as she sat in her own nightgown. She kept half an eye on the dressing-room door and watched Marie retie the bow under her ear and prance about some more.

"Oh, you are a vain little flirt," she teased finally, and crawled into bed. She held up the covers for Marie, who jumped in, lively with the pleasure of a new outfit, even if it was just another's nightgown. "You have to help me with flowers tomorrow, so let us sleep."

Marie cuddled close to her, and she sniffed deep the fragrance of the little girl and the spice in which Mama had packed her old clothes. "I cannot help with the flowers," Marie said finally, drowsy and warm in Audrey's embrace. "I promised to help Cook with more biscuits tomorrow."

"Oh, my, you are in good hands then," Audrey murmured. There was no answer. She smiled into the dark, silently blessed Cook, and closed her eyes, trying not to think of the major in her dressing room.

He left it some time before morning because he was gone when she woke. She thought she knew when he left; those warm fingers on her cheek couldn't have been her imagination, or the hands a dream that tucked the covers closer about her and patted her hip in a gentle gesture she could only call husbandly.

* * *

She spent the day in the church, arranging and rearranging the flowers that came, expensive and pampered, from Bath succession houses. It was one thing to put them in tall vases, but quite another to determine if the effect was pleasing to the viewer. She longed for Marie Deux's discriminating eye and even Major Redpath's comfortable presence. She knew if he were there he would contribute no more to the project than stretch himself out in one of the pews and agree with whatever she wanted. And he would do it with that slight smile on his face that she was familiar with, the one that made her want to kiss him and see what developed.

The brevity of their acquaintance made no difference to her. This was the man she loved. She could know him two days or two years, and it would be the same. "Well, in two years, I would probably know if he picks up clothes or leaves them strewn about, or if he objects to changing baby's nappies," she murmured into the roses. "I know already that he is kind and honorable, fond of children and artillery."

She laughed out loud, then looked around to make sure that the vicar was not about. *I have it from unimpeachable sources that his guns are his chief delight,* she thought. *I wonder if he would give them up for me. And if he will not, I wonder if I could follow the guns like Marie Deux, uncomplaining and flexible, inured to hardship and sudden death.*

It may not come to that, she thought, grateful suddenly to Napoleon for having the good sense to abdicate and change his address to Elba. *Now John Redpath is merely to be stationed in Belgium, and what can come of that? Living on a major's income will be no hardship,* she decided, *even if he has no other money of his own. I have my inheritance, and we can rub along on that. Thank goodness I never told anyone but Emmeline that I would never marry into the military again. It astounds me how fast the right man can change one's mind.*

"Then, sir, I think you must propose," she said, getting up off her knees and lifting the vase to the stand beside the prie-dieu. "It is your fate. We will be Marie Deux's parents."

John and Audrey Redpath and Marie Deux. *How well they go together,* she thought, as she tacked satin rosettes to the pews. *We'll have children of our own, I am certain, but Marie Deux will be loved as much as they.*

There was more to do, but she was hungry for luncheon and the sight of Marie and the major. She walked home at peace with herself, admiring the blooming hawthorn and wondering if Emmeline would consider it too plebeian to poke here and there among the roses. She sighed over the increase in carriages and strange servants at the house, and decided that lunch in the kitchen would be more comfortable.

It was, except that the major was nowhere about. She sampled Marie's biscuits and smiled over Cook's praise, as proud as any mother. As she ate lunch, she listened in delight to Marie's description of the biscuit-making process, told in her breathless combination of English and French, with the occasional Spanish word to give it flavor, hands gesturing in Gallic emphasis. Audrey's heart ached a little as she thought of the hollow-eyed young girls in the foundling home, scurrying from baby to baby. *Not for you, Marie, and thank goodness for that*, she thought, pulling the child close for a kiss on the top of her head. *Of course, I am depending on the major to propose.*

Marie looked at her in surprise. "I love you, Marie Deux," she whispered, then got to her feet and held out her hand. "Come with me to the church this afternoon. I need your good opinion."

"Sister, I must borrow Marie Deux," said Emmeline from the doorway.

Audrey turned around with a smile. *See there, Emmy*, she thought in triumph, *you are not immune to Marie Deux's charms.* "Well, I don't know," she said in a teasing voice.

"Marie has already promised me she will show me where the tablecloths came from," Emmeline explained, joining them at the table and accepting a biscuit from Marie. "Um, good! You and the major were one short yesterday." She made a face. "Silly me! I broke the pitcher when I was taking it from the crate. Marie said she can show me where to get another." She kissed Audrey. "See there! You have to share!"

"If I must," Audrey teased back. "Does Ed go with you?"

"No, the wretch, I get only a footman! I have sent Ed and the major to hunt gifts for the groomsmen and then see about some really good blacking for their boots. Oh, Audrey, think how magnificent they will look tomorrow

in their regimentals!" she sighed, then put her arm around
Audrey and gave her a squeeze. "It is going to be a perfect
wedding."

"I don't doubt that for a moment, Emmy," Audrey said
as she rose to go. "I will see you all later this evening then,
at the rehearsal." She blew a kiss to Marie Deux. "Emmy,
send some nieces and nephews to help, if I cannot have
Marie."

"You cannot," Emmy replied with a smile. "And yes, I
will send them!"

Her heart light, she spent the afternoon with what the
vicar, dear old man, called "relative assistance." *I think
that when the major finally proposes, we will dispense with
flowers and too many relatives*, she thought, as she separated nieces, nephews, and quarrels, and attempted to
turn their energy to good use.

Hunting the wild hawthorn proved to be a sensible
diversion. She sent them into the trees by the church
armed with dull pruning hooks so they would take lots
of time and give her the calm she craved. She was joined
by the organist, who added to the serenity of the church
and her own peace of mind by liberal applications of
Bach, Handel, and Purcell. Soon she abandoned the flowers altogether and seated herself in a pew, happy beyond
words for Emmeline and Ed. *Only treat Emmy well, Ed,
and I will forgive you for distancing yourself from your major
and your little embarrassment*, she thought. *Why must
people think the worst of those whom they should love and
admire the most?*

She perked back into action when the nieces and
nephews tromped in, dirty from climbing the trees but
laden with flowering hawthorn. She thanked them, sent
them back to the house to clean up, and barely finished
arranging the last sprig among the roses before everyone arrived for the rehearsal. In perfect charity with her

relatives, she endured the scolds from her sisters-in-law for the disrepair to their children. She looked about for Marie Deux and almost asked about her, but thought it best not to remind her relations of gossip fodder.

Emmeline was splendid, even in an ordinary dress. She waited with what Audrey considered remarkable forbearance for her fiancé and the best man to arrive from their expedition to town for boot blacking. "They may have had to go farther afield than they originally intended," was her only comment as she arranged her bridesmaids to her liking, waved the vinaigrette about for poor Mama, and indulged in a little mild flirtation with the groomsmen.

And then they were there, Ed all smiles, and Major Redpath keeping his own counsel, as usual. He joined Audrey in the pew. "Don't know why we had to go to the ends of the earth for blacking," he grumbled. "Everyone will have their eyes on Emmeline tomorrow." He glanced sideways at her with a look so warm that her throat went suddenly dry. "And you."

Say on, sir, she thought, but he was looking about the sanctuary now. "Where is that little scamp?" he asked.

"I thought perhaps she would come with you," Audrey said, getting up when her sister motioned to her. "Emmeline needed her help to buy another tablecloth."

"Ed and I came right from town," he explained, rising too.

"Then I must assume that after she and Emmy returned, Cook found her totally indispensable," Audrey said with a smile. "Onward, now."

Emmeline surprised her with her serenity. Audrey minded her steps, took her place near the altar below the best man, and remembered her own nerves eight years ago. *Dear sister, you are obviously made of sterner stuff*, she decided as she watched Emmeline, on the arm of her eldest brother, glide up the aisle. *I was quaking in my shoes*, she remembered with amusement, *afraid of the person I loved the most.*

She thought of Matthew Winkle and the great care he had taken of her tentative love. "I thank you for that, Matthew," she whispered, her lips barely moving. *Your grace in love gives me confidence to try again.* Tears welled in her eyes, the last she would ever cry for her late husband, as she contemplated Emmeline and Ed standing together at the altar. With a glad heart, she folded the memories of Captain Winkle deep within herself and knew without a qualm that all was well.

The feeling persisted as she strolled home with Major Redpath, even though he did not take the opportunity to propose, as she had hoped. In fact, he was strangely subdued. "I still do not know what to do with Marie Deux," he said finally as they approached the house and both of them slowed their steps.

Propose to me, you slowtop, she thought, *and this will resolve itself promptly.* After a moment's hesitation, she put her arm through his, leaning against him a little—but only a very little—as they stood in the driveway. Surprised, he looked down at her, his smile uncertain, which puzzled her.

"Audrey Winkle, I never took you for a tease," he said, gently removing her arm from its comfortable niche within his. "I know I owe you a great apology for what happened in the storage room. You must think me a thoroughgoing rascal, particularly in light of your own inclinations. I hope you'll forgive me."

"I . . ." *I what?* she thought in sudden irritation. "My own inclinations?" What do you mean? She felt her newfound serenity dribbling away and decided that she did not know what to think. He was moving again, and she moved forward with him, wanting instead to tug at his arm and dig her heels into the gravel of the driveway and talk to him. *He must think I kiss men like that all the time*, she thought in misery.

She was about to grab him by the shoulders and tell him that she loved him when the door opened and Mama called to her. She looked around in real irritation, uttered a strengthy oath under her breath that she had overheard from Captain Winkle, and hurried up the front steps.

"Mama, what is it?" she said, hoping that her misery did not show, and longing for her own room.

"You know you should not linger so long in the night air," Mama scolded. Her chin quivered and she burst into noisy tears. "Audrey, Emmeline is my baby!"

Audrey sighed and let Mama cry. "There, now, I'm here," she soothed, all the time her own heart was breaking. *And I'll be here a long time, it seems, because a certain Scot is less interested than I thought*, she considered. "Now, blow your nose, Mama, and remember that Emmeline will be with Ed in Ostend, or Brussels, and you have always wanted to visit the Continent."

"You'll come too?" Mama asked anxiously.

No, I will not, she thought. *I could not bear to see the man I love again, especially since he seems so little inclined to love me.* "Oh, Mama, someone will have to watch the house here," she managed, on the edge of tears herself. "Now, what can I do for you before I go to bed?"

Mama blew her nose again, thought a moment, then nodded her head decisively. "Count the silverware in the dining room one last time." She leaned closer to Audrey. "One can't be too careful with ragamuffin French army leavings about."

"Mama! Marie Deux would never steal anything!" Audrey exclaimed in exasperation. *Only my heart, and Scots majors of artillery are equally adept at that*, she thought, as she directed Mama back to the sitting room and went to the dining room.

Everything was there, of course; she counted every knife, fork, and spoon twice. Even in the middle of her misery, she was able to admire the elegance of the dining room, all set up for the wedding breakfast after the ceremony. The crystal goblets that Major Redpath had purchased sparkled even in the low light as servants hurried to lay down the last place setting. She glanced at the extra glassware still sitting on the serving table and looked closer, frowning.

There were two pitchers now. *Odd*, she thought. *Emmeline told me she broke one and that she had to buy a new one this afternoon with Marie Deux's help.* She came closer, picking up both pitchers. They were the same. "Emmy, why on earth would you tell a fib, then pick up another pitcher?"

I shall ask Marie, she thought, as she closed the door behind her. *And come to think of it, I have not seen her all day.* She went slowly up the stairs, stopping halfway up when the front door opened, and resisting the enormous urge to turn around and see if it was the major. *No, Audrey, you're not so hard up for a husband that you need to fling yourself at a man who obviously just wanted to flirt. Try for a little dignity.*

She hoped that Marie would still be awake and lying in her bed, but the bed was empty. Quietly, she tiptoed to the dressing room and leaned against the doorjamb, smiling despite her unhappiness. "Worn out, are you?" she whispered, looking into the gloom at the child who slept on the cot, hair tucked tidily into her sleeping cap. She closed the door quietly. *I do not know what Major Redpath plans to do with you, but you must certainly take my hand-me-downs with you*, she thought. *And my heart.*

* * *

I wonder if I can break myself of this stupid habit of rising with the roosters, Major Redpath thought with irritation as he lay on his back and stared at the ceiling. *Probably not*, he decided. *I have been at war too long to change anything after all, I suppose. What I thought was something new yesterday is just the same old routine today*, he decided. *I wake up early, and there is no one here beside me to play with. I dress, and there is no one who needs me to button her up the back. I eat, and I see no pretty face across the table, buttering toast for me or asking my opinion about mundane household duties. And when I go to Ostend in a month, I will go by myself. After a long day of gunnery drill, there will be no one to incline me to skip an evening of cribbage and think up creative excuses for an early bedtime.*

There will not even be Marie Deux. I will have to find an orphanage for her, no matter how I despise the idea, he decided as he got up, stood at the window, and regarded the beauty of the morning. It struck him as remarkably short-sighted of the Lord to provide so lavishly for this wedding day when he, Major John Redpath of His Majesty's Royal Horse Artillery, was sunk in such misery.

"Dashed inconsiderate, I call it," he said as he washed, shaved, and dressed in his regimentals. He usually took some pleasure in putting on the handsome uniform, serene and somewhat arrogant in the knowledge that none of the other services looked half so good as the artillery. This time, once he got past the doeskin breeches so white that he squinted, everything reminded him of Marie Deux. As he buttoned it, he remembered that the frilly shirt was the only dress shirt she had permitted him to pack. He remembered with a pang her fingers gentle on the rows and rows of gold braid that spanned the breast. He knotted the scarlet sash about his waist, shrugged into the jacket, and glowered at himself in the mirror.

As he pulled on his boots, shined with care and a good thing too, considering how long he and Ed had chased about finding blacking, he wondered if his old housekeeper at home could keep Marie. He sighed. Maudie McCormack must be past seventy now. *I simply have to do what I said I would,* he told himself, *and resign myself to the unalterable fact that I am every bit as soft-hearted and mush-brained as those wretched, magnificent gunners I command. Of course they should have left Marie Deux to die in the heat and waste of the ruined French artillery. Now we have saved her for an orphanage or a workhouse.*

He hesitated a moment outside Audrey Winkle's door. *I could fling it open, throw myself at her feet, tell her to please overlook that she does not wish to marry into the military again, and propose. I could assure her that goodness, no, a major of artillery runs no risk of death, but that would be a lie, and she is not stupid. She is a wise woman who does not wish to throw herself away twice on dead meat, and I cannot fault her for that. But, Audrey, take a chance on me!*

It was stupid, and he knew it. He went to breakfast, glared at the relatives assembled, and played with his food, hardly looking up when his lieutenant, all jitters and bloodshot eyes, came to sit beside him.

"Well, Lieutenant, you look terrible," he said finally, as the assembled relatives tittered.

Ed said nothing, which surprised him into a closer look. Lieutenant Sir Edmund Parkhill had all the appearance of a man about to change his mind. *I can see being uneasy at the contemplation of marriage . . . no, no, I can't,* he contradicted silently. *I can imagine no joy greater than the thought of splicing myself body, soul, and heart to Audrey Caldwell Winkle Redpath. Ed, what is your problem?*

He did not ask, of course, deciding that all men face the eventuality of wedlock differently, and it was Ed's right to suffer, if he chose. He sat there indecisive, of half a mind to go in search of Marie Deux, or run upstairs, rip out his heart, and throw it at the widow's feet, when the door opened.

Redpath looked around hopefully and met the frantic eyes of the butler. He stared in surprise, knowing that he had never seen a butler look like that before. "Ames, are you well?" he asked, as the other relatives and mends gathered there swiveled around too.

Ames was not. He opened and closed his mouth several times, uttered strangling noises that could have been speech in an earlier anthropologic age and stepped aside for the constable.

"Major John Redpath?" said that worthy.

"Yes?" Redpath answered, his voice wary, as the relatives all leaned closer. He contemplated his various sins and decided they did not fall within the provenance of a constable at law. "What can I possibly have to do with you?"

The constable drew himself up taller, as though he could hardly wait to unburden himself before such an audience. "Mrs. Audrey Winkle wishes me to inform you that she is being detained by the law and hopes you will bail her out."

Redpath blinked. Audrey's brothers gasped out loud. One of the sisters-in-law began to wave about her vinaigrette as the other gathered her children close and tried to clap her hands over their ears. Uncle Eustace let out a whoop and Aunt Agatha seemed to have trouble breathing. The others began to chatter among themselves.

"May I ask what she did?" Redpath questioned, even as Ed cleared his throat. He was on his feet now, towering over the constable, who backed up into the jam cart.

"It's not my doing!" the man protested as he wiped at the seat of his pants. "I think she's one part lunatic to try to get some little waif out of a workhouse! Created a real scene, she did! But we've got her locked up now, and the child's right where nature intended her." He smiled at the astonished assemblage, the picture of legal complacency.

"Blast it," Redpath said, his voice perfectly toneless, his mind traveling a thousand miles an hour. He felt a chill run down his spine and then back up again as he thought of Marie Deux and all his promises of a good family. *Someone has put you in a workhouse and I let it happen.* He picked up the constable by the front of his jacket and held him against the wall. "How did the child get into the workhouse?" he asked quietly.

"Sir, I can—"

"Shut up, Lieutenant," he snapped. "I want to hear from this gentleman. Tell me now," he repeated as he lowered the little man to the floor again.

"You don't need to get violent about it!" he declared, brushing off the greasy front of his jacket. "The beadle told me a blonde-headed lady brought her by yesterday afternoon, and that's all I know!"

Suddenly it was all clear. *Someone sent Ed and me on a wild-goose chase for bootblacking*, he thought, as he turned around slowly to contemplate his lieutenant. *And didn't Audrey tell me that Emmeline borrowed Marie for some last-minute shopping?*

"Sir, you know we were only postponing the inevitable." Redpath stared at his lieutenant, who blanched under his gaze.

"You were determined to find fault with every single orphanage we looked at in Land's End," Ed continued, his face pale but determined. "We had a duty to discharge, and heaven knows enough tongues were already wagging about Marie Deux . . . and us."

"And you," Redpath amended. "You see, Ed, I didn't mind the gossip because I knew it wasn't true."

"Perhaps you should worry about such things, Major," the lieutenant replied. "Think how all this reflects on the Caldwells."

"It reflects on no one but hypocrites," he declared roundly, "people who are happy enough to have us keep them safe from Napoleon, but who have no charity for the weakest among us, the children of war, whatever side." He ignored the gasps of indignation around the table.

Ed had nothing to say.

"Do tell me this, Lieutenant Parkhill," he asked formally, "was this your idea? I would have thought better of you."

Parkhill hesitated. "No, it was not," he said at last. "I knew what she was doing, however, and—"

"And dragged me all over creation for bootblacking." The major looked around the table. "If you all will excuse me, I have to bail a lady out of jail."

He left the breakfast room, taking the stairs two at a time back to his room to retrieve his hat and wallet. *I wonder how much it takes to bail out a lady?* he thought, finding himself amused now that he did not have to look at her relatives.

Uncle Eustace waited for him at the bottom of the stairs. "I'm coming, too," he said. "No, I am!" he insisted when the major shook his head. "She's my niece, and by Gadfrey, sir, you might need some help to spring the little'un from the workhouse."

He stopped in his headlong rush from the house, touched by Eustace. "It doesn't bother you that I am ruining the perfect wedding?" he asked.

Eustace flipped up his eye patch, scratched, and lowered it again. "I'm tired of so much perfection among the Caldwells. Lead on, Major!"

From the glances, stares, and titters that followed them from the edge of town to the center of Bath, the major could only assume that people would have plenty to talk about through the coming summer and likely well into autumn. Everyone seemed to have business at the magistrate's that morning, he thought, shouldering through the crowd that parted like ripples around a boulder, then closed in again after the two of them. Knowing that he looked perfectly intimidating in his best uniform and much over six feet tall with the hat on, he strode to the magistrate's desk and slapped his hand on it.

"I'm here to bail out Mrs. Audrey Winkle," he said. "She's matron of honor at a wedding in"—he paused and pulled out his pocket watch, the one that had seen duty in battles less important to him now than this one—"in forty-five minutes."

The magistrate blinked and tugged on his wig. He settled himself behind the high desk but was unable to achieve much intimidation, because the major appeared even more formidable. Elaborately he looked at the notes in front of him until Redpath itched to grab him by the wattles of his fleshy neck.

"She was disturbing the peace, General," the magistrate said finally and looked over his shoulder. "Bring out the prisoner!"

As the major watched appreciatively, Audrey Winkle was led forward, distracted, flushed, militant, and beautiful all at the same time. Her lovely hair was independent of any braids or pins, and he felt himself growing weak in the knees.

"Twenty pounds!" declared the magistrate.

The crowd gasped. Eustace flipped up his eye patch again for another scratch. "'Pon my word, niece, what did you do?" he asked. "Kill two or three of them and burn down the place?"

"I wanted to," she said, her voice firm and not in the

least repentant. "And it's a dashed good thing it wasn't the Foundling Home!"

The magistrate looked at the ledger in front of him. "Says here, Mrs. Winkle, that you swore a round oath, threw an inkwell at the beadle, and then beat him with his own mace when he would not produce a waif named Marie Deux."

What a woman, John thought, as he tried not to laugh.

"The beadle is an idiot, and I don't scruple to tell you so," she replied, biting off each word, a tigress fighting for her cub. "I would do it ag—"

"She'll be silent now," the major said, with a warning look. He opened his wallet. "Twenty pounds? You'll release her to me?"

"Depends, General," said the magistrate. "What's her relationship to you?"

He took a deep breath, grateful that the men of the Second who looked to him for guidance, wisdom, and leadership, were not there. "She's my lover from the wars and the mother of our unfortunate child you have so wrongly allowed to be incarcerated in the workhouse!" *My, that was a stunner*, he thought, as soon as he uttered it. *Who'd have thought I had such an imagination?*

Apparently the citizenry of Bath who frequented magistrate's halls had no quarrel with his declaration. Admiring glances from some of the more lived-in looking women and ugly murmurs from the men directed toward the magistrate assured him that his cause was just among the lower class of Bath. There was scattered applause.

"I have come to claim that which is mine alone to claim!" he declared in ringing tones, liking the sound of it all, and wondering just briefly if he ought to throw over the army for a career in Commons. "I demand justice!"

He would have said more—he was just warming

up—except that Audrey took him by one arm and Uncle Eustace by the other.

"Quite so, lad," Uncle Eustace said. He looked at the magistrate. "When does my plaguey niece have to reappear?"

"Quarter sessions!" the magistrate said, banging down the gavel. "Unless she can wheedle the beadle into dropping charges."

The crowd seemed to like his assonance and applauded him too. The magistrate beamed down on them, the soul of benevolence again as he waved the major away.

"That was stunning," Audrey told him as they hurried along, hand in hand. She looked over her shoulder at the crowd following them to the workhouse. "Do you realize every Caldwell within shire boundaries will be snickered at from now until at least the next century? My reputation is gone."

"Yes, isn't it? You may have to move," he said, all complacency as they hurried him along.

The beadle was less trouble than any of them anticipated. One wary eye on the crowd and the other on Audrey Winkle, he listened to a reiteration of Major Redpath's speech, blanched, and summoned Marie Deux from the bowels of the workhouse. "I had no idea," he murmured over and over.

Neither did I, Redpath thought. *This is turning into such an interesting day.* He glanced at Audrey, who stared back, then startled him by running her tongue over her lips and giving him such a look that he wished—not for the first time—that it was his wedding in thirty minutes now.

Then Marie Deux was there, hesitating in the doorway, poised to run if the chance developed. She rushed toward them with a shriek and a cry that brought him to his knees. Audrey was beside him, trying to gather as much of Marie into her arms and catching him too, until his uniform sleeve was quite wet with someone's tears. They could have been his.

"Terrible mistake," Audrey was saying into Marie's ear, except that it was his ear, and her lips made him tingle all over. "My darling, forgive us. We had no idea this would happen yesterday."

Even the beadle appeared to be affected by the scene before him, dabbing his eyes with the handkerchief Uncle Eustace offered him. While they could only hug Marie in love and relief, Audrey's uncle proved his worth.

"Now, there, sir, you don't really want to bring charges against this lovely lady, who only wanted to reclaim her child?" he asked, ignoring the startled look Marie Deux gave him.

"Well, no," the beadle agreed, his eyes going to the ink-stained wall behind him. "But there are damages . . ."

"Which I am certain this will cover," Eustace murmured. There were guinea-sized sounds and then silence as the coins disappeared in the beadle's uniform jacket. "Come, niece," he said. "There's a wedding in half an hour, I would remind you."

Eustace hurried ahead while the major and Audrey Winkle followed, each clutching tight to Marie Deux's hands. "When did you find out?" Redpath asked.

"I'm such an idiot," Audrey said. "I thought she was sleeping in my dressing room on that cot, but it was one of my nieces! I confronted Emmeline, told her what I thought, then ran to the workhouse." She looked down at Marie and stopped her long enough to kiss the top of her head. "Emmy took her to town yesterday on those errands as an excuse to pitchfork her into the workhouse, and I was none the wiser! I could kick myself."

Redpath sighed. "I fear my lieutenant was in on the whole scheme, even though he did not plan it. I suppose I cannot fault either of them too much. We were supposed to find that orphanage for Marie Deux, and your sister did want the wedding no one forgets. Things change."

I wonder if you can change enough, he thought, as they hurried up the steps of the church. "I know how you feel about military men—" he began, then stopped as Mrs. Caldwell, her face a shade of gray not found in nature, yanked Audrey away from him and Marie and hurried her inside, scolding and trying to brush her hair at the same time.

He sat on the steps of the church with Marie between his long legs. "My dear, I suppose we will have to go to Belgium, after all."

Marie looked dubious. "I do not think Mrs. Hurley will have room for me."

"I will, Marie Deux, I will," he said. "I'm not exactly the family I promised you, but . . ."

It was his turn to be hauled away, this time by Uncle Eustace, who told him that Lieutenant Sir Edmund Parkhill was already standing at the altar, and from the looks of him, in need of support. Eustace slapped a ring in his hand. "Don't lose this," he muttered. He took Marie Deux by the hand. "You can sit with me and Aggie, m'dear, and hang the relatives."

He whisked her away. Major Redpath took a moment to run a comb through his hair, pull his sash back around where it belonged, tuck his hat under his arm, and walk slowly and deliberately to the front of the church to stand beside his lieutenant, who had been weighed in the balance and found decidedly wanting.

"I hope you will forgive me, Major, for being an idiot," Parkhill said out of the corner of his mouth as the triumphal entry began, everyone rose, and the flower girl strewed rose petals down the aisle.

Audrey came next, her hair in order now and under a beautiful headpiece of roses that made the major's heart beat even faster. The bridesmaids followed, and then the bride, a vision of purity, loveliness, and irritation as she caught his eye and he made a face at her. *I feel better now,* he thought.

"Sir?"

"Ed, this is not the time for remorse or conversation," he whispered back. "Save it."

"But, sir. I need advice—"

"Ed!"

And then it truly was too late for conversation. Audrey stationed herself a few steps below him. He looked down on her and wondered how much fun it would be to unbutton that dress. *I wonder if she knows what I'm thinking?* he asked himself with amusement, as he noticed the flush spread around her neck. He directed his eyes forward then and knew that he would have to take his chances with Mrs. Winkle. He thought about Marie and came to the startling conclusion that with such a wealth of love and friendship, he could possibly even do without his guns. And there was a good-sized estate near Dumfries that could use his attention, after so many years of neglect dictated by war.

"Sir? I have to—"

"Ed, really!" he whispered back. "Stow it!" He nudged Ed forward to take his place beside Emmeline, who continued to glare at him.

He half-listened to the vicar go on and on, his mind seeking courage to propose to Mrs. Winkle. The majestic phrases of the Church of England wedding ceremony unfolded around him, pausing at the memorable question when the vicar asked if anyone had any objections.

"I do, sir."

It was Ed. He was stepping away from Emmeline awkwardly as she gasped and tried to tighten her grip on her fiancé. The major blinked in surprise, as his lieutenant started toward him. "That's what I was trying to tell you, sir! I don't think Emmeline wears well in a crisis."

He may have been well-trained to plot the course of canister, case shot, and shell through clouds of battlefield smoke, but Major Redpath knew he would be hard-put to remember the precise sequence of what followed next. It was possible that Mrs. Caldwell leaped up from her front row pew with a scream worthy of Boadicea, but that may have been after Emmeline, fire in her eyes, grabbed one of Audrey's lovely vases of rose and hawthorn and slammed Lieutenant Sir Edmund Parkhill over the head with it. That was when Ed dropped like a clubbed mullet onto the steps leading to the altar and the vicar leaped back and fell over the prie-dieu behind him. The acolyte performed a juggler's act with the book that went flying in the air, lost, and started to laugh, which seemed to be the cue that set off the entire assemblage.

To their further entertainment, Emmeline threw off her veil, snarled at Redpath as though he was to blame for the whole turn of events, and stalked down the center aisle. Her dress must have caught on a nail or something, because he heard a fearful zip. It sounded enough like a Congreve rocket misfiring to make him drop to his knees out of instinct and pull Mrs. Winkle down with him. It would have been a good time to faint or die—which would have suited Emmeline—but he was made of sterner stuff. He started to laugh instead, sitting on the steps and wiping his streaming eyes.

He was still sitting there a half hour later. Uncle Eustace had taken pity on Ed and carted him off to a nearby inn, figuring that his appearance in the house of his former loved one would cause only mayhem. "I tried to tell you, sir," Ed managed to gasp as Uncle Eustace summoned two groomsmen to carry him off. "Emmeline's changed, or . . . or maybe I have."

The soul of equanimity now, Major Redpath nodded and patted his subaltern. "Best go on to Ostend right away, Ed. You might be safer with the Channel between you and the Caldwells."

The major stayed where he was, content to breathe the scent of roses and hawthorn that filled the almost-empty church. He glanced over at Marie Deux, who rested her head against Audrey Winkle's legs as she sat on the steps too. *If Ed is brave enough to speak his mind, I should take a page from his book and try it.* He opened his mouth to speak, but Audrey was whispering something to Marie, who nodded, added a little earnest commentary of her own, then walked to him and sat down. He touched her hair and smiled at her.

"Mrs. Winkle thinks you should marry her."

He stared at Marie, and then at Audrey, who was grinning at him as she twirled her nosegay of roses around her finger. He leaned toward Marie, "Well, tell her . . . oh, this is silly. Audrey, I have it on good authority that you have sworn never to marry a military man," he said, lifting his voice to be heard above the organist, who, through some musical perverseness, had continued to play doggedly.

"I never . . ." she began, then her eyes became militant again. "I could strangle Emmeline," she said.

With a sigh that went all the way down to his well-blacked boots, he leaned back against the chancel rail and regarded his dearly beloved. "You didn't mean it?" he asked. "Emmeline told me."

"Emmeline should be taken out and shot," Audrey said, getting to her feet and brushing off her dress. She came to his side of the church and sat down well within range of his arm. "I said that once, a few weeks after Captain Winkle died. I think it was an understandable reaction."

He pulled her close. The organist stopped, assessed

the situation, and began a tentative replaying of the wedding processional.

"You don't mean it, then?" he asked, hardly daring to imagine his good fortune.

"Of course not. I love you," she said, so matter-of-fact that tears came to his eyes. "And how else will I ever get Marie Deux as my daughter, if I don't marry her father and my lover from the wars! Really, John, who'd have thought you to tell so many tales in one morning? I own I didn't."

He didn't answer because he was busy kissing her. *Pretty soon I can do this anytime I want*, he thought, his brain busy. *And other stuff, which will probably mean I won't spend much time at trout streams this month. Lucky fish.*

"Very well, then, I'll do this but once. Audrey Winkle, I love you . . ."

". . . even more than your guns?" she teased.

"You know, I think so. Will you . . . will you marry me?"

"Yes," she said immediately, and gathered Marie Deux into the embrace. She laughed into his shoulder. "I think Ed even has an unused marriage license."

"Nope. It's registered in his name," the major informed her. "I'll tell you what. If you can pack quickly—I'm sure Emmeline will help—you and Marie and I can be in Gretna Green sometime tomorrow. I'll marry you promptly like a good Scot, over the anvil, with a proper Church of Scotland ceremony." He fished Ed's ring out of his uniform front. "As the wife of a frugal Scot, you won't cavil at wearing this ring, will you? I'm sure Ed won't need it anytime soon."

She kissed him this time, seriously troubling his breathing, his mind, and his body. "That sounds irregular, vulgar, and calculated to send my mother and all the other Caldwells into spasms," she said, her lips close to his. "You're right, of course. It's certainly the least we can to do make this a wedding day that no one ever forgets."

"Just as Emmeline wanted," he added.

"And you can write to General Picton and tell him that you were a clunch and couldn't remember the name of that orphanage, and tell him that Marie Deux is ours now."

"It was St. Pancras at Austell," he said promptly.

Audrey pulled away from him, looked into his eyes, and burst into laughter. "You rogue! You never forgot it!"

He got to his feet and pulled his women up with him. "No, I didn't. I just couldn't give her up." He bowed to the little girl elaborately, as she clapped her hands in appreciation. "And now, Mademoiselle Marie Deux, will you do me the honor of becoming our daughter, now that I have a wife promised?"

As pleased as he was with himself, there was something new in the look that Marie Deux gave him that brought tears to his eyes. She observed him solemnly, and he realized with a pang how much of his heart he had already lost to her. *And now I will have a wife and a daughter*, he thought. *This is something new, indeed, for I did not know there was so much love in the world. I am a lucky son of the guns.* He picked up Marie so he could look into her eyes. "Well?"

She patted his cheek. If she had just said *oui,* or *si,* or yes, he would have managed, but the huge sigh that came up from her toes, and the way she nestled against his chest filled his cup to overflowing. He could only sit down on the steps again and hold her close.

Audrey, bless her, sat beside him, resting her cheek against his arm, her hand light—but possessive—on his thigh. "I think Marie and I will both give you sufficient reason to stay in Scotland," she said, her soft words tickling his ear. He suddenly knew with all his heart that she was right.

After a moment, Marie pulled away enough to look at him. "It is a good thing, Major," she said, her hand gentle on his face. "Someone needs to tell you when to throw out shirts."

Audrey laughed. "I had thought I could help there, Marie," she protested, her eyes bright with amusement.

Marie regarded her. "Perhaps," she allowed cautiously, "but I have been looking in your wardrobe, and I think you could use some advice too." She made that dismissing gesture with her hand that Redpath was already familiar with and which Audrey was destined to discover now.

Audrey laughed and kissed them both. "John, I fear we are in the hands of a tyrant!"

"Aye, my bonny love," Redpath agreed, totally at peace with the idea. "I believe the French are well known for that, wouldn't you say?"

THE BACKGROUND MAN

⌒

IT WAS ON DAYS LIKE THIS—WHEN THE rain poured from sodden skies onto slate roofs, to roar down over taxed drainpipes—that Charles Mortimer missed the heat of India. Naturally, through some cosmic conspiracy, such days seemed to collaborate with Mondays. Chin in hand, he stared out the front window across the lobby, watching London's workers hurry along the sidewalk, staying well back to avoid spray from the coaches and carts.

His honesty required an amendment; Mondays made little difference to him. As manager, he lived at the Grand Hotel, and while he was granted days off, he generally had nowhere to go and nothing to spend his money on. Mrs. Wheelwright, the housekeeper, had quizzed him once about his solitary life. "A day off to you only means coming to the front desk two hours later than usual, is that it?" she asked, and he had agreed.

And here we are, open on July 1, right on schedule, he thought, *even though I cannot get into my rooms behind the lobby because they are still full of boxes that I suspect belong in that other hotel my employer is opening in Kent.* He sat up straight and frowned. *And the carpenters are still banging away in the upstairs linen closet. I suppose that Sir Michael Moseley will poke his head in the door now to declare that Mr. Simmons has recovered from the gout, and I can return to deputy manager instead of manager.*

I should be a prophet, he thought, startled, as the footman opened the entrance door upon the owner himself. Charles held his breath while Sir Michael Moseley let the footman remove his many-caped cloak. *Now if only my employer will be hard of hearing*, he thought.

Sir Michael was not. "What do I hear, Mortimer?" he asked, his voice thundering across the great and elegant space between door and desk.

Charles sat up, his Monday morning reverie at an end. "That, sir, is the sound of hammering," he stated. "The carpenters forgot to line the linen closet shelves with cedar."

Sir Michael sniffed, and then sniffed again. "Paint? Paint? Do I smell paint?" His face was long and lined, and when he turned it upon Charles, it seemed to the hotel manager that he bore a remarkable resemblance to a basset hound. "I was led to believe by Mr. Simmons—from his bed of pain, mind you, where all men tell the truth—that the Grand Hotel was finished."

"I believe it will be by six of the clock, Sir Michael," Charles said, "or so the workers have promised me." He managed a slight smile. "Sir, there are always kinks to work through." He coughed, wondering at his own presumption. "But you know that far better than I do, Sir Michael. Is this your sixth hotel?"

"It is, Mortimer." The owner made his stately way across the lobby, pausing to stare at the muted blue and yellow tones of the wallpaper as though for the first time, even though Charles had it from Mrs. Wheelwright that the man had been making a nuisance of himself with the workers for the past month. "You would think he had never built a hotel before, Mr. Mortimer," she had confided over tea belowstairs last night.

I will allow my employer his idiosyncrasies, Charles considered. *He has employed me in his other hotels since my return from India, and I have observed—and endured—his bluster.*

Sir Michael stood before him now, on the other side of the marble-topped front desk. "I worry when things are not done and guests are already arriving. Is my trust well placed in you, Mortimer, to run one of my establishments?"

Should I be humble or honest? "Yes, it is, Sir Michael," he replied.

"Then the workers will be gone tomorrow?"

"If the Grand Hotel is done, and not one moment before. I have standards too." He waited for the blast to come.

Sir Michael glared at him. "So you will not bow and scrape and tell me lies, eh?" he asked.

"I shouldn't think so," Charles murmured. "It's not my usual pattern."

The owner rested his elbow on the desk. "It is just that you seem somewhat meek, Mr. Mortimer, and that will never do. Your position requires a certain dignity, combined with an element of humility and deference." He waved his arm. "Let them know who is in charge, but at the same time . . ." He paused.

Lick their boots? Charles thought in wry amusement. *I've done that aplenty in twenty-five years of the working world. Bow and defer and speak softly and arrive at solutions to problems they have not even voiced? I am an expert. Make suggestions that guests far grander than I can adopt without any nagging sense of plagiarism? I am your man, Sir Michael.*

"Sir Michael, you may be certain that the Grand Hotel is in good hands," he said. It was prosaic, but entirely what he should say.

"I'll judge that, won't I?" his employer stated. His words only avoided being menacing by the fact that most men who look like basset hounds cannot be thought sinister, or so Charles reasoned.

"To be sure, Sir Michael."

Sir Michael continued to regard him. "We shall see. I hope I have not misplaced my trust by making you a manager at last," he said, then looked behind him. "And now you have a customer. Good morning, madam." Sir Michael bowed to someone behind him that Charles could not see, then turned again. "Mortimer, I will be checking on you." He turned from the desk in an elaborate motion worthy of the regent himself and headed for the grand staircase, obviously intent on exploration upstairs. *Go in peace*, Charles thought with fervor and turned his attention to the lady who stood before him now.

He wasn't surprised that he had not noticed her behind Sir Michael's impressive bulk, because she was short. And Charles couldn't be surprised that he had not noticed her entrance when he was occupied with his employer, because there was nothing about her calculated to attract attention. She was one of hundred, no thousands and millions of women who inhabited the world in quiet, possessing no air to make a man look twice, or maybe even once.

That is, unless the right man took time out for a second perusal, Charles Mortimer decided as he looked again at the lady before him. No question in his mind: She was a lady. She had a pleasant face with a sprinkling of freckles across her nose and a cleft in her chin. Her brows were thick, and her eyes lively. Her face was wet, which surprised him, because she carried an umbrella. *I wonder if she dislikes those as much as I do*, he thought as he cleared his throat and then smiled at her.

When she smiled back, he took a third look, and for

the first time in forty years of ordinary living, surrendered himself to someone he did not know. He could not credit the strange way he felt as he continued to smile at the lady. *My word, she is beautiful*, he thought. *How is this?*

She cleared her throat this time, and he knew he should say something. He continued instead to smile at her, even as his brain protested somewhere inside his skull that he was looking stupider by the half second.

"Excuse me, sir, but I believe I have a reservation," she said. "Millicent Carrington, from Edgeley, Kent."

"Oh, yes, of course," he told her and dragged his attention to the card box where all reservations nestled in precise alphabetical order. *Oh, please don't let her be encumbered with something as distasteful as a husband*, he thought. *I will have to remember how to shoot and then call him out.* "Millicent Carrington," he declared, holding up the card as though she were the first visitor of his life, and not one of thousands. "Mrs. Carrington?" he asked, remembering his manners and hoping for information that would prevent the purchase of dueling pistols.

She shook her head. "Miss Carrington, if you please." He could have fallen in a heap behind the desk, such was his relief. *I am being stupid*, he told himself as he smiled back and was rewarded with a smile of her own that made her blue eyes fairly glow at him. *I wonder if she smiles at every man like that*, he thought with a jab of sudden jealousy. *A man can only fight so many duels in one lifetime.*

She cleared her throat again. "Sir, is there a register I sign?"

Register. Register. "Yes, of course, Miss Carrington," he replied. "Things are so new here that I seem to have misplaced it."

"Um, I believe it is right here in front of us," she said, after a moment's pause.

"Heavens! There it was, all the time!" he said,

looking down at the book that rested on a prominent stand between them. "And open to Monday, July 1," he said, wincing at his inanity, he who was the most unflappable of men. "Fancy that."

She leaned forward to sign the register while he admired the top of her bonnet and the faint fragrance of lemon that rose from her skin. He could hear her breathe. Miss Carrington looked up at him then. "Sir, is there a key?"

A key. A key. Now why would . . . of course there was. He glanced at her card. He had planned to put her in 301, at the opposite end of the hall from his own temporary quarters, but he took the key to 318 from the pigeonhole next to his own. *Why am I doing this?* he asked himself. He handed her the key, then motioned to the other footman positioned by the grand staircase. "Devost will take your bags and show you to your room, Miss Carrington." Was that *his* voice cracking? Good heavens, he was nearly thirty years from his voice change.

"Thank you, Mr., Mr. . . ."

"Mortimer, Charles Mortimer," he replied. "If I can do anything for you, you need only ask." *Oh, please do*, he thought. *Tell me that you think Devost is a scoundrel and you'd rather that I carried your bags upstairs. Anything.*

To his dismay, she seemed to have no qualms about his footman and surrendered her luggage with good grace, pointing to the portmanteau by the front entrance that the hackney driver had deposited there. "This is your first hotel, Mr. Mortimer?" she asked while she waited.

I must seem greener than a Spanish lime, he thought with a wince. "The first hotel where I am manager, Miss Carrington," he said. He hesitated a moment, wanting to tell her more, wondering if she expected it. "Actually, I have worked for Sir Michael Moseley for over ten years . . . ever since my return from India." There. That seemed enough, without being too much.

She looked at him with what he hoped was real interest. "India? My brother was with the duke's own Thirty-third. We shall have to talk about India, Mr. Mortimer."

She nodded to him then and followed Devost and her luggage up the stairs. He watched until she was out of sight at the stairs' turning and wondered if she was seriously interested in more conversation with him. Reason told him no, that she had only been filling time until the footman should return with her baggage. And yet. After another moment, he braced himself and returned to his duty.

By the time his day ended hours and hours later, Charles had convinced himself that no, he was not relapsing into malarial fever, and yes, he was a foolish fellow. It was an easy conclusion to arrive at, considering that in his forty years on the planet, he had never been overly concerned with women. It wasn't that he didn't like them; he did. The problem was a matter of simple ciphering: As the ninth of ten children of an earnest vicar unencumbered with either a good living or money of his own, the necessity of earning his bread had somehow always superseded any attempts at wooing.

I suppose I could have chosen a different venue to begin my career, he thought, not for the first time. Clerking for the East India Company had plunked him down in a corner of the world that while exotic offered little opportunity for matrimony with a proper British lady. And come to think of it, the Hindu women hadn't been eager to give him any of their time, either. The Mogul ladies? They were only a rumor, shadows on the street in their head-to-toe wraps, and otherwise kept behind high walls like mad uncles in England. India wasn't the place to find a wife; he might as well have lived on the moon.

He thought about the matter while he ate dinner in the kitchen belowstairs and reread, "On the Proper

Administering of Hotels," Sir Michael Moseley's primer on hotel management, with its plethora of do's and don'ts. He had returned to England with Wellington's Thirty-third; brought out of the country by the direst necessity, afflicted as he was with malaria. He wanted to die at Port Said, but the vessel's surgeon wouldn't hear of it; he had no alternative but to live.

The attacks of malaria were less frequent now, but he could never deny that they held him back from advancement in Sir Michael's hotel empire.

Or had until now, when Mr. Simmons's gout had reached such a degree of agony that the poor man yelped when anyone even walked close to his foot and stirred up a breeze. He glanced up from the rule book to see Henri DuPré eyeing him across the cutting board. "Excellent chicken soup, DuPré," he said, never quite sure what to say to a French chef with more than his share of arrogance.

"Monsieur! It is soup à la reine! Can't you taste the almonds and veal stock?" the chef snapped, banging down his French knife and decapitating an entire rank of unsuspecting carrots. "Chicken soup! Chicken soup! You might as well call Napoleon a private on half pay!"

"Yes, I might," Charles said under his breath. "Excellent soup, DuPré," he repeated. "Almonds and veal stock, you say?" *I suppose that is my problem*, he thought as he returned his attention to the rule book. *I don't have any imagination in the kitchen.* He smiled into the bowl, so DuPré would not see. *Still tastes like chicken soup to me.*

He did take a turn around the dining room after he finished his dinner, pausing to bow to the few guests already assembled and listen to their complaints about the banging and clanking and strong smell of paint that lingered still. He made a mental note to send them each a box of Copley's Crunchy Toffee. Nowhere did Sir

Michael mention it in his pamphlet, among the admonitions and caveats, but Charles knew from long experience that giving people something to eat that they didn't pay for invariably reaped dividends. *I should write my own booklet*, he thought. *Actually, I should run my own hotel.*

Miss Carrington came into the dining room just as he was completing his circuit and mentally girding himself for a diplomatic discussion with the carpenters. How nice, if only for a moment, to tuck away the upcoming unpleasantness and look upon a pretty woman.

In the soft light of midsummer that streamed in the tall French windows, Miss Carrington did not disappoint. He moved closer, as the maître d'hôtel seated her, then cleared his throat, not wishing a repeat of his adolescent falsetto earlier that afternoon. "Miss Carrington, would you wish to be seated with another lady? Some of our single guests request it."

She smiled her thanks but shook her head. "No, Mr. Mortimer. I prefer to sit alone." She smiled again. "Would you think me terribly ill-mannered if I read while I am waiting? Father never allows such liberties at home."

She could have done a fandango on the table and he wouldn't have objected. "Not at all, Miss Carrington," he assured her. "I always read when I eat."

"Then we are two dull dogs, indeed," she told him, and he laughed out loud. The maître d'hôtel looked at him, his eyes wide. *Yes, Washburn, I do laugh*, he wanted to say. *I've even been known to want a woman, although it's been a while.*

She took a small book from her reticule, so he could think of nothing else that would keep him by her table. He bowed and left the dining room.

The carpenters occupied him to the utmost levels of diplomacy for another hour. Patiently he listened to their catalog of troubles and delays, accepting blame when nothing else would work and offering gentle admonitions of an avuncular nature when that seemed apropos.

The carpenters left at ten o'clock, cheerful again, armed with his quietly voiced suggestions and ready to finish in the morning. He relieved the night clerk at the desk so the man could eat and indulge in a restorative nap, and then spent the next two hours catching up on correspondence, filing reservations, and forwarding invoices to Sir Michael at his office on Oxford Street. When he looked up again it was midnight. Another day gone. When Chaseley returned, refreshed from his nap, Charles Mortimer went to his room.

He opened the door and sighed out loud. Everything was jumbled where he had left it that morning, when he vacated his rooms off the lobby. He moved a few boxes to one side, located a towel for his morning bath, and then carefully arranged his clothes across a chair. *This inconvenience will last for two weeks*, he thought, *or three at the most, until Wellington's big party ends.* He sat on the bed, smiling to himself, and thinking suddenly of his father, that worthy man, and his sermons.

"The sermon," he said out loud, that homily on inconveniences and problems, the sermon that had shaped him more than he knew, until he had applied it at the worst moment of his life. He lay back on the bed, his hands behind his head. "Yes, Father, how I wish I could have told you," he murmured and closed his eyes, thinking in odd, telescoping fashion backward to India, and then the Deccan, and Assaye, and Kaitna Ford, and then smaller still to the cannon where he passed ammunition all the hot afternoon, until the moment when he was the only one left to fire the gun. And then he was touching the punk to the hole, his entire energy focused on that effort, and kept from fear by the certainty that this was a problem and not merely an inconvenience, and how refreshing it would be to tell his father that he knew for himself now.

I promised myself then, Father, that if I avoided being cut into bite-sized chunks by those Mahratta swords that I would always know the difference between an inconvenience and a problem, he thought. *Father, malaria is an inconvenience; a problem is having only one canister remaining to fire at a foe grudgingly sharing the same spit of land between two rivers.*

It hadn't been a problem for long. Wellesley himself (this was long before he was Wellington) brought him canister shot from the rear that was only the rear because it was twenty yards farther back. They had stared at each other for the briefest moment, Wellesley muttered something about East India clerks expanding their repertoire, and then he mounted his horse again.

After the battle, when Charles amused himself by the realization that he was still alive, he sat down on an ammunition box, only to find himself joined on another by Wellesley again, the man as black from powder as he was and as exhausted. Wellesley sat there with his elbows on his knees, his head far forward, his eyes closed. After a long pause, he turned his head slowly, as though every part of him ached. "Mortimer, are you ready to return to pushing a quill across a page at Fort William?"

"Can you doubt it, sir?" he replied.

Wellington grinned suddenly, his teeth amazingly white in his black face, and then gave that horse's laugh of his. "You're welcome anytime to serve my guns, Mortimer," he said. "Thank you with all my heart."

"You're welcome," Charles said as he lay there on his bed in the Grand Hotel. "Why didn't I tell him that? Why did I just blush and mumble?"

He opened his eyes and glanced at the night table next to the bed, then sat up, looking around. The table was there, of course; there was always a night table at a Moseley hotel. The manuscript was missing. In a moment he was on his feet, searching for it. He retrieved it from the neat folder of hotel business that he kept in his room, and placed it on the table. *Wellington in India*. He knew it was a simple title, but he had never managed a better one. He ruffled the pages, his evening's work for many years, secure in the knowledge that the manuscript would be complete soon enough to present it to the great man during the summer's fetes.

"And so I shall," he murmured, tired now and ready for the release of sweet sleep.

He slept peacefully and well—the times of nightmare were long over—and woke to the sun coming in the window and then a scratching at his door. "Come, please," he said, alert now and ready for the day's first emergency, early as it was.

Betty the 'tween stairs maid opened the door, peeking in to make sure that he was dressed, he thought, then pausing outside when she saw that he was still in bed.

"Oh, come in, Betty," he said, sitting up and tucking the blanket around his waist. "I'm probably twenty times more harmless than Mr. Simmons, if I can believe rumors. Is there a problem?"

She smiled at him then and came into his room, although no farther than the wall by the door. "Mr. Mortimer, there's trouble with the drain in the public bath, down the hall. The lady in there thought you should know."

He frowned. "It's not draining?"

"That's what she said." Betty grinned. "She was awfully nice about it. Oh, haven't we seen some guests flutter up into the boughs over little?"

Oh, we have, he thought, then waved her away so he could dress. *Everyone expects perfection in a Moseley hotel.*

While buttoning his trousers he looked at his manuscript, knowing that there wouldn't be any time to write this morning. India would wait.

There were two public baths on the third floor, unlike the second floor, which had private baths in each chamber. Even though he was certain that the lady would not have remained there, he knocked.

"'Make thee an ark of gopher wood,'" he heard a woman say in a deep voice. He laughed and knew without knowing that Miss Carrington was on the other side of the door.

"I'm coming in, Mrs. Noah," he said and opened the door to gaze upon Miss Carrington clad in a perfectly respectable but entirely fetching robe, her hair wrapped in a towel, her feet bare, her ankles so fine.

"You know your Genesis," she began, not rising from her perch on the side of the tub, or her contemplation of its recalcitrant drain. The steamy room smelled radiantly of that exultant lemon essence she wore.

"I am the child of a vicar," he said, coming closer to join her in staring at the drain.

"Are you?" she asked, the interest evident in her voice. "Then you must be well acquainted with the entrancing delights of waiting your turn for the tub."

He laughed again. "I am the ninth of ten, Miss Carrington. Not only did I queue up for the tub, I usually got hand-me-down water."

It was her turn to smile and twinkle her eyes at him. "That was not my intention in summoning you from sleep, sir," she replied, then blushed, probably from the suggestion of her reply. "I followed the time-honored ritual of lifting the stopper, but as you can tell, the result was less than satisfying."

"Shall I send a dove for the plumber, Mrs. Noah?" he asked.

"By all means, sir," she said and rose gracefully. "As if you did not have one hundred other pesky duties incumbent upon opening a hotel. I can wait here for the plumber, if you wish."

He did not overlook for one moment that he could summon Betty back or call for the underfootman, but he nodded. "I will bring you tea," he said.

"'An ever-present help in trouble,'" she quoted.

He thought a moment. He felt the years drop away in that peculiar fashion that happened among friends, but never with a woman before or someone he scarcely knew. "'. . . Though the waters thereof roar and be troubled.'"

She clapped her hands. "Mr. Mortimer, you are amazing! That is even the same psalm!"

With a nod to her, and a feeling of real satisfaction at his own wit, he hurried belowstairs to summon the plumber. He ordered a pot of tea and biscuits for the third floor west bathing room, which brought such an elevation to Mrs. Wheelwright's eyebrows that he feared for her hairline.

He was not destined for an immediate return to the third floor. The carpenters had arrived and needed his soothing ministrations. He supervised the changing of the guard at the front desk from a bleary-eyed Mr. Chaseley to the much more alert Mr. Kipling. One foot on the stairs, he was recalled to solve a complaint of an Italian guest who had misplaced either her husband or her dining table—he couldn't be sure which, because Charles Mortimer's Italian was untested ground. She did seem happy to see a peculiar-looking dog when it strolled into the lobby, and even happier when it was followed by a little boy. He smiled, bowed, and resolved to consult his Italian grammar that evening.

He did so hope that Miss Carrington wouldn't have exchanged her robe for a dress and shoes by the time he returned to the third floor, but time had passed; she was dressed and seated by the tub, this time with a sketch pad in her lap. She looked up and smiled when he came in, gesturing toward the plumber.

"Do you know, Mr. Mortimer, that water swirls counterclockwise above the equator and clockwise beneath it?"

He wondered if she had any idea how entrancing she was, sitting here in a rectangle of sun from the skylight, her hair still damp and spread like a fan across her back. "I don't know that I ever considered the matter, Miss Carrington," he told her.

"Mr. Wilson here tells me that it is so," she replied. "Do you know that he was an able seaman on one of Captain Cook's voyages of discovery to the South Seas? I am astounded at what a person can learn, watching a drain. And here my father told me that I would find London a bore."

He shook his head in amazement. *I have never met anyone like you*, he wanted to say. "Wilson, wasn't it two voyages with Cook?" he asked.

The plumber looked up from the drain, where he was snaking down a pliable copper rod. "It was, sir."

Miss Carrington gazed upon him with what he hoped was admiration. "You know your employees, sir."

He felt faint surprise at her comment. Of course he knew those who worked for him, right down to their birthdays. "Miss Carrington, I worked with Wilson in Harrogate. When Sir Michael was building this hotel, he moved the manager and me down to run it, and some staff chose to follow."

"That speaks well of you, sir," she said.

He knew he was blushing when Wilson laughed. "Ah, miss, don't make 'im get all flustery!"

She smiled and inclined her head toward him. "My apologies, Mr. Mortimer, but Sir Michael must certainly repose some confidence in you."

The plumber snorted and returned his attention to the drain. "I say it's high time!"

"Oh, Wilson, leave off," Charles protested, more amused than irritated.

The plumber forced the snake farther down the drain. "Miss, it's only Mr. Mortimer's little souvenir from India what holds'm back."

"Malaria," Charles said when Miss Carrington gave him an inquiring look. "It comes back like unwanted relatives." He tried to make light of it, because it embarrassed him to be talking about himself. "It's hard to run a hotel with the fever and shakes."

"So you're always second-in-command?"

"It works better that way, Miss Carrington. Except what does Mr. Simmons do but contract the gout? I am now manager by default."

"There are some of us what didn't mind that, either," Wilson muttered under his breath.

Charles was spared any further discourse by the plumber, who grunted in satisfaction as the snake stopped. He tugged gently, turned the snake, and then pulled out a glob of plaster. "There y'are, Mr. Mortimer. Happens all the time with new construction."

"Excellent, Wilson. Do have a biscuit."

"I believe I will, sir," the plumber replied. "Any of that tea left, Miss Carrington?"

"Just enough for you," she said, pouring him a cup. "Since you didn't come back, Mr. Mortimer, I knew you wouldn't mind if Mr. Wilson used the other cup."

"Of course not." Charles sat down on the stool at the dressing table. He looked at the sketch pad in her lap, thought about all the rules in Sir Michael's book that he and Wilson were probably fracturing, and set them aside. "Are you an artist, Miss Carrington?"

"I pretend to be," she said, passing the teacup to the

plumber, who sat on the lip of the tub and took it from her as nicely as though the three of them inhabited a drawing room. "It's hard to draw water swirling, and here was my perfect opportunity to practice a sketch." She smiled at the plumber, who smiled back. "And what does Mr. Wilson do but regale me with stories of watching the transit of Venus and cannibals in Fiji. I had no idea that Moseley hotels could be so . . . so entertaining. I have been totally diverted."

"Best not breathe a word of this to Sir Michael," Charles said after a moment's pause. "He would probably wonder what any of us are doing taking tea in a bathing room at nine in the morning."

"Absurd, isn't it?" she agreed. She stood up and closed her sketch pad. "I don't know why this is, but I always seem to stumble into the most agreeable situations and meet the most interesting people. Good day to you both. I had better be about my business."

He watched her go, then turned to regard the plumber. "Wilson, did you ever?"

"Not me, sir," Wilson said, then chuckled. "But you know, I think she meets interesting people because she asks questions, and glory be, she *listens*!"

"How rare in a guest," he said.

He went about the duties of the day then, knowing how busy he would be soon, with the grand fete for Wellington approaching. However shy of visitors the new hotel was, he knew that the Moseley reputation for order and efficiency would soon fill it. It was his duty to make things run smoothly. "Each employee must be polite, thoughtful, and capable," or so the rule book stated. *I am all those things*, he reminded himself as he was tempted to contemplate Miss Carrington.

Maybe even a little bloodless too. Mr. Simmons had accused him of that once; or maybe it wasn't so much an accusation as a comment on his subdued personality. He had thought about his supervisor's comment, mulling it about during a solitary walk (the only kind he ever took), and then deciding that he was not so much bloodless as he was resigned. He had decided years ago that certain things in life—a wife, children, a home—would never be his. His breeding was good enough, except that it was unmatched by even the smallest inheritance to grease his way. He had never regretted, until now, his personal honesty that had never allowed him to cheat his way to a fortune in India, as many other clerks in the East India Company had done.

He knew he was a quiet man, one not inclined to trumpet himself to the notice of others. He liked his solitude, relished it even, after a long day of dealing with the petty inconveniences of spoiled hotel guests. In time, he had come to prefer it. If that resigned him to a bloodless existence, then so it was. He had found his niche—even if it was a step or two down from what his breeding should have allowed—and tailored it to suit himself, the perfect existence.

Except that suddenly it wasn't so perfect. Somehow between yesterday and today, a page had turned in his book of life. He had been mindful of a page turning at Kaitna Ford, when he went from youth to man in one horrific afternoon. Time had passed and more pages had turned, but now they seemed to be turning back to a chapter he had skipped, overlooked, or simply ignored, because the possibility of fulfillment was so remote. The rain thundered down again that afternoon, and he knew, with despair in his heart—that place where he usually felt nothing—that he wanted not only a wife and little ones, but also that he wanted Millicent Carrington.

The thought jolted him. He knew from long practice that he could get rid of it; enough work and worry over this opening and Wellington's fete would push Miss Carrington so far back in his mind that he would soon forget her. He had the ability, except that this time he hesitated to dismiss her from his brain, and most certainly from his heart. *I am being absurd*, he told himself as he greeted guests, spoke with them in the lobby, let Mr. Kipling check them in, and summon the footmen for their luggage. He knew Mr. Kipling was wondering at him, wanting to ask why he was not squirreled away in his office as usual, doing the hotel's paperwork, like the super-efficient clerk he was. He could never tell his day clerk that he, Charles Mortimer, was waiting like a mooncalf for Millicent Carrington to appear in the lobby. He wished he had the nerve to ask her day's business.

To take his mind off Miss Carrington, he looked through the reservations for the month and was gratified to note members of Parliament, clergymen, and military officers. He sighed. And royalty. "Oh, mercy, we must bow, we must scrape," he murmured as he fingered the card with the name of Princess Henrika Hafkesprinke.

And Americans, apparently. He held up a card, marking the place in the file box with his finger. "Malachi Beach, Boston, Massachusetts, the American Society for Abolition," he murmured, then replaced the card and picked up the next one. "Mountrail, Lady Augusta. Heaven help us." He replaced it quickly, remembering her from previous visits to the Grand Vista in Harrogate, a lady tottering on the brink of death—or so she told everyone—who lived only to torment his staff. "'The guest is invariably correct,'" he murmured to himself, quoting Sir Michael's first rule.

He hoped, as he always did when he saw her name, that she would forget to arrive, or die, whichever seemed more convenient to her. As the morning wore on and his stomach began to gnaw itself at the prospect of her arrival, he thought he would circulate a warning throughout the hotel, rather like that fellow in the colonies who warned the Minutemen. As it turned out, there wasn't time.

She came as she always came, preceded by her dresser, a thoroughly cowed woman who, if she could have, would have flattened herself against the wall and slithered in, so as to escape all possible notice. Charles Mortimer, who had faced sword-wielding Mahrattas, stared down malaria, and survived ten years in Sir Michael Moseley's employ, felt his courage sink to cellar level.

"You have Lady Mountrail's reservation, I trust," the dresser asked, her voice scarcely above a whisper.

He could easily have turned the matter over to Mr. Kipling, but one glance at his day clerk's pale face told him that it would be useless. Lady Mountrail could smell fear like a bulldog. "Certainly, Smith. We have placed her in the Grand Garden Suite on the second floor. Here is the key."

He looked up then while the dresser registered for her mistress, knowing that Lady Mountrail would make her entrance now.

The riders from her post chaise came first, bearing her luggage, to be followed by the lady herself, bundled in fur and turbaned to guard against a chance bit of chill air on a July morning. Under her arm she carried a lapdog with a pushed-in face registering the same utter disdain as her mistress. Lady Mountrail was thin and wizened like an apple forgotten in the bottom of the bin. Mr. Simmons claimed that she knew everyone and forgot nothing. As Charles gazed on her, he felt icy fingers down his back: the guest from the nether regions, where it was always warm.

She moved with surprising grace for one of such antiquity. For all he knew she may even have been a gazetted beauty at one time, perhaps during the earlier days of the

Roman Republic. He smiled at the thought, then wiped the grin from his face when she skewered him with a stony stare.

"Mortimer, is it? I thought we had seen the last of you at Harrogate."

"I was transferred here, my lady," he managed. Out of the comer of his eye he saw Millicent Carrington descend the staircase and then pause.

"Let us hope that you have not brought along your typical mismanagement," she snapped, slamming her walking stick down on the desk, coming within inches of his nose. "I have not forgotten that time you checked me into a room where the sun struck my face at ten in the morning! Or the time you—you, Mortimer—allowed them to serve me Darjeeling tea instead of Lapsang souchong!"

"How could I do that?" he murmured, wishing that Miss Carrington would hurry on and not stand there to witness his humiliation.

"I trust you have learned something in the six months since our last conversation."

"I trust I have, my lady," he agreed and bowed. "Smith has your key, and you know that we are at your disposal."

She slammed down the stick again, and Mr. Kipling, cowering by the reservations, began to tremble visibly. "Simmons always shows me to my room, Mortimer," she said in an awful voice that made his hair rise on the back of his neck. "Have you *already* forgotten?"

Without a word, he came around the desk and extended his arm for Lady Mountrail. The lapdog snarled at him, but Lady Mountrail gave a vicious jerk on its diamond collar. "That's enough, Teddy," she growled back. "Save it for the footman!" They started across the lobby, followed by underfootmen with luggage and the dresser. Progress was slow, with the witch on his arm keeping up a steady diatribe about the weather, the general nastiness of London drivers, the odor of new paint in the lobby, the height of the carpet in the corridor, and the way the sun glanced off the windowpane and reflected in her eyes. Charles didn't think she paused for a breath.

He knew the suite wouldn't be to her liking: the windows too tall, too short, too wide, too narrow; the bed too soft, too hard, or both; the bell pull too far from the chair he sat her in. He fled the room as soon as he could, after promising to send up a footman to walk her nasty dog.

Miss Carrington still stood in the lobby, frowning. "Heavens, Mr. Mortimer, do you ever contemplate a different career after her visits?" she asked as he came near.

"Every time."

She touched his arm, which brought some measure of peace to his heart. "Do you know, if there are any Sicilians in town for the duke's fete, perhaps you could arrange an accident?"

He laughed out loud and amazed himself by clapping his arm around her shoulder and giving her a squeeze. She looked at him in delight, but he remembered Sir Michael's rule book and released her just as promptly. He wanted to ask her to luncheon in the dining room, something also forbidden he knew, but she nodded to him and bid him good day.

He didn't know it was possible for a day to extend itself as this one did. His darted glances at the clock in the lobby only frustrated him because the dratted timepiece seemed to be on some cosmic pause, once Miss Carrington left the building. He knew his job better than anyone; he greeted guests, solved problems, coaxed the carpenters to unimagined heights of efficiency, while all the time some corner of his brain waited to astound Millicent Carrington with his wit upon her return.

Lady Mountrail did not reappear in his lobby, but a

footman came and went with the dog. On his return, the man muttered that next time he would push the little beast into oncoming traffic. His best upstairs maid came down to him in tears because the cucumber sandwiches she had served with tea weren't all the same length, and Betty the 'tween stairs maid had fled in terror when Lady Mountrail accused her of staring at her. "Honest, Mr. Mortimer, all I did was sweep a little coal dust from the hearth!" she declared as she sobbed and he patted her shoulder.

As the dinner hour came and then went, he wondered if he had missed Millicent Carrington somehow. He thought about asking the footmen, but they would want him to describe her, and what could he say about someone who looked as ordinary as she did, except that she was wonderfully, magnificently original, qualities that didn't show?

The dining room had been empty for an hour and shadows were lengthening across the lobby when the footman opened the door for Miss Carrington, looking a little blue-deviled. He was sitting down at the desk behind the counter where he knew she could not see him. He leaned back in his chair and watched as she crossed the lobby in silence, with only a nod to the footman, until she stood before the great vase of flowers that Sir Michael Moseley mandated for all his lobbies. As Charles watched, fascinated, she slowly untied her bonnet, lifted it off, and set it on the bust of Sir Michael that was also de rigueur in each Moseley hotel. Mr. Chaseley at the desk started forward.

"No, Chaseley," he said, his voice low, "leave her alone."

"But, Mr. Mortimer," he began. He took another look at the bust with its bonnet and deep green tie. "Does look festive, doesn't it?"

"Most certainly," he agreed. "It's a wonderful hat. I'm certain she'll remove it eventually."

After another long look, Chaseley busied himself putting letters in pigeonholes. Charles got up quietly and stood at the front desk, his eyes on Miss Carrington. She had returned her attention to the vase, which she surveyed for a moment, then began to rearrange the flowers. She worked with a sure hand—a rose here, a gladiolus there, more baby's breath bunched in one corner—until she was satisfied. She stepped back again, and he noticed that the high lift to her shoulders was less pronounced.

Without looking at her face, he could tell that she had reached a certain equanimity. *Writing does that to me, Miss Carrington*, he thought. *After a dreadful day, I can return to India with ink and paper. You do it with flowers.*

She stood admiring the much-improved arrangement, and with a sigh that he could hear across the lobby, she removed the bonnet from Sir Michael. On impulse, Charles left the desk and crossed the lobby. "Miss Carrington, would you like some tea?"

One foot on the step, she turned around; he watched her smile center itself somehow in her eyes. He couldn't help but smile back and wonder, just for a second, about the many ways a woman was beautiful. *I can't be the first man to have noticed this about Miss Carrington*, he thought. And then, *I wonder if other men feel this way about their dear one?* And then, *I am presumption personified.*

"I think I would like tea more than anything, Mr. Mortimer," she replied to his heart's delight, he who was self-contained, regulated, and sufficient unto himself. "It might just keep me from throwing myself under a dustman's cart or prevent me from taking the king's shilling."

The idea of Miss Carrington enlisting was so amusing that he laughed out loud. "Surely your day has not been so terrible," he said as he walked her into the dining room and seated her.

She relaxed visibly. "Mr. Mortimer, I came into your hotel positively long-jawed this evening, and you kindly let me arrange the flowers! I shall have to tell Sir Michael that he was wise to transfer you here . . . that is, if I knew him."

He ordered tea and biscuits. "Would you like anything else?"

She shook her head. "No. The activities of this day have quite caused my appetite to vanish."

That was an opening if ever he had heard one. *She is a guest, Mortimer,* he reminded himself. *She surely cannot want you to delve into her life. She can't mean you to pry.* "That bad?" he asked, mentally tearing up the rule book and scattering the pieces around in his brain.

But she was regarding the ceiling now with that same degree of interest she had reserved for the bathtub drain only that morning. "Do you know, Mr. Mortimer, I rather think that I would duplicate that ceiling design around the top of the wall there," she said, not shifting her gaze. "It would make such a declaration, if you bring down the blue and yellow from the ceiling medallions."

He followed her gaze. "I believe you are correct," he said, after considering the matter. He took a deep breath. "You've changed the subject, Miss Carrington. Why was your day so horrible?"

The tea came; she took a sip, and then another before answering him. He had the strangest feeling that she was measuring him. "Such a restorative! Mr. Mortimer, I am a clergyman's daughter. I will be thirty at Michaelmas." She paused and moved her chair closer to his, which gratified him to no end. "Papa would gladly support me forever, and my brothers are already clamoring for me to visit them." She returned to the tea, took another sip, and then stared into the cup as though she planned to read her fortune there.

"Then you are probably more fortunate than most of England's females." Charles felt himself on firm ground. He worked with women every day who were compelled by necessity to labor outside of their own hearths.

"I don't want to burden my family," she said simply. "I told Papa I was coming to London to find myself a position as governess. I speak Italian, play the pianoforte, know the rudiments of grammar and history, and I can sketch. Do I not sound like a governess already?"

"You sound like an accomplished lady to me," he replied. "If you don't need to seek employment, why do it?" He took a deep breath and retreated further from Sir Michael's book of rules. "I do not understand why you have chosen not to marry, Miss Carrington."

"No one ever asked me, Mr. Mortimer," she said simply. "My marriage portion is respectable, but I've never been fond of losing at chess, just because it's the ladylike thing to do, or agreeing with a man, even if what he says is stupid." She looked at him then, and there was some color to her cheeks. "I'm sorry, Mr. Mortimer, but do you know, you have an air about you that rather invites me to speak my mind."

"Do I?" he asked, startled. "This is certainly a mutual discovery."

She returned her attention to her tea, and there was a look of sudden confusion about her that he found entirely endearing. She blushed then, and he turned his attention to the ceiling again. *Bless her*, he thought. *She might like me to think she is more confident than is really the case. It must be a daunting thing for a lady to go to an employment agency.*

"No luck at the agency, Miss Carrington?"

She took another sip, then sighed and settled back in the chair. "On the contrary, sir, too much luck! Every lady, between here and Galway Bay seems to want a governess to educate the young. I have only to pick and choose."

He frowned. "Where is the difficulty? If there is a dearth of intelligent men willing to propose, and you don't want to become the aunt-in-residence, have you changed your mind about . . . about governing?"

She laughed. "I have not! It is merely this, Mr. Mortimer, plainly put: I had wanted to spend at least a week in London, just enjoying the place, before I chose a position." She leaned forward. "But I find that I do not have enough money to remain at the Grand Hotel." She put her hand on his arm for a moment. "Oh, I will never escape in the middle of the night, sir! I have enough for last night and this night."

He found the notion of Miss Carrington shinnying down a rope hugely appealing; he had not a doubt that she could do it. He shook his head. "No, my dear, you would have to knot the bedsheets together, and I am not certain that the height of the building from your window and the length of the sheets are entirely compatible. You might be a floor short of success." He frowned again, wondering why someone as well dressed as she should be short of funds after so brief a stay in London.

"And now you are wondering why I am at such a low tide," she said, and he was struck again how they seemed to read each other's thoughts. "When I was returning here, I happened by a family that had been evicted. There they were, sir, with their belongings all around them on the street." The reminder seemed to galvanize her, and she shook her finger at him. "Mind you, such a thing would be unheard of in my father's parish!"

She didn't need to say any more. "So you emptied your reticule on them?" Charles asked.

"It's what any Christian lady would do."

Oh, you're a green one, he thought. *Totally dear, but a green one all the same.*

He studied the matter a moment, thinking to leave it

alone, but knowing that if she was plainspoken, he should be too. "Was it off Bayswater Road?"

"Why, yes. Are all landlords there so unfeeling?"

"Miss Carrington, there is a family in that vicinity whose career in life is to gull passersby from out of town."

She said nothing for a long while. While he did not look at her directly, he could watch her expression from the corner of his eye, and how it went from shocked disbelief, to argumentation, to real embarrassment, and then— ah, relief—to humor.

"And no one but visitors stop, is that it?" she asked.

"Precisely. Everyone else who knows the scam just walks by. Eventually someone will tattle on them and the Runners will show up."

"But by then they've packed their bundles and are off in search of another street corner," she finished, her expression thoughtful. "And they are probably well acquainted with the Runners and their habits."

"Can you doubt? Rumor has it that they have put one son through medical school in Edinburgh on the strength of that dodge."

She groaned, made a face at him, and drank the rest of her tea. "I depend upon you not to tell anyone!"

"The thought never crossed my mind," he replied, the helpful hotel manager again. He touched her hand this time, intensely aware of what he was doing, but unable to resist because of the doleful look on her face. "If it's any comfort, I fell for the same dodge when I arrived here two months ago."

"You?" she asked in amazement.

He smiled at her then, his fingers still light on her arm. "Miss Carrington, I am a clergyman's child too." He was relieved to see the frown leave her face.

"Better to be cheated than to have passed up an opportunity to relieve suffering?" she asked in a low voice.

"Of course."

She shifted slightly in her chair, and he withdrew his hand quickly, only to discover that she was moving closer, and not farther away. *Let it go, Mortimer*, he told himself.

"So I will march back to the Steinman Agency tomorrow morning and engage an employer, then return virtuously, pay my bill, and leave," she told him.

"I could loan you some money," he offered. *Sir Michael, have I now broken* every *rule?* he asked himself.

"I wouldn't accept it."

"You could write your father."

"And tell him what I have done? He would know that I am a babe and unfit to be loosed on an unsuspecting world."

"Then I suppose we are at *point non plus*, Miss Carrington."

"Well, I am, at any rate," she replied. "It's not your problem." She rose then, and he rose too. He wished there were some way to detain her longer in his empty dining room, but thought of nothing. "Good night then, sir," she told him. "I suppose I was unfair to unburden myself like that."

"Just one of the many services we provide at Moseley hotels," he teased, even as he understood in his heart how seriously he had just flouted his own rule of disinterest, not to mention all of Sir Michael's.

"Oh, I doubt that Sir Michael is concerned about much beyond the last entry in the ledger, Mr. Mortimer," she said. "Good night."

She left him then but looked back at the ceiling as she stood in the arched doorway. "Yes, if I ran this Moseley hotel, I would bring down that color. Good night, sir."

When he returned to the lobby, glum-faced he was sure, Chaseley looked up from a London *Times* some guest must have left behind. "Miss Carrington, sir?" he asked.

"Yes. She had some slight problem and needed a little advice."

"Could you help her?"

"No."

"That's not like you, Mr. Mortimer." Mr. Chaseley leaned his elbows on the counter, which Charles should have frowned on, but overlooked instead. "I know we have not known each other long, Mr. Mortimer, but do you know what a reputation you have throughout the Moseley enterprises?"

This was turning into a day of surprises, Charles decided. He came closer to his assistant, even though the lobby was as empty as the dining room, and lowered his voice. "I don't know what you mean."

The younger man gave him what he thought was a charitable look, the kind he, as a young man, would have reserved for elder statesmen. "Everyone knows how good you are at solving problems. Haven't you ever wondered why Sir Michael moves you around from place to place?"

He had never considered the matter before. "I've always assumed it was because he couldn't find me a niche, but that I was too useful to sack."

"Goodness no, Mr. Mortimer!" Chaseley exclaimed. "You are the perfect background man. You do everything right and by the book." He leaned closer. "Sir Michael told me so himself, when he moved me up here after he replaced Mr. Simmons with you. 'Study him,' he told me. 'He's the kind of employee every entrepreneur wants—the perfect background man.' Honest, Mr. Mortimer, that was what he told me."

Charles wondered if this was a compliment, then decided that it must be, or he would have been sacked years ago, after that first reoccurrence of malaria had rendered him immobile and sweating for days in decidedly untropical Glasgow. "'Pon my word, Mr. Chaseley."

His assistant must have decided that he had over-stepped his bounds, because he mumbled something about needing to file some reservations and returned to his duties. He looked up long enough to say good night and add something about "too bad you couldn't help Miss Carrington."

It was too bad, he decided as he sat down later in his room, his manuscript open before him. Sir Michael Moseley had always made it perfectly clear that any guest who could no longer pay his bill at a Moseley hotel must be invited, nay, urged, to leave. He had certainly done his share of ejecting through the years, but Miss Carrington needed no encouragement to vacate. Tomorrow she was going to cheerfully pay her bill and vanish from his life into some estate schoolroom, where she would likely be underappreciated. If he thought it would have made a difference, he would have dropped a wad of his own money—after all, what did he ever spend it on?—in front of her door, except that he knew she would merely return it to the front desk and encourage the clerk to find the rightful owner.

Moody now, he rested his chin on his palm and stared down at the manuscript, which only awaited that final chapter chronicling the last string of victories that put the seal on Wellington's years in India. After returning to Fort William after Assaye, he had admired the great man from a distance, hearing from others of the victories at Argaum, that steaming plain, and then the fortress of Gawilghur, sieged and then taken at so little cost. Ordinarily the mildest of men, Charles had not even flinched at the stories of Mahrattas thrown alive from the battlements of Gawilghur to break apart on jagged rocks far below. He had fought them at Assaye and had earned his cynicism.

How far away it all seemed now as he sat in his quiet

room. He wrote too late, or at least until his eyes began to feel sandy. Leaving the last page open to dry, he stood up, stretched, and went into the corridor. He stood a moment, hands in his pockets, shirt open at the collar, then did what he always did every night. Weary with writing—why was it that something so sedentary could wear him out so fast?—he took off his shoes and walked quietly through his sleeping hotel. In a few hours, the maids would be rubbing slumber from their eyes as they came down from the attic. Chef DuPré would coax the kitchen fires into life again and shoo his assistant outside with orders to return with only the freshest produce from London's great open-air market.

He went into the dining room and stood for a moment by the table where he and Miss Carrington had taken late-night tea. *I would like to sit here with her again*, he thought, then shook his head at the impossibility of it all. He pushed open the French doors and strolled onto the terrace that overlooked a most pleasing vista of Kensington Park's new-planted shrubbery. The view was handsomer in Harrogate and he wished himself back there, even as assistant manager again. London was too large, and when Miss Carrington left it, he knew it was going to be too much trouble.

After a moment breathing in London fumes, he shook his head and closed the French doors again. He was halfway up the back stairs and headed to his bed when he suddenly decided that some of Sir Michael Moseley's rules deserved to be broken. *I wonder if Miss Carrington will agree*, he thought as he walked quietly down the carpeted hall, his eyes on that angle where wall met ceiling. Who better to bring down the color than the guest who suggested it? Why should this London hotel look like all the others? The paint could certainly come out of his own pocket; the painters, too, for that matter. And if Sir

Michael sacked him, well, he could find another job. He returned to his room, wrote a quick note, then tiptoed next door to 318 and quietly secured the note to the door with a tack, something never done at a Moseley hotel.

He was up early as usual, despite his late night. A glance outside his door showed him that the note was gone. He listened then, a smile on his face; someone was humming in the bathroom, and he didn't think it was the plumber. He dressed quickly and hurried downstairs. He stayed long enough at the front desk for the changing of the guard from Mr. Chaseley to Mr. Kipling, then went into the dining room to wait for Miss Carrington.

She did not fail him. She made herself comfortable and looked at him expectantly. "Your note said you had a brilliant idea."

The imp of self-doubt bounded into the room like a Gibraltar ape and hoisted itself onto his shoulder. *This is insane*, he thought in sudden panic. *What was I thinking?*

He knew he was just sitting there staring at her, and he wouldn't have been surprised if she left the room without a backward glance. To his amazement, she only smiled and nodded. "I've had brilliant ideas that turned a little soggy by morning too," she said. "Oh, and here is some tea. May I pour you a cup?"

He nodded, touched by her charity. He took a sip and reminded himself that he was forty-one years old, and by most reckoning an adult. He had faced down hundreds of Mahrattas, each intent upon killing him; surely he could make a harmless suggestion to a pretty woman?

He thought he could, but the issue hung in some doubt. The only thing that made it possible for him to speak finally was the utter conviction, coming from where he knew not, that Miss Carrington took him seriously. "Miss Carrington, would you consider accepting a temporary position at the Grand Hotel?"

He could tell that he had surprised her by the way her eyes widened. "Doing what?" she asked finally.

"Painting and arranging flowers," he replied, after listening with super-sensitive ears for some wariness in her voice, and finding none. He looked over her shoulder to the wall. "I like your idea of adding color to the walls there. You're not afraid of heights, are you?"

"With three brothers and an apple orchard? I wouldn't dare be," she said. She paused a moment, and he crossed his fingers that calm good sense would not overtake his lovely companion. "You are serious, aren't you?" she asked.

"Never more so, Miss Carrington." He cleared his throat. "And both Mr. Kipling and I observed yesterday that you have a superior talent with roses and . . . and whatever those things are."

"Gladioli," she said, her eyes lively again.

"Of course, I wouldn't recommend another bonnet on Sir Michael's bust," he said.

"No, he's more a turban man, I should think," she said promptly, then held out her hand while he laughed. "I do so want another week in London. Let us shake on this, Mr. Mortimer, before either of us changes our mind!"

Shaking her hand, he almost asked her why she wanted another week in London. He knew his own reasons, however skewed they were: He wanted another week to enjoy her presence before she left his life forever. Of course, he reasoned, there was always the chance that she could register at his hotel again someday. He also knew how awful it would be if she came as a guest someday with a husband in tow, and two or three children. Which would be worse, he wondered as he watched her drink her tea and look thoughtfully at the opposite wall, to see her married or see her still single?

It was food for thought far less nourishing than breakfast, he decided after he finished taking ham and eggs with Miss Carrington. He left her there in the dining room because she wanted to think about the wall. Her only request was a tape measure, which he procured from the laundry room. By the time he returned with it, she had already cajoled someone on his staff into locating a ladder. He felt a knot growing in his stomach as he sent the footman on an errand to summon the painters again. His anxiety was not without cause. When the painting crew arrived, all gloomy with sullen looks and filled with pointed disfavor, he knew it was time for a brave front. "Ah, and here you thought you were done," he began, wincing at the trio of sour expressions.

"We were, Mr. Mortimer," the chief painter said. "Do you have any idea how busy every painter in London is right now? We might decide that we don't want to help you."

"You might," he agreed, totally in sympathy. "I would understand. Would you just follow me into the dining room? I'll let you judge for yourselves." He started for the dining room, hoping the men would follow. To his relief, they did.

He opened the door, heard the crew chief sigh, and knew that the painters were his. Tape measure draped about her neck and chin in hand, Miss Carrington perched on top of the ladder, staring at the wall. She gave him a cheery smile—at least he thought it was directed to him—that made the chief painter sigh again. "Reinforcements?" she asked.

"Pardon me, ma'am, but you shouldn't be there," the crew chief said, hurrying forward to grasp the ladder. "Tell me what you want, and I'll do it."

Charles could only stand there with his arms folded and hope that his own countenance was sober, should the crew chief decide to look at him (and which seemed unlikely in the extreme, especially since Miss Carrington's fine ankles were just so discreetly evident).

What a lady, he thought as she gave the painter a look of vast understanding. "You are kindness itself," she told the man, who had been joined by the other two painters, each of whom now had a grip on the ladder. "What I want to do is stencil this edge to approximate the furbelows in the ceiling." She looked down, the picture of good humor. "And then it would be our task to paint the design." She who was anything but helpless gave Charles a helpless look. "Of course, I can imagine that you are so busy right now, and probably weary of the thought of one more day here at the Grand Hotel."

A chorus of nos, followed by vigorous headshakes and general murmured disagreement, came next, and Charles could only look away and consider the lilies of the terraced lawn and how they grew. *Men are clay and putty*, he thought. *There are probably even some of us who think we rule the world. Idiots.* Standing behind the painters, he grinned up at Miss Carrington and winked.

With only the barest glance in his direction, she gazed down at the painters. "Of course, you may have already decided not to take on this picayune project."

"We have oceans of time for this little thing," the crew chief declared, perjuring himself, Charles knew, beyond all hope of redemption. "We will tell you what we need, and Mr. Mortimer can arrange delivery."

Unwilling to ruin Miss Carrington's diplomacy by any words of his, Charles bowed and left them to work, feeling more satisfied than in many a week. All afternoon he wanted to return to the dining room, but every glance he made in that direction seemed to be intercepted by his day clerk. "Mr. Kipling, what is your problem?" he finally asked in exasperation as the day dragged on. He must have startled Kipling; he knew he startled himself. *I'm rarely that rude with my staff*, he thought.

Kipling was all fumbles and stammerings then, and

Charles felt instant remorse. "I was only thinking that it . . . it is a good thing that . . . that Sir Michael doesn't know what Miss Carrington is do . . . doing."

Let us pray he never finds out, Charles thought. *He'd have my guts in a bucket if he knew I had bartered work for a room fee. There is nothing in the Moseley hotel hand-book that even comes close to this subject.* "You're so right, Kipling," he said. It was lame, but at least Kipling stopped his fluttering.

The painters, all smiles still, left in midafternoon. "She's finishing the stenciling now," the crew chief told him, handing over a list of supplies. He leaned closer. "I didn't want to disappoint her, but we do have a project to complete tomorrow. She seemed quite agreeable when I told her we would be back tomorrow evening to work."

Am I in some sort of handyman heaven? Charles asked himself as he took the list in nerveless fingers. *Did some-one in the construction business actually* tell *me his plans for the next day?* He thought of all those strange disappear-ances of painters and carpenters through the years—here one day, gone tomorrow—and could only marvel at the effect of a pretty lady with nice enough ankles. In a daze, he gave his regards to the painters, handed the list to the footman, and went into the dining room before anyone else could waylay him with demands that ordinarily would never ruffle him, but which right now would cause him some irritation.

Miss Carrington had traded the ladder for the floor and, using a rule that the painters must have left, was busy outlining a stencil. He watched her from the door-way of the empty dining room, inching her way along the floor as she drew the design that would be stenciled onto the wall. His viewpoint was all a man could ask for, he decided as he felt the duties of the day slip from his shoul-ders. *Miss Carrington, you have a lovely backside indeed.*

He must have made some noise (he hoped he wasn't breathing hard) because she looked around, then scooted sideways quickly. "Mr. Mortimer, what do you think?"

In an amazingly short time he thought of many things, most of them involving no one but him and Millicent Carrington. He walked closer to look at the floor. "This is the center section," she said, sitting back now. "We've already stenciled the corners."

He looked where she pointed. With obvious skill, they had replicated the curlicues and furbelows from the ceiling onto the top of the wall. "The painters—oh, Mr. Mortimer, they are such *nice* men!—said they would be back tomorrow after the dining room closes and we will paint."

He was going to sit down, but she held up her hand to him, so he pulled her to her feet. Standing so close to her, he wished there was some reason to continue holding her hand. He could think of none, so he released her, cursing his lack of imagination or maybe his want of backbone. He could only look at her and smile.

She smiled back, then stooped to pick up her chalk and stencil. "I think I will prefer working at night, because that will give me time in the day to view London's attractions. What would you recommend I see?"

"The Elgin Marbles," he said promptly, thinking of an editorial he had read in the morning paper about the disgraceful way the Greek treasures were housed. "I believe they are stored in some kind of shed, somewhat open to the elements. You could draw them," he suggested, warming to the topic. He took a deep breath. "I could escort you there tomorrow morning, if you wish."

There now, I have fractured another rule in Sir Michael's handbook on hotel management, he thought. *Make no attempt, beyond polite, unvarying service, to encroach upon the personal lives of the patrons.* He could see the words emblazoned on the page in his mind's eye.

"I think that is a perfectly wonderful idea," she told him. "Do you have the time?"

"I believe tomorrow is my day off," he replied.

"How fortunate." She smiled at him. "Mrs. Wheelwright will be so pleased."

"Mrs. Wheelwright?"

"Your housekeeper," she reminded him gently. "She took us belowstairs at noon for a sandwich and confided that you never take a day off."

He laughed, pleased that Mrs. Wheelwright was also breaking Sir Michael's rules. A guest belowstairs? Unheard of. "I suppose I don't take many days off," he said. "There's so much to do to get ready to open a hotel."

"That may be," she said, "but Mrs. Wheelwright claims that you are legendary at Sir Michael's hotels for *never* taking a day off. What is so fun about neverending toil? I live to be lazy."

He doubted that, but he did find her reply amusing. "Miss Carrington, I have no one on whom to lavish time." There. It sounded bald to him, but he hoped not pathetic.

"You don't even have a diversion?" she asked.

"One." He had never told anyone about his manuscript, but something told him that she would be interested. "I am writing a history of Wellington in India. It is nearly done."

She leaned toward him in that confiding way of hers that he was already finding indispensable. "I think that is marvelous, Mr. Mortimer. Perhaps you would let me read it?"

"You're serious?" he asked, surprised.

"Never more so." She leaned closer. "In turn, I could show you my sketches of India. I told you my brother was with Wellington's Thirty-third, didn't I?"

He nodded. "Did he describe India to you?"

"He did in his letters, and then I looked at books. He

gave me some constructive criticism during his last furlough." She sighed. "Perhaps you could tell me how accurate they are."

"Just ask him," he said.

"I would if I could, but he died of the fever a year later in Madras." She touched his hand before he could mumble any platitudes. "Stay right here. I'll go get my sketches."

She hurried from the room. The Grand Inquisitor himself with a staff of thousands could not have budged him from the dining room. He sat down and willed himself to relax, letting the day slide from his shoulders.

When he opened his eyes, Miss Carrington was sitting beside him. "You'll think I am lazy," he said in apology as she removed her drawings from a large folder.

"I think you are a man who needs to take a day off now and then," she replied. "Tomorrow I will require nothing more strenuous than that you carry my sketch pad. Here they are."

She spread her sketches before him, and he was enchanted—graceful women in saris, an ox pulling a big-wheeled cart, sun shining through a pipal tree, entrepreneurs in turbans squatting in an open-air market. "Rob thought I had captured the look of India," she told him, "but I credit his descriptive letters. What do you think?"

"They make me want to return to India," he said simply. He picked up a sketch of a boy with a monkey on his shoulder, the long tail curling around the child's neck. "I liked it there."

"So did Rob," she said, her voice soft, as though she did not wish to interfere with his memories. "Are they accurate?"

"For the most part." He ran his hand over a water buffalo on a road lined with tall grass. "I should rather tone down the size of that beast through the shoulders here, and elongate the horns a little. Yes, right there. And Indian women are a little narrower through the waist and wear more bangles on their arms. They are beautiful people, Miss Carrington." *But not as lovely as you*, he wanted to add.

"Now you must share your manuscript with me," she said, after another long moment as the dining room sank into deeper shadow.

"Very well, Miss Carrington." He stood up. "It is a work in progress." *And so am I*, he reasoned with himself, discarding forever the notion that he was mature, ordered, and prepared for any of life's eventualities. "Wait in the lobby if you wish. I will bring it down."

When he returned, she was seated on one of the overstuffed sofas in the empty lobby, her legs tucked under her. He stopped on the stairs to watch her a moment, struck by the serenity of her appearance. "I think it will put you to sleep," he told her quietly.

She held out her hands for the pasteboard box that contained his labor of four years. "It might," she agreed, "but I doubt it." She looked at the first page. "Your handwriting is so legible," she told him. "Of course, you were a clerk. It should be readable."

If another lady had said that, he reasoned, it would have sounded like a setdown. From Miss Carrington, it was only an affirmation of his life's work, almost conspiratorial, as though she said, "See here, you were a clerk and I am a painter of walls and soon a governess."

He gave her the manuscript with a bow, ushered the startled Mr. Chaseley off to a late dinner belowstairs, and sat at the desk basking in their camaraderie, even though she was halfway across the lobby from him. In a few moments he was engrossed in reservations. She minded her own business, looking up at him occasionally—he was aware of her every glance, even as he concentrated on his work—as if taking his measure in this history. "You were at Kaitna Ford," she commented once. When he nodded, she said, "So was Rob. Desperate work."

She did doze once or twice, resting her head along her arm. The lobby was so quiet he could hear the clock ticking. The few guests returning from late-night ventures took their keys from him in silence, almost as though they did not wish to disturb Miss Carrington, either. When Mr. Chaseley returned to duty, Charles sat down next to her on the sofa. She opened sleepy eyes. "It is not boring," she assured him, "but I think I am ready to retire for the night." She held up the few chapters remaining on her lap. "Trust me with it?"

"Of course. Good night, Miss Carrington. When do you wish to begin our expedition tomorrow?"

"By nine o'clock at least," she said promptly. "That will give you time to manage any number of crises and still feel virtuous about leaving for a few hours." She laughed. "Do I understand you, sir?"

"Quite well, Miss Carrington. Good night."

It was an easy matter to walk upstairs with her, but harder to just let her go into her room next to his and shut the door on him, after a good night smile. He was awake a long time that night.

In spite of little sleep, Charles Mortimer was up early enough to console himself with a quick bath and a quicker bowl of porridge belowstairs with Mrs. Wheelwright, who informed him that Sir Michael Moseley had already made his stately way through the kitchen that morning. Charles sighed and took a firmer grip on his coffee cup. "I suppose he is upstairs waiting to pounce?"

Mrs. Wheelwright observed him over the top of her spectacles. "As sweet as you please, I told him it was your day off, and what does he do but laugh? Mr. Mortimer, you're going to have to take a day off one of these days."

"Today, as a matter of fact," he told her. "I am escorting Miss Carrington to the Elgin Marbles." He held up his hand. "I know, I know! Sir Michael's rule book says this is a great misdemeanor."

"But you're also employing her, or so she told me," the housekeeper said, leaning closer. "Good for you, I say, Mr. Charles Mortimer."

He blushed, which only made his housekeeper laugh. "You might mention that I'd like her to arrange two vases of flowers in the cooling room before you drag her to look at some dusty marbles."

By now he was at the door, coffee cup still in hand. "She is a pretty thing, isn't she, Mrs. Wheelwright?"

"A real bloomer, sir, a real bloomer." She winked at him, and he felt the color rush to his face again, he who had given up blushing years ago for Lent. "I think you ought to find her all kinds of walls to paint."

Sir Michael paced back and forth in the lobby, which apparently had flustered Mr. Kipling into dropping a file of reservation cards. They littered the floor in front of the check-in desk, and there was his deputy manager, on his hands and knees gathering them. "Steady, Mr. Kipling," Charles murmured as Sir Michael broke off his distempered pacing and bore down on the desk. "Mustn't show fear."

"There you are!" Elaborately, Sir Michael dragged out his watch and glared at it. "I can't imagine why you would trust the front desk to this . . . this butterfingered lackey who calls himself a deputy manager!"

"It's my day off, sir, and I have complete confidence in Mr. Kipling," he said calmly. "Hurry up there, Mr. Kipling."

Now or never, Charles thought. He strolled over to his employer with what he hoped was an air of supreme confidence. "Sir Michael, I want to show you what we are doing in the dining room, at the suggestion of one of our guests." He led the way into the dining room, which was inhabited by a few patrons who relished breakfast, that unfashionable meal. He pointed to the stenciled outline high on the wall. "She suggested that we could duplicate the colors from the ceiling and achieve a thoroughly pleasing look. I agree with her."

Sir Michael stared at him in amazement. "This has never been done in a Moseley hotel!"

Charles Mortimer had no idea where his huge vat of confidence was coming from. "Well, you might want to consider it for your other hotels. I think the effect is going to be quite charming. I would urge you to return in a day or two and see."

It seemed to Charles that Sir Michael stared at the stenciled outline long enough for Napoleon to have made his retreat from Moscow half a dozen times, with room in between for the entire Tilsit negotiation. After another long moment, Sir Michael clasped his hands behind his back and began to rock on his heels slightly. "You could be right, Mortimer," he said finally. "A guest suggested this, you say?"

He nodded, scarcely daring to breathe. "A lady from Kent, daughter of a vicar, I believe. Bit of a painter herself."

Another pause. Sir Michael chuckled. "'Pon my word, Mortimer. I don't know that any other hotel manager has ever gone to so much trouble to please a guest."

"I am not any other hotel manager, Sir Michael," Charles assured him, in voice quiet, then nearly fell over backward at his own temerity. "And this is no ordinary hotel."

Sir Michael was smiling now. He unclasped his hands and allowed Charles to walk him from the dining room. "I might refer you to my rule book for hotel management, Mortimer," he admonished, but there was no sting in his words. "A vicar's daughter from Kent, you say?"

"Yes, indeed."

"Well, carry on then! I'm flat amazed that you could cajole a crew of painters to help. I think every journeyman in town is touching up something or other for the duke's festivities."

"They're coming at night, sir."

"And not charging you dear?"

"No."

"You must have amazing powers of persuasion that I have been unaware of all these years, Mortimer," Sir Michael said when he recovered himself.

"I rather think it was a good look at the vicar's daughter," he offered in all honesty, and his employer burst into laughter.

"Heaven help us, Mortimer!" he said when he could talk. "You are amazingly diverting!"

"Not as much . . ."

". . . as the vicar's daughter!" the two finished together, completely in charity with each other.

Pinch me and wake me up, Charles thought. "Do trust me, sir," he said.

"I suppose I must, considering that someone has stenciled the dining-room walls." Sir Michael looked at the footman, who started forward with his hat and cane. "Oh. One thing more: Here's a little tidbit for your chef. The duke himself will be early at Carlton House at the end of this week to judge a pastry contest, of all things. It is some harebrained scheme of our regent. The hotel that makes his grace's favorite confection will have his patronage during all future visits to London. Do you think that scoundrel DuPré can manage to not embarrass us?"

"Certainly, sir," Charles replied. He accepted a broadside from Sir Michael. "These are the rules of the contest?"

"Yes indeed. See that you give them a little more

consideration than you have given my rules of hotel management, Mortimer."

"Certainly. Good day, Sir Michael."

He was content to finish more hotel paperwork while Miss Carrington, blooming as a posy herself, went belowstairs to arrange flowers. She wore the prettiest blue muslin, almost a Wedgwood color that set off the rose and cream of her English complexion. *So you are rising thirty*, he thought as he watched her go. *Thirty never looked so good to me. Are blondes still in fashion? How should I know? I love brown hair. And freckles? Miss Carrington, I love those too.*

When she came upstairs with a rose tucked in the roll of her hair where she had gathered it low on her neck ("Mrs. Wheelwright insisted," she told him, not without a blush of her own), he showed her the broadside Sir Michael had left. "I suppose you know his grace the duke better than some," she teased. "What does he like for dessert?" She put down the paper and her expression changed. "Oh, Mr. Mortimer, what a time you had in India."

"Do you like the manuscript?"

She nodded, looking him in the eyes long enough to start a curious feeling in his stomach. "It's a wonderful work. I want you to finish that last chapter as soon as you can. I will insert my sketches, and you can give the whole thing to the duke."

The peppery fragrance of the rose in her hair mingled with the lemon cologne on her skin and he felt himself going quite light-headed. He hoped it wasn't a malarial relapse. "What a lovely idea, Miss Carrington," he told her. He had the strongest notion to kiss her right there across the front desk, but it was midmorning, and there was Mr. Kipling. "But now I think we had better locate the Elgin Marbles before some dustman carts them away, Miss Carrington."

"Or you find yourself trapped into working through another day off."

After some days of rain, the sun shone so brightly that he squinted, then almost regretted the necessity of securing a hackney. He helped her in, again captured by the sweet smell of her. They rode in silence, not so much because he was tongue-tied this time, but because she seemed as content as he to enjoy without words the pleasure of an extraordinary July day.

"Do you know," he said finally, "I am convinced I know precisely what will win that pastry contest."

"I thought you would."

"Plum duff."

She looked at him in delight. "There is no more plebeian dessert that I know of," she said at last, leaning forward in that way of hers that gave him her complete attention.

"He always asked for it in India." He sat back and laughed. "Henri DuPré will suffer a major convulsion if I suggest it."

"But you will, I hope. I believe I could even make plum duff, if he chooses not to." She shook her head. "No one else in London will even think of it. Mr. Mortimer, you are the most clever of hotel managers."

He only smiled and looked out the window again, content to bask in the warmth of her approbation.

The Elgin Marbles were no anticlimax, despite his sole interest in the woman who shared the hackney with him. After paying a small fee, they picked their way among the rubble and weeds to gaze in silence at a caryatid from the Erechtheum. Miss Carrington sighed and leaned against his arm, completely caught in the magic of the fluid robes and grace unexpected, even in marble. He held his breath, hoping that she would not notice what she was doing. Casting all caution away, he put his arm around her shoulder. She only leaned closer, to his unimaginable delight. She was a short woman, but not tiny. Her shoulder felt strong.

Bound together, they strolled toward a collection of three figures, one headless woman reclining in the lap of another, which must have formed the most acute angle of the pediment. "Look at the lines, Charles," Miss Carrington murmured, his name sounding like music to him. She touched his hand that rested so lightly on her shoulder, so he knew she was aware of him "Oh, they are glorious. Please, can we stop here?"

He did as she said, removing his arm from about her and handing her the sketch pad he carried in his other hand. Eyes on the figures, she seated herself on a column fragment. He sat down to watch her sketch.

She sat for a long time with her hands folded in her lap, looking first at the caryatid, and then the group of three. As he watched in pleasure, and then growing disquiet, her expression changed. She frowned. She shifted on her marble perch. In another moment, he saw her dab at the corner of her eyes.

"Miss Carrington?" he asked, uncertain of himself. "Millicent?"

She looked at him then, and her eyes, to his horror, filled with tears. "These should have never been taken from the Parthenon," she said in a low voice. "Oh, Charles, think how beautiful they must have been on the Acropolis! What was the matter with Lord Elgin?"

He didn't know what to say, so he handed her his handkerchief. The moment was so personal, and she had said his name again. In another moment he perched himself beside her on the marble slab, his arm about her again as she sniffled into his handkerchief and blew her nose.

He knew he shouldn't have, but Charles kissed her hair and sat in silence, thinking about India and

Wellington, and Napoleon on Elba now, and change, and death. "Better we should stay on our own little island and never bother anyone else, eh?" he asked softly. "Better the Turks should use these figures for target practice and blast them to rubble? The world's a complicated place, Miss Carrington, isn't it? The older I get, the fewer answers I have anymore. And here I had hoped to be wise someday."

In the circle of his arm, she rested her head against his chest. "You must think I am silly," she confessed.

He chuckled and drew her closer. "No, none of it. I think you're sensitive to waste." He sighed. "Maybe I am, too. I work in a hotel that is utter perfection, with everything planned out for the total accommodation of pampered people. I move around quietly in the background, seeing that things are always done right." He sighed. "For dreadful creatures like Lady Mountrail"

She pulled away a little to look at him. "And have you constructed a life out of always doing things quietly for others? Is it enough?"

"Not anymore."

She touched his face. He knew it was an amazingly intimate, forward gesture on her part, one he never expected, but he was overwhelmed with a feeling of protection. *I am safe with this person*, he thought as he kissed her.

He couldn't recollect that he had ever kissed a woman before, and he enjoyed the moment as none other in his life, even more than moments of greater intimacy with lesser women. Her hand pressed against his neck at his hairline and her fingers were as warm as her lips. She murmured something low in her throat and the sound made his lips tingle in a pleasant way. He kissed her again when she pulled away slightly, and she made no objection. He heard the sketch pad slide from her lap and onto the ground, as the sun shone on his face, and mingled with the fragrance of lemon on her skin. Every feeling and sound seemed to magnify itself into a moment of total completeness. He kissed her and understood awe, and it had nothing to do with statues or vistas, or battles won and celebrated. It had only to do with him and her.

And then the moment ended; he thought they both pulled away at the same time. He was relieved to see no wariness in her face, no revulsion. She only watched him with that same expression of amazement she had first reserved for the now-ignored triumphs of Greek civilization that stood or reclined in the weeds of a forgotten yard.

"I . . ." He shook his head and waited another moment. "I should apologize, Miss Carrington, except that I do not wish to."

She smiled, and his heart began to circulate his blood again. "It's Millie." As he sat beside her, still so close, she picked up the sketch pad, and with fingers that shook a little, drew his own face. Surrounded by wonders of the ancient world, she drew his face.

On the ride back to the Grand Hotel, he wanted to tell her he loved her, but he was as silent as she. Quiet, they sat close together hand in hand. He realized with a jolt that throughout his life he had never put himself forward except once at Kaitna Ford in India, and all his doubts returned.

They went into the lobby together, standing farther apart now, calling no attention to themselves. He stopped her at the entrance. "Miss Carrington, I must have been out of my mind," he said quietly.

If he had disappointed her, she did not show it. "I doubt you ever take leave of your senses, Charles," she told him.

How serene you are about all this, he marveled as she

continued her graceful way through the lobby, a slight smile on her face.

They hadn't taken more than three more paces when Mr. Kipling left the desk and hurried to him. He bowed to Miss Carrington, and all but plucked at Charles's sleeve. "I thought you would never get here," he whispered.

Charles felt himself on sure ground, except that he could almost feel himself blending into the background again. "What could possibly be the matter, Mr. Kipling?" he asked.

With only the slightest gesture toward the desk, the deputy manager inclined his head. "Do you see that man there, that man of color?" he whispered. "He is trying to check in!"

"He's not a servant?"

"No! He claims he is a free man from Boston in Massachusetts and actually wants to stay in a second floor suite!" He noticed Miss Carrington. "Begging your pardon, ma'am," he said.

"This has never happened before," Charles said. He could see Sir Michael's book of rules in his mind. Page three, column one, he thought wearily.

"I've tried to direct him back to the docks—those hotels take anyone—but he says his money is good." Mr. Kipling was wringing his hands now. He looked at Miss Carrington. "Ma'am, you wouldn't think a black man would have so much gall, would you?"

Charles was almost afraid to look at Millie. "Really, Mr. Kipling," he murmured. "Let us leave our guest out of this. Excuse us, Miss Carrington."

I know what to do, he thought as he walked to the desk and went behind it. *I know what Sir Michael expects.* "May I help you?" he asked. "I am Mr. Mortimer, the manager."

"I have a reservation, sir," the man said. "Malachi Beach of Boston. From the American Society for Abolition." He leaned forward, and there was no mistaking the exhaustion on his face. "Actually, I made a reservation at every good hotel in London, and you are my last stop."

Mr. Kipling must have taken out the card from the file box because it lay between them on the desk. Charles picked it up, then looked at the man in front of him, someone about his own age, tired, with travel worn clothes. *I could send him on to a lesser hotel, where he will get the same rude treatment*, he thought. He has obviously spent the better part of a day looking for a room. *Or I could step out from the background.*

He glanced at Millie Carrington, who had quietly come closer, and could not overlook the concern in her face. The thought came to him—it was an odd, stray thought—that he wasn't sure if she was concerned about Malachi Beach or Charles Mortimer. He smiled at Malachi Beach, then turned to the key rack as Mr. Kipling sucked in his breath.

"Here you are, sir," he said and handed the man a key. "I am sorry you had to wait." He nodded to the footman, who stood as still as Parthenon marble. "Devost here will take your bags. Dinner is served from six to nine, if you do not have another place to dine." He laughed quietly and was relieved to see his guest smile. "Even though we've barely opened, we're already going through some renovation in the dining room. What can I say? I hope you enjoy your stay."

"I believe I shall, Mr. Mortimer."

He watched Devost take the man's bags and lead the way upstairs. Charles ignored his deputy manager's tug on his sleeve. He rested his elbow on the check-in desk, contemplating nothing more than the marble on the counter. *I wonder why I did that?* he thought first, and then, *How soon before the news travels to Sir Michael Moseley?* He waited for dread to set in, but nothing happened.

This has been a strange day, indeed, he thought. *I wonder what else will happen?*

"Mr. Mortimer, you know what the rule book says!"

Charles turned to gaze for a long moment at his deputy manager. "Do you know, I think it's a foolish rule, Mr. Kipling. Don't you? We're running a business, Kipling."

From the way he blinked his eyes, Charles could see that Kipling had never considered the stupidity of some of Sir Michael's rules. And did Kipling seem to regard him with a degree of deference he hadn't noticed before? Strange indeed.

"Well done, sir," Millie said as Kipling turned away to distract himself with interminable filing.

"Thank you," he said, pleased to note that his plain speaking had somehow driven away any shyness regarding Miss Carrington.

It was her turn to lean toward him across the counter that separated them. "Aren't you a little fearful of losing your job if Sir Michael finds out?" she asked.

He considered her question and shook his head. "Likely I could find another, Miss Carrington." *I love you, Miss Carrington*, he wanted to add, but he knew he hadn't the courage.

The painters arrived in the evening after the dining room was empty of patrons. He stood in the doorway, charmed with the effect of the blue and yellow design now making its way around the top of the wall. Millie smiled at him from her perch on the scaffolding that the painters erected.

He would have invented some reason to stay and watch, but he strolled into the lobby in time to nod good evening to Mr. Kipling and welcome aboard Mr. Chaseley for the night shift. Restless, he paid a visit belowstairs. He asked himself how Henri DuPré would feel if he broached the subject of plum duff for Wellington as the Grand Hotel's entry in the dessert contest.

His suggestion was met with the disdain he expected, as well as a sprinkling of "bahs!" and "sacré bleus" until he found himself—he, the mildest of men—gritting his teeth. *Frogs*, he thought as DuPré raved on, flinging his arms about. *I do not know that I would miss the French, if some rare disease suddenly swept them from the earth. I doubt anyone would, come to think of it.*

"It was only a suggestion, sir," he said when the chef paused to take another breath. "You're certainly welcome to make your entry. It's just that I know the duke, and he . . ."

Oh, dear, that was unwise of me, Charles thought in dismay as DuPré burst into derisive laughter.

When DuPré collected himself, leaning against the counter to hold himself up and wiping the tears from his eyes, he elaborately offered Charles a chair. "I think you have been touched by the sun, Mr. Mortimer," he said, and Charles almost winced from the disdain in his voice. "If you know His Grace, the Duke of Wellington, then I am Caroline of Brunswick!" He started to giggle again.

Charles regarded the chef for a long moment. "No, I don't see any resemblance. Her mustache is lighter than yours," he said softly, more to himself than to the chef. "Well, monsieur, you won't mind if I make a little plum duff anyway, will you?"

The chef gave him a dark look. "Only if you place it far, far away from my meringue *glaces*"—he held up a bony finger and struck a pose—"soaked in raspberry sauce. I will call it Triomph de Toulouse, in honor of his final victory over Napoleon, that most misunderstood of men."

"No one will ever know our recipes came from the same kitchen," Charles assured him. "I'll never tell the duke." He left the kitchen, disgruntled and dogged by DuPré's laughter. *DuPré is an idiot, but I wonder if Wellesley will remember me?* he asked himself as he went upstairs again. *He's never really seen me with my face devoid of black powder. If my plum duff wins, I will take the opportunity to present him with the manuscript. And Miss Carrington has promised her sketches.*

The painters were leaving when he came upstairs, and the lobby was quiet. Mr. Chaseley looked at him and smiled, raising a handful of letters. "Sir, I do believe that the Grand Hotel will be full to the rafters in two weeks for the celebrations."

"Excellent, Mr. Chaseley. And by the way, let me compliment you on the way you handled that rather intoxicated patron last night."

The night clerk beamed at him. "Oh, I've just watched the way you handle'um, sir."

Well, what do you know, he thought. He looked in the dining room, hoping to see Miss Carrington, and there she was, standing on the terrace, breathing deep of the night air. She turned around when he approached, and without a word, embraced him and raised her face for a kiss, which he willingly shared with her. They stood in the circle of each other's arms. "This is beyond belief," he said finally.

"I know," she agreed but made no move to leave. But she did move finally, standing away from him until he lowered his arms. Before he could feel too disappointed, she took his hand and led him to a table. "Let's sit here a moment," she said. "There's something . . . something I have to tell you." She looked down at the table. "I don't think you'll like it very much."

Here it comes, he thought, willing himself numb before she began to speak. *True, we are both the children of gentlemen, but as in India, there are many layers to our British castes. Say on, lady, I knew this was coming.*

She couldn't look at him for the longest moment, and as she opened her mouth to speak, Mr. Chaseley flung open the dining-room door he had so carefully shut and stood there, obviously searching for them in the dark.

Alarmed, Charles leaped to his feet. "Chaseley, I am here," he said. "What is it?"

There was no disguising the urgency of the night clerk's voice. "Mr. Mortimer, you have to hurry. Lady Mountrail. Second floor."

He took the stairs two at a time, Miss Carrington right behind him, after admonishing Chaseley to stay at the desk. He pounded up the stairs and looked down the long corridor to see Lady Mountrail's dresser, that meek woman, kicking Betty, the 'tween stairs maid. "Oh, I say, please stop!" he insisted as he ran down the hall.

He wrenched the sobbing child from the dresser's grasp just as the door swung open and Lady Mountrail stood there. "She was snooping around this door!" she shrieked.

Heads popped out of other doors. "Please don't concern yourselves, ladies and gentlemen," he said as he held Betty close to him. "Please, Lady Mountrail, may I come into your room to settle this in quiet?" he asked, his voice low.

"Absolutely not!" she declared. "I'm a lady!"

I have my doubts, he thought, in a rage. "Hush, Betty," he said, and gave her a little push toward Miss Carrington, who folded Betty in her arms. "Very well, Lady Mountrail, we'll talk right here in the hall like commoners."

She gasped and yanked him into her room with a grip he hadn't expected. Miss Carrington followed with Betty, giving the dresser such a look that Charles wanted to cheer.

"What happened here?"

Before he could stop her, Lady Mountrail reached

forward and gave Betty's hair a sharp tug. Miss Carrington turned to shield the child. "Don't you touch her again, you dreadful woman," she warned.

"Please, Miss Carrington. Watch your tongue," he said, his voice sharp. He flinched inwardly at the look she gave him.

"Lady Mountrail, what has happened?" he asked again.

"That gutterscamp was lurking around my door," she screamed, all but jumping up and down in her fury. "I am certain I am missing half my jewelry!"

"I sincerely doubt it," he said quietly. "Betty, what were you doing?"

He took Betty by the arm and Miss Carrington reluctantly released her grip. "Come, now. How can I help you if you won't talk?"

"Help her? Help her? *I* am the injured party!" Lady Mountrail insisted. She sank into a chair and the dresser began to fan her.

Betty burst into tears and sobbed into Charles's shoulder. He held her in a firm grip, patting her back. "Come now and tell me, my dear," he murmured.

"Mrs. Wheelwright said I was to close the draperies and turn down the bedclothes," she said finally, speaking through the handkerchief he had given her and dabbing at her nose. "She said the other maids were busy, but they don't like coming in here any more than I do!" She looked at him, and he was appalled to see the hopelessness in her eyes. "I was afraid to go in, so I . . . I walked up and down trying to get my courage. Mr. Mortimer, I would never steal anything."

"I know you wouldn't."

She stood on tiptoe and spoke into his ear. "I'm afraid of her too, Mr. Mortimer."

He would have smiled, if the situation had been different. "I am, as well, Betty." He took a deep breath and turned to Lady Mountrail. "Perhaps you should examine your jewel case now."

"She just said she didn't steal anything!"

He looked around, surprised at Millie's outburst, then filled with shame that she should see any of this. "I have to ask, Miss Carrington. It's my job."

"Part of the rules?" she snapped.

"Yes, as a matter of fact. Lady Mountrail?"

The woman made a gesture to her dresser, who brought the jewel case and set it on her lap. Heads together, the two women brought out each bauble, while Betty shook and sniffled in his arms and Miss Carrington stared stonily ahead.

After they had sorted through the little pile twice, he asked, "Well, Lady Mountrail?"

"I think there is a pearl necklace missing."

He noted the confusion in her eyes now and felt the tiniest twinge of sympathy for the old harridan. "But you're not sure if you may have left it behind on your estate?" he suggested gently.

Lady Mountrail said nothing for a long moment. "I am not certain, Mortimer, not certain! You'll turn her off though, won't you?"

"Yes, I will," he replied, dreading the explosion from Millicent Carrington, even as he tightened his grip on Betty, who sobbed in earnest now.

"How can you?" she said, her voice low with scorn, which he decided was worse than all of Lady Mountrail's ravings.

"It is one of Sir Michael Moseley's rules, Miss Carrington," he said. "Any suspicions are dealt with this way."

The next sound was the door slamming. *Oh, well*, he thought. *Oh, well.*

He left the room fast enough himself, after assuring Lady Mountrail again that Betty would be let go. His arm around the young girl, he led the weeping child down the backstairs to the kitchen, where he sat her down at the table to a good cry, tea, and Mrs. Wheelwright's combination of admonition and sympathy, which helped the tears stop.

"I didn't pinch anything, Mr. Mortimer," Betty said again, when her eyes were dry.

"I know you didn't," he said quietly. "It's not in you to steal. I still have to let you go, but let me tell you how I'll do it."

She listened in fear, and then, to his relief, relaxed when his quiet explanation began to make sense. "You're an orphan, I know," he said, "and maybe you'd just like a change of scenery . . . at least until this ill wind blows somewhere else."

"The manager at Harrogate will take me in?"

"Positive. I know him well, and what's even more to the point, he's suffered through a visit or two from Lady Mountrail himself." He rose and stretched, wondering what time it was. "I'd never just turn you off, and I don't care what Sir Michael Moseley says."

'Tween stairs maids don't have many possessions, and Betty was packed by the time he had finished his letter to the new Harrogate manager, a dependable man he had shared the front desk with when they both worked in Glasgow. He took the child in a hackney to the closest mail coach stop, paid her wages (and a little more from his own), bought a ticket, and gave her the letter.

He walked back to the Grand Hotel contemplating his evening's work and his own hypocrisy in keeping some rules and flouting others, and the obvious loss of Miss Carrington. He beat himself with a few more stripes, then reminded himself that she had been about to let him down anyway when Chaseley intervened with Betty's crisis. "Some things just aren't going to happen," he said out loud as he stood in front of his hotel, looked at its magnificent facade, and found himself sadly wanting. And his head was starting to ache.

It was too late to go to bed and too early to rise, so he sat down in his room to finish *Wellington in India*. The narrative warmed him as it always did and gave him comfort as he wrote steadily, consulting his voluminous notes. He was sweating so he opened his window and leaned out to get a breath. *I don't know that I like London so well, myself,* he thought as he rested his arms on the windowsill and tried to breathe deep. *Simmons's gout can't last forever, and I will gladly recommend Chaseley for a promotion to my position. Maybe Harrogate needs a night clerk; it's all the same to me now.*

He finished the last chapter just as he heard the maids coming downstairs to begin their morning's work. He went to add it to the other pages in the pasteboard box, but remembered that Miss Carrington still had possession of his manuscript, unless she had dumped the whole box outside his door or in the nearest dustbin. In a few days he would begin a fair copy of the whole thing and present it to Wellington somehow before the conclusion of the upcoming festivities. *Then what will I do?* he asked himself as he lay down on the bed, his hand to his head. *I have no other diversions.*

It took him a long time, but he finally summoned the energy to put the final chapter in front of Miss Carrington's door, then crawled into bed. He managed to sleep for an hour, until Mr. Kipling, all aflutter that he was not at the desk, pounded on his door and woke him. In a haze—his head was pounding now in good earnest— he washed and dressed and took his usual place at the front desk.

He was seated at his desk behind the check-in counter when Miss Carrington left the hotel. When he noticed her in the lobby, he thought she might slam her key on the desk, but she didn't. In fact, she had no luggage, so he knew she wasn't leaving. He reasoned that she would never leave the dining room half-painted and had to thank her for that, at least.

She returned less than an hour later carrying a package. He wanted to say something to her, but she refused to look at him. *And what would I say?* he thought. *Please excuse me for being a hypocrite? I'm sorry I fell in love above my station? I could at least tell her that Betty wasn't out wandering the streets and hungry.*

He didn't see her for the rest of the day, but there was plenty of work for him. He was aware of the painters arriving that evening, and despite the buzz in his ears, heard her laughing with them in the dining room. He could only stand up now when there was something to lean upon, and he knew his temperature was shooting through the roof. Any moment the chills would begin, and his semi-annual malarial relapse would be firmly under way. *Drat the luck,* he thought. *My Indian friend, my cursed companion, couldn't you have waited another month until the festivities for Wellington were over?*

He watched the painters leave, and then Millie followed after a time. He wondered if she had lingered in the dining room for him but dismissed the idea. When she crossed the lobby, he thought she hesitated. He couldn't be sure; his entire goal was already focused on climbing those same stairs and hoping he could make it to his room.

But first he had to see the dining room. He knew that Chaseley had been watching him all evening since he came on duty, staying close as though ready to offer assistance, and he was grateful for the man's perspicacity. *I certainly shall recommend that he fill my position here,* he thought.

It wasn't so hard to cross the lobby because there were

enough sofas and chairs to lean upon. The expanse from the last chair to the dining-room door was daunting, but he had faced worse inconveniences. *Just inconveniences, Father,* he told himself. *The only problem I have now is that I will spend a lifetime without Miss Carrington, and I cannot bear that.*

Someone, probably Millie, had left a lamp burning in the dining room. With a force that made him stagger, he started to shiver. He pulled up a corner of a tablecloth to wipe the sweat that poured off his face and then stared at the wall trim. Despite his discomfort that was growing by the second, he smiled. *Miss Carrington, you were so right,* he thought. *It is beautiful. You have a flair.*

That was his last conscious thought before the convulsive shivers reached his legs. He clutched the tablecloth as though it could hold him up, then sank to his knees when it didn't, and sagged against the table. From miles away he heard it crash and then remembered nothing more.

The relapse followed its usual, dreamy course. One moment he was staring intently at Mr. Chaseley's mouth as the man slowly, slowly formed words. Another moment, and he was wishing the people in his room would not rush about too fast for his eyes to keep up with them. He was colder than a naked man on an ice floe; he was hot, sweating, and in the humid Deccan again. Someone raised his head enough for him to swallow bitter medicine, and then his ears began to ring, even as his shivering slowed.

Was it days? Was it minutes? He finally opened his eyes on a nearly normal world, except that Miss Carrington sat beside his bed. He knew that was a hallucination, especially when she rose, put a cool hand to his forehead, and then darted from the room. He closed his eyes again and let the tears slide into his ears.

He kept them closed, even when the door opened

and someone held his wrist. He heard a watch case snap, and after a year or two, someone spoke so loud that he flinched.

"Well, Mr. Mortimer, you've given us a scare, you have. Are they always this severe?"

He nodded and went back to sleep. The doctor released his hand, but someone else with lemon-scented skin pulled the blanket to his chin when he started to shiver again. In another moment there was a cloth-covered hot water bottle at his freezing feet, and gentle hands rubbing his legs.

He felt better when he woke again. He had a sense of time now, and he knew without opening his eyes that it was afternoon sun that rested on his hands folded across his stomach. He panicked first. *They're laying me out,* he thought, then raised a cautious hand to his cheek. *No, even a London undertaker wouldn't bury me with this much stubble on my face.*

"You're a little hairy, but you were shaking too much to shave."

He knew the voice and opened his eyes anyway. "Millie. Why?" he asked, frustrated because the words in his head weren't coming out of his mouth. "The painting. Done. What day?"

"Four nights ago Mr. Chaseley came to your rescue in the dining room," she said, leaving her chair to sit on the edge of his bed.

"Four. Who in charge?"

"A sentence! Hooray!" she said in all good humor. "Mr. Chaseley. Mr. Kipling wasn't up to it, so Mr. Chaseley staged a coup d'état. I thought it was a good idea. I kept Uncle Moseley out of it, but he will be here tonight and . . ."

He couldn't have heard her right. "Uncle?"

She must have leaned closer, because the next thing he

knew, she was rubbing her smooth cheek against his stubbly face. "Heavens, Charles, you reek. I told you I had something to tell you that you wouldn't like very much."

He closed his eyes and slept.

When he woke it was darker, and his room was lit with a soft light. He managed to raise his head off the pillow. He wanted to lean on his elbow, but it was still made of melting wax so he didn't try. He lay back and Millie propped a pillow behind his head.

Sir Michael Moseley paced back and forth at the foot of his bed. Millie's chair was pulled up as close to the bed as she could contrive it, and Mr. Chaseley grinned at him from his perch on the window ledge. Mrs. Wheelwright, daring him to object, ran a warm cloth over his face, and then down the front of his nightshirt and under his arms. He wasn't about to object; it felt wonderful. "When we think you won't drown, the footman will help you bathe," she told him.

"Sir Michael, I am sorry," he said finally.

This was all the opening his employer seemed to require. He stopped his pacing and leaned on the foot rail of the bed, pointing his finger. "You have been deceiving me," he began.

Charles opened his mouth to agree, but Sir Michael was pointing his finger at Millie. Charles looked at her with a question in his eyes. She took his hand. "That's what you won't like, Charles. I'm Sir Michael's niece. He's married to my father's older sister. I almost hate to say this, but he planted me in the hotel to see what kind of a manager you were."

"Millie!" he said, unable to hide his disappointment.

"Charles? Millie? Oh, worse and worse!" Sir Michael thundered. "For more than a week now, Niece, you have told me that everything was going fine here at the Grand Hotel! You're a positive viper in an uncle's bosom!"

Charles started to shiver again. Millie leaped to her feet and right into her uncle's face, a wren squaring off against a great blue heron. "Don't shout!" she shouted. "He's still in a weakened state!" She put her hand to her mouth. "Oh, I'm sorry, Charles."

He only smiled. "Sit down, Millie." She sat. "First things first," he said, looking at his night clerk. "Betty?"

"I got a letter two days ago from Williston at the Grand Vista," Chaseley said, coming off his window perch. "She's fine and working as an underhousemaid. It seems Williston was short-staffed."

"Thank heavens. Lady Mountrail?"

With a glance at Sir Michael, and after a deep breath, Mr. Chaseley spoke. "Would you believe that she discovered that her dratted necklace had never been packed in the first place?" Mr. Chaseley ran his finger around his collar. "I . . . I told her what I thought." He glanced at Charles. "I suppose I rather thought that's what you would do."

Charles smiled.

Millie glared at her uncle as though daring him to speak. "Uncle Moseley, the guests are *not* always right. Sometimes you have to trust your manager not to be a slave to rules."

This is daffy, he thought. "Sir Michael, you *planted* Millie?"

"I always do that with new managers," he said, speaking softer now. "Well, not Millie." He glared at her. "Never again Millie! She was here in town to secure a position as governess—if that wasn't harebrained enough—and I thought I could use her." He threw up his hands and started to pace again. "And what does she do but encourage you to break all kinds of rules!"

"They were stupid rules, Uncle," Millie insisted.

"Your father's not a vicar?" he asked.

"Oh, yes!" she declared. "I wouldn't lie to you . . . well, about that."

He couldn't help grinning. "No wonder no one's ever dared to marry you, Millicent Carrington."

"Sir!" she exclaimed, but she was smiling, too. "Oh, Charles, it just so happens that we are a wealthy family. It's a . . . a blasted nuisance."

"Millie!" her uncle said, shocked.

"I said I would stay at the hotel and find out if you were a good manager." She gave her uncle a long, measuring look. "Oh, Uncle Moseley, Charles Mortimer is imaginative, kind to his staff, listens to them, knows a good idea when he hears one, and . . . and isn't afraid to let people stay here who you might not consider . . . consider . . ."

"Kipling tattled to me about the man of color from Boston," Moseley said. He cleared his throat. "Were either of you aware that Mr. Beach was invited to London to address Parliament about enforcing that 1807 law against the slave trade in our empire?"

"No!" Millie said. "He never said that."

"I had a visit from Lord Dickinson only this morning, thanking me for extending him the hospitality of the Grand Hotel. It seems that Mr. Beach was quite eloquent."

"Good," Charles said.

"Everyone's been giving me an earful," Sir Michael growled, except that this time he sat on the end of the bed. "Who should come to me in tears but that wretched chef Dumb . . . Dumb something . . . no, no . . ."

"DuPré," they all said together.

"It seems he entered a pastry with some froggy name in that contest last night, and it met with foul play." He sighed. "Millie, are you responsible for this too?"

"I'm not sure," she said uncertainly. "Charles, don't you dare laugh! What . . . what kind of foul play?"

"Oops," said Chaseley from the window. "I'll tell what I did if you'll tell what you did, Miss Carrington."

"I don't want to hear it!" Sir Michael said, throwing up his hands.

"Mrs. Wheelwright distracted him, and I slipped cream of tartar in the raspberry sauce," she confessed. "It probably tasted awful."

"I'm to blame then, because no one ever tasted it," Chaseley admitted. "It seems that at Carlton House, DuPré tripped over my foot and landed face first in the Triomph de Toulouse. *Sacré bleu,*" he concluded solemnly, and Millie burst into laughter, which she quickly smothered with a corner of Charles's bedsheet.

"What entry won?"

"Why, Mr. Mortimer, can you doubt? Millie's plum duff, of course," Chaseley said. "His Grace said it was always his favorite dessert." He looked at Mrs. Wheelwright. "Don't you just love military men and their total lack of culinary curiosity?"

"That is uncalled for, you young chub!"

Surprised, everyone in the room turned to look toward the door, except Charles, who knew that voice. *Oh, I am weak*, he thought. "Your Grace," he said, raising his head up from the pillow again. "Do come in and join the rest of London in my room."

His Grace, the Duke of Wellington, resplendent in his uniform and fairly bristling with medals, entered the room. Millie quickly stood up and offered the great man her chair, which he accepted with a nod. He looked around. "I do beg your pardon. I hate to squelch a perfectly rousing donnybrook—it must be the Irish in me—but I only have a few minutes before the next silly event begins and I wanted a word with Charles."

Sir Michael's eyes fairly popped from his head. "May the Almighty preserve us!" he exclaimed in a strangled tone.

"Oh, no," said the duke calmly. "That title of Almighty belongs to our first minister, if rumor suffices." He turned his attention to Charles. "You look fit for a midden. Could you use some more quinine, or have they dosed you with too much? Ears ring?"

"I think I'll survive, Your Grace."

"Thank goodness for that." He glanced at the door. "Crauford, give over that manuscript, if you would. Thank you." He placed the pasteboard box on the bed. "This came with the plum duff. I read it last night—stayed up far too late, drat you—and came here to ask your permission to send it round to Epping and Stanley."

"The publishers?" Millie asked in a whisper, her eyes wide.

"The very same. By the way, is this your handwriting? You have quite an elegant fist."

"Thank you," she said. "It's only partly copied, Your Grace," she said to Wellington. "I can finish it in a week." She looked at Charles. "I started copying it that morning after I was so rude to you."

"Which morning was that?" he teased.

Her eyes filled with tears. "Oh, I am so glad you can quiz me about it now. I thought you were going to die." She came closer again to dab at her eyes with the bedsheet. "And that would never do, because I love you."

Sir Michael groaned in despair. "Millicent, this is extremely unsuitable!"

"Far from it, Uncle," she replied calmly. "I love this man. As I am your favorite niece—don't deny it—we will accept the gift of a hotel on our wedding. Don't you think Charles and I could run a fine hotel? I recommend the Grand Whatchamacallit in Kent. Isn't it opening soon?"

Sir Michael Moseley winced, then thought a moment. "It is. You may be right."

"Sir Michael, if I may," Chaseley began, after clearing

his throat. "I think I can vouch that any staff member where Mr. Mortimer has served will be happy to follow him to the ends of the earth." He looked at Charles and shrugged his shoulders. "You may deny it, but you have a certain something."

"There you are, Uncle," Millie said.

"Charles, you are a lucky dog," Wellington said. "Let me put my oar in. Everyone's been after me to write my memoirs, and dash it, I haven't the time. *Wellington in India* will do for starters. Perhaps you and I will collaborate on the Peninsular Wars. The illustrations are excellent, by the way. Miss Carrington, when you have copied it entirely, send it round to Epping and Stanley. They are expecting it." He looked up at Sir Michael. "Charles Mortimer is talented. What can one expect from a man who served the guns so well at Kaitna Ford? He probably has many hidden talents. How lucky you are to employ him, Sir Michael."

"Yes, Your Grace."

The duke looked at Millie. "These are your drawings, are they not?"

She nodded. "I did them for my brother, Major Robert Carrington."

"I remember him well, my dear." He paused, remembering. "You're a pretty thing. Has Charles Mortimer proposed yet?"

"Not yet," he said from the bed. "I thought the matter was hanging in some apprehension."

"I doubt that," the duke replied, after a long look at Millie's blushing face. "My dear, Charles Mortimer is just a late-bloomer. I was one, myself. Perhaps you are too?"

She nodded.

"Give him a week, and he'll be on his feet again." The duke looked toward the door and sighed. "Crauford is dancing around and nervous that I will be late to the next event. Miss Carrington, take the manuscript so you can continue." He took Charles by the hand. "Thank you again for Kaitna Ford."

"You are welcome, Your Grace. I . . . I have wanted to tell you that."

Without another word, the duke kissed his forehead, stood looking at him for another moment, released his hand, then left the room. He must have sucked all the air out with him; exhausted, Charles closed his eyes and slept.

Charles left the Grand Hotel on a stretcher the following morning, bolstered by another dose of quinine, and Millie standing close. He had tried to protest, when she stayed by his bed all night, but he couldn't really form any words until morning. He didn't think she would have listened, anyway.

He hadn't the energy to voice any objection to Millie's plan to take him to Kent and the vicarage for a full recuperation, but no objection had occurred to him. *Perhaps the vicar will marry us*, Charles thought. *I shall ask him, when I am able. While I am not precisely a father's dream of a husband for his wealthy daughter, Millie likes me.*

Millie loves me, he amended as dawn approached and his strength returned. His words still came out halting and disjointed, especially after that next blast of quinine. She seemed to consider "Love you," and "Marry me?" as complete sentences of amazing eloquence, and responded to both in the affirmative.

He would have preferred to exit the Grand Hotel as a normal biped, but he couldn't manage to get the mattress off his back. Mr. Chaseley, totally in charge now, directed the footman to put him—"Gently now!"—onto a stretcher.

Their slow progress across the lobby halted when a familiar voice hailed him and he opened his eyes.

"Mr. Mortimer, call it Providence; my gout is better."

Simmons swam before his eyes, then came into focus. True, the man was leaning on a cane, but there he was, none the worse for three weeks off his pins. "Glad to hear," Charles said, wishing that his voice was not so faint.

"The first thing to do is remove those boxes from my rooms behind the lobby, Mr. Mortimer," the manager said, shaking his cane at his former assistant manager. "Really, Charles, if you were only more forceful, so much would be accomplished." He sighed. "If only you were a man of action."

Charles smiled and closed his eyes. *Charles Mortimer, man of action, that I am,* he thought in amusement as he managed to wave good-bye to his staff (and remind Chaseley to plan for a move to Kent soon as his new assistant manager), then take Millie by the hand as she walked alongside his stretcher. *I am a detail man, a background man, and soon a husband and lover.* He put his hand on Millie's arm as the footman prepared to lift the stretcher into the carriage. "Feel lucky?" he asked.

Right there in front of the Grand Hotel, with his whole staff looking on and Mr. Chaseley cheering, Millie kissed him thoroughly and well.

ABOUT THE AUTHOR

Photo by Marie Bryner-Bowles, Bryner Photography

CARLA KELLY IS A VETERAN OF THE NEW York and international publishing world. The author of more than thirty novels and novellas for Donald I. Fine Co., Signet, and Harlequin, Carla is the recipient of two RITA Awards (think Oscars for romance writing) from Romance Writers of America and two Spur Awards (think Oscars for western fiction) from Western Writers of America. She is also a recipient of Whitney Awards for *Borrowed Light* and *My Loving Vigil Keeping*.

Recently, she's been writing Regency romances (think *Pride and Prejudice*) set in the Royal Navy's Channel Fleet during the Napoleonic Wars between England and France. She comes by her love of the ocean from her childhood as a Navy brat.

Carla's history background makes her no stranger to footnote work, either. During her National Park Service days at the Fort Union Trading Post National Historic Site, Carla edited Friedrich Kurz's fur trade journal. She recently completed a short history of Fort Buford, where Sitting Bull surrendered in 1881.

Following the "dumb luck" principle that has guided their lives, the Kellys recently moved to Wellington, Utah, from North Dakota and couldn't be happier in their new location. In her spare time, Carla volunteers at the Western Mining and Railroad Museum in Helper, Utah. She likes to visit her five children, who live here and there around the United States. Her favorite place in Utah is Manti, located after a drive on the scenic byway through Huntington Canyon.

And why is she so happy these days? Carla doesn't have to write in laundry rooms and furnace rooms now, because she has an actual office.